...by the people...

The Novel

by

William M. Schmalfeldt

To Gail — for hanging in there.

FIRST EDITION – 2004

ISBN 0-9748410-1-3

1

"Oooooooh! You so strong!"

This utterance had just the effect she wanted on the naked man she was riding. His body tensed. His rhythm quickened. He grabbed her hips and clenched.

Good, she thought. *He'll be finished soon.*

Hatsuko (she told him it was "Suki," as Americans seemed to like that name) looked down into his face. For an American, he wasn't all that disagreeable. This one had a full head of thick, gray hair. He was clean-shaven and smelled pleasant. He wasn't fat, and he didn't slobber, like so many of his barbarian compatriots.

She knew nothing about the man, other than his apparent wealth and power. The phone call a couple hours before made it clear that this was not just another businessman on a Japanese junket. The familiar voice told her to wait in the hotel lobby and wear something sexy.

"This is a very important American. You will make him feel relaxed and welcome. You will give him happy memories. You will make him think favorably about Japan."

"Oooooh. You make strong sex!" she moaned, doing her best to lobby for her country. "You make such strong fucking!"

The naked man grabbed her buttocks, as if to indicate his agreement.

This was another thing she found distasteful about Americans. They liked it when she talked like a gutter whore. It was so unbecoming. Most Japanese men preferred their women to tremble in fear and awe at the potency of their godlike onslaught. It didn't matter if the trembling was feigned.

But even so, a girl had her limits. She had been bouncing up and down on this gaijin for almost a half-hour without even a hint of him reaching "the moment of wind and rain."

She continued to watch his face, hoping to see the narrowing of eyes, or the popping neck cords that would signal the end of her job. Instead, his eyes were wide open. He grabbed her buttocks even harder and pumped faster.

Time to end this, she thought, and then arched backwards, held his ankles for support, and brushed her silky black hair against his feet.

"Ooooooh, yesssss!" she moaned. "Oooooooh! You so BIG!"
The man continued his viselike grip on her left buttock. He rubbed her small, tight belly, snaking up her smooth skin to her petite breasts. His breathing had become a series of hoarse pants. Before he could reach her breasts, his left hand clenched. Then loosened. Then clenched again. Then it dropped to the mattress. His right hand released her buttock, leaving red fingerprints on her white flesh.

"Aaaaaaah! Mygaaaaah! Ohhhhhhh. My God! Mygaaaaaaaaaa…"

Good for you, she thought. With any luck, her business with this fellow would soon be finished, and she'd be able to join her friends for coffee at the Blue Note. She shut her eyes and pumped her hips for all she was worth.

The man spasmed once, then again. His whole body seemed to clench. Then it went still.

Something was missing. She didn't feel the warm splash of wetness that usually accompanied such enthusiastic expressions of delight. She leaned forward and studied his features. His face was beet red. His mouth was open and wet with drool. *It's not just the fat ones after all*, she mused. His eyes were open, but they weren't pointed in the same direction. The right eye had drifted outward, and was now the color of

2

blood.

"Hey," she said, poking his chest. "You okay? Huh?"

He didn't answer.

She put a finger under his nose but could feel no air. She leaned forward and placed her ear against his chest.

"Not again," she whispered in Japanese.

Six months earlier, a businessman as prominent as he was elderly breathed his last exuberant breath under her ministrations. His unfortunate demise paved the way for a young successor — one whose ideas were considered to be "more forward-thinking" by those in a position to care. Those in Hatsuko's circle bold enough to whisper about the event dubbed her the loveliest murder weapon in Japan.

She eased forward, disengaging herself with just a bit of difficulty, as if a slight amount of suction had been generated by their frenzied end-game. If the rest of him looked limp and dead, she noted, one part of him still looked swollen and eager to complete its business. She walked to a nearby chair and lifted a red silk kimono, easing it over her shoulders. She tied the belt around her waist and surveyed the situation.

She fought back a wave of faintness by pinching the bridge of her nose with her thumb and index finger. When the room stopped swirling around her, she proceeded to the bedroom door and slowly opened it.

Two men, white Americans (gaijins), were seated on the couch. Another, a black American (a kokojin), was watching a baseball game on television. A Japanese man, the one who picked her up and drove her to this penthouse suite, was smoking a cigarette, exiting the kitchenette area with three bottles of Asahi Beer. All four men eventually noticed her standing in the doorway. Politely, she waited until she had their attention before speaking.

"Gomen nasai," she apologized in her native language. Then she spoke in English. "Please excuse me. I am very sorry. The gentleman is not well. I fear he may be dead."

The two white Americans drew automatic pistols from their shoulder holsters. They rushed into the bedroom, pushing Hatsuko out of the way. She steadied herself against the door jam. The kokojin followed his colleagues, invoking the name of his Christian god in a loud, anguished voice. The Japanese man looked at her with a stunned expression. Then he sank to the couch. He covered his face with his hands and, after a moment, started giggling.

***

The large black man practically filled the doorway. He watched as the two Secret Service Agents conducted a visual sweep of the room, their weapons drawn and ready. After checking under the bed and looking in the closet, they directed their attention to the man on the bed.

There, on the rumpled sheets, lay Eugene Walters, vice president of the United States of America. His thick, gray hair was scattered all over his head. His face was pale, save for several smears of bright red lipstick. Both eyes were open. So was his mouth, although there seemed to be the slight suggestion of a smile. Yet the first thing one noticed about the body of the man who had recently been just a heartbeat away from the presidency was the erection — still quite vigorous.

One of the agents stood and watched as the other checked for a pulse on Walter's left wrist. Then he laid his head on Walters' chest. He looked at the large man standing in the doorway and shook his head.

"Aw, Jeeez!" the large man moaned.

Don Franklin, who had been the vice president's chief of staff, was now technically unemployed.

He had arranged this trip as a "trade mission" to the Far East. He had explained to their hosts that the vice president would likely "see things favorably" if he had a chance to "relax" before the next morning's discussions. And now his employer lay five feet away from him, naked and dead.

"It must have been a heart attack," said the agent who had checked for a pulse.

Franklin moved closer and examined the face.

"Nah, I think it was probably a stroke. Look at that eye." He pointed to the one that seemed to be filled with blood. "I was constantly reminding him to take his blood pressure pills."

The two agents began to perform CPR. One agent climbed onto the mattress and straddled the vice president's hips while delivering rhythmic compressions to his sternum. The other clamped his lips over the lipstick-smeared mouth and blew into the man's lungs — one breath for five of his partner's compressions.

Akihiro Tanaka, the little trade group's official liaison to the Japanese government, walked into the room. His eyes widened as he saw the agents performing CPR.

"Ah," Tanaka said. "It would seem Suki-chan was correct in her most unfortunate observation." He stopped suddenly, taking notice of the vice president's erection.

"Honto! My goodness," he whispered.

Franklin turned to his host and noted the direction of his stare. "Tell you what, Tanaka-san. Would you do me an incredibly big favor and wait — out there?" He gestured toward the sitting room. "And is there a hotel doctor or someone you could call?"

"Oh, hai," Tanaka said a little too briskly, as if snapping out of a trance. "Yes, I will call him right away."

He hurried to the door, looking back over his shoulder as he went. Franklin waited until he could hear him speaking on the phone, then walked over and quietly closed the door. He turned to face the two agents, still working on the vice president. Walters was starting to turn blue.

"Boys, that there has got to be one of the jolliest looking dead men I've ever seen." Neither agent seemed to find the remark amusing. After a few more minutes, the agent performing the compressions paused to check for a pulse. He shook his head. "I'm no doctor, but I don't think he's coming back."

The agent providing the artificial respiration looked at his partner. The first agent nodded, giving him permission to stop. The second agent exhaled tiredly and lifted his head. The lipstick smears had transferred to his own face.

Franklin walked toward the agents and put his large hands on each of their shoulders.

"Now, fellas, I need you to hear me on this. I am not going to tell you how to report this. That would be wrong. I am, however, going to tell you what I'm going to say about it. And I think my version will be in the best interest, not only of our country, but of the memory of this fine public servant laying in stately repose on the bed."

"You want us to lie," said the first agent, matter-of-factly.

"No! Heavens no! I'm not going to lie either! When I speak to the White House, I will give them all the details. But with the media... merely the basics. Vice President Walters had either a heart attack or a stroke. That's the truth. He died in bed. That is also the truth! Any embellishment of these very basic facts would go above and beyond the nation's need to know. Do we really want to serve up the memory of this fine man to the snickering jackals who'd love nothing better than to besmirch him and everything he stood for? I think not!"

"When you put it that way..." the second agent said.

There was a knock on the door. "Mister Franklin?"

"We'll be out in just a minute, Tanaka-san," Franklin shouted over his shoulder. He turned and addressed the agents. "Now, gentlemen, shall we make our vice president... presentable? Why don't you fellows see if you can straighten out the bedroom a little. I'll go have a word with our friend. Then I'll be right back."

The agents looked at each other, shrugged their shoulders, then set about straightening the room. Franklin opened the door, closed it quickly behind him, and went to where his host was sitting. The girl sat on a couch, looking at her hands folded on her lap.

"The doctor, he will be up directly. He was having his dinner, so he may be a moment. Should I call him again and ask him to hurry?"

"I don't believe that will be necessary, Tanaka-san," Franklin said."

Tanaka jumped to his feet and stood ramrod straight. "I most humbly regret this incident," he said, bowing low. "And, if you should so desire, I will take immediate measures to ensure that the young lady does not say anything to anyone about this."

Franklin looked at the girl. She was pretty. He supposed there were infinitely worse ways to die. Then he realized just what his host was suggesting.

"No, now wait a minute," he stammered. "If you're talking about doing something to this young lady, then I must strongly..."

Tanaka looked confused for a moment, then his eyes brightened.

"Oh, my goodness, please forgive my inadequate use of your language," he said with a smile. "I meant only to say that she will be richly compensated and relocated at our expense — after promising to keep what happened here a matter of the utmost discretion. Suki-chan is a wonderful girl. A special girl. And a professional! It would not do to destroy such a beautiful flower in the full bloom of youth, neh?"

"Fine," Franklin said, relieved. The girl just sat on the couch, her face impassive.

"Tell you what," Franklin said, after an awkward silence. "Why don't you see what's keeping the doctor? I'll see if the fellows need a hand."

He returned to the bedroom. The agents had done good work. Walters was lying on his back, under the covers, eyes shut, hands folded over his chest. He looked peaceful, as if he had died in his sleep during a pleasant dream. The only thing that seemed out of place was the tent-pole effect of his erection on the bedspread. Franklin supposed the morticians would have some secret remedy. The lipstick smears had been wiped from the vice president's face.

Franklin realized that something else would need cleaning.

"Did you fellows wash his..." Both agents shook their heads vigorously.

Franklin sighed. *Well*, he thought, *he'd done worse during his time in government.*

"That's okay, you guys did a great job. Wanna wait outside with Tanaka-san?" They both exited.

Franklin walked to the bathroom and soaped up a washcloth. He grabbed a clean towel and walked toward the bed, exhaling in a long, whistling sigh. He had one more duty to perform for his boss. Then he would call Washington.

Neither job was particularly appealing.

2

Jim Englund wouldn't normally have been worried about his boss.

Since 1975, when Englund had his own gall bladder removed, the procedure had come a long way. Back then, the surgery involved an incision of nearly twelve inches, running from the sternum to the bottom right side of the rib cage.

Nowadays, thanks to the endoscope, it was a much simpler procedure. Three punctures, the abdomen is inflated, and the endoscope does the trick. A nip, a snip, a suture, and the inflamed gall bladder is hauled out through one of the holes. The patient is up and around in hours.

But there were complications with this one. The doctors wouldn't tell him much about it, but his boss, lying in a post-surgery bed, was more than happy to fill in the blanks. To hear his boss tell it, the doctors had stumbled upon a blocked common bile duct. The duct was infected, and there was a fluid backup. The endoscopic procedure had to be abandoned in favor of the more invasive method. And, as long as they were in there anyway, they decided to take a look around. That's what explained the large, inverted V-shaped incision right below his ribcage.

"Nothing to worry about," his boss had said. "I'll be up and kicking keister in no time."

But when your boss is the president of the United States, it's hard not to be worried about everything. President John DeWitt seemed to be recovering from the operation at his own speed. And that speed, Englund observed, was none too quick.

Still, the president was working his way back to a modest daily routine. That meant Vice President Walters would soon return to his regular duties, while DeWitt reassumed more and more of the burdens of office.

Englund looked at his appointment calendar. Walters was due back from Japan that evening. The president planned to invite a select few of the White House Press Corps into the Oval Office the next afternoon for an informal chat that would signify his return to full-time duties.

It was early, not quite seven a.m. The caffeine jolt from his first four cups of coffee hadn't hit yet. But his bladder ached for release. Just another penalty for getting older, he mused.

The secure phone on his desk chirped insistently. Given the early hour, this was unusual. He picked up the receiver.

"Yes?"

"Jim? Don Franklin. Trouble."

Englund grimaced.

"Please, Don. Do tell. Did the vice president eat some bad sushi and do a 'George Bush' on the Prime Minister's lap?" He smiled at the memory.

"Beats me," said Franklin. "I'd ask him, but he's dead."

***

"Will the gentleman yield?"

"No, the gentleman will not yield," said the congressman from Texas. "This is my time, and I will be heard! The majority party is bent on defining this debate in terms of dollars and cents, without giving a thought to the devastating effect this legislation will have on the people who count on this program."

"The gentleman's time has expired," said the Speaker of the House. He delivered a perfunctory bang of his gavel.

10

Congressman Roberto Huerta stood silent, his mouth open in disbelief.

"Mr. Speaker, I understood we each had ten minutes…"

"The gentleman's time has expired," said the speaker, this time with a slightly more vigorous whack. "The chair recognizes the gentleman from Kentucky."

"Thank you, Mr. Speaker." Speaker Albert Orwell Wantner raised a gray, bushy eyebrow in recognition of his colleague's gratitude.

"I'm not surprised that my first-term colleague from Texas is having a difficult time comprehending the gravity of this issue. After all, he's a Democrat. And what my friends on the other side of the aisle all seem to fail to realize is that we are not here to throw around the people's tax money on programs that do little more than ensure the never-ending cycle of government dependency."

Yada yada yada, Wantner thought. Once again, he found himself fighting the urge to doze. There was a time when he would have expressed his boredom aloud on the House floor. But those days were behind him. Now he had to be a leader. He just thought it would be more exciting than this.

Congressman Wantner, Republican from Charleston, South Carolina, did not become Speaker of the House by virtue of being a nice guy. Rather, it was the culmination of a long, tedious, sometimes dirty climb through the congressional hierarchy.

Like so many Republicans, Wantner spent the first part of his career as a member of a party that seemed doomed to permanent minority status. During his first six terms, he labored as a party functionary on minor committees, doing favors for others, storing up markers for later repayment. His true ascendancy began in the early 1990s, when Republicans began to whittle away at the Democratic majority. Although far from being the most senior GOP congressman, Wantner was definitely one of the most outspoken. He did not shy away from making outrageous statements. At one point, he even advocated withdrawal from the United Nations, saying that the agency was involved in "covert planning for a paramilitary operation that will threaten our very sovereignty."

At first, the more mainstream elements of the party laughed away such pronouncements. But when the ranks of GOP members swelled, it was with newly elected representatives who, by and large, shared Wantner's "us vs. them" view of the world.

Eventually, in the same election that swept the doddering geriatric and his fornicating fool of a vice president into the White House, the far right wing of the Republican Party finally had enough power to appoint someone of their own bent to the speakership. That man was Albert Wantner of the Palmetto State.

At the moment, Albert Wantner was bored to distraction. He wouldn't normally even be in the chamber (it was a minor debate on an obscure agricultural funding bill), but he figured he could just as well be bored in the speaker's chair, where his face might show up on TV, than be bored in his ornate, anonymous office.

He realized he was learning a lesson learned by all revolutionaries. Once the revolution is over, the victor must govern.

Without a challenge, things were coming too easily for Wantner. Victory piled up upon victory. Sure, the senile fool in the Oval Office had veto power. But the House had nearly enough congressmen who voted with Wantner to override any veto. Too bad the nimrods in the Senate didn't have the same kind of backbone.

Wantner looked at the timer and realized the hayseed from Kentucky had overstayed his ten minutes. Then he decided he really didn't care. The place was pretty sparsely populated anyway — perhaps only 20 or so legislators in the chamber, jockeying for their few minutes on C-SPAN, maybe even a little soundbite for the voters back home.

Wantner's attention – such as it was – was suddenly diverted by one of the nameless, faceless House pages who climbed the steps to the speaker's podium with a folded piece of paper. Wantner nodded a cursory recognition and took the paper from him.

He unfolded the note and read what was printed on official White House letterhead. His face went slack. He felt his lips beginning to tingle, and momentarily forgot to breathe. As soon as he felt steady enough to do so without staggering, he rose to his feet.

"Would the gentleman from Kentucky yield?"

"Why of course, Mr. Speaker. I'm always happy to..."

Wantner ignored him. "My fellow members," he said, as calmly as he could. "I have just received some very unsettling news. As this news comes from the White House, we must assume it is official."

The members in attendance stared silently at the speaker.

"I have just received word that our vice president, the honorable Eugene Walters, has died of an apparent stroke during his trade mission to Japan. I'm sure you will all join me in a moment of silence."

The assembled members of Congress bowed their heads, as did Wantner.

Providence, he thought.

After a suitably respectful period, Wantner raised his head and banged the gavel once again.

"The House stands adjourned until eight a.m. tomorrow."

Wantner climbed down from the podium and hurried to his office. He had phone calls to make.

***

ASSOCIATED PRESS BULLETIN

TOKYO – (AP) – May 10: Administration officials have confirmed that Vice President Eugene Walters has died from an apparent stroke. He was 62 years old.

According to Donald Franklin, the vice president's

chief of staff, Walters died in his sleep in the presidential suite of the New Shinjuku Hotel.

Walters was in Japan on the final stop of a seven-day Asian trade mission that took him first to Hong Kong and South Korea before arriving here in Japan.

The vice president's body was flown by helicopter to the Yokosuka Naval Hospital at the U.S. Naval Base south of Tokyo. After an autopsy, the remains will be flown to Washington, D.C., where funeral arrangements are pending.

***

The large man on the toilet cursed himself – perhaps for the thousandth time – for eating Italian sausage the night before. The sausage had an unsettling affect on his digestive system.

He blamed his older brother for getting him hooked on the habit. There was a time when just regular spaghetti and meat sauce would suffice. That was before having dinner with Jack a year or so earlier.

"You don't know what you're missing," Jack Anniston said. Being two years older than Stan and having a better-than-average sense of birthright, he had no qualms about making all manner of suggestions regarding his little brother's lifestyle.

"It just ain't spaghetti unless you got some tasty saw-seech with it," Jack would say, slicing a lordly hunk, impaling it with his fork, twirling it in spaghetti and sauce, and sticking it in his mouth.

"Good eatin'!"

And Stan had to admit, his brother was correct. Too bad, he discovered, that this delicious addition gave him a case of what Grandma Genny used to call "the greenapple quickstep." It was a hazard a morning radio announcer could ill afford — especially if the aforementioned announcer was the host of a semi-popular local talk show. The typical "disc jockey" was in a better position to accommodate such gastric events. Songs like Gordon Lightfoot's "The Wreck of the Edmund

14

Fitzgerald" and Don McLean's "American Pie" were the stuff of legend in the world of the small-market broadcaster. Talk was, whenever one heard either song, it meant the disc jockey was in the "library." They'd never have gotten the airplay necessary to launch them to the top of the charts if they weren't longer than five minutes,.

No such luxury was afforded the host of a big-city talk show. Music was used sparingly, if at all. Anniston's job was to keep the calls coming in. The sausage, however, necessitated a momentary change in format. At the moment, the record playing in Stan Anniston's studio was Johnny Cash's version of "The Legend of John Henry's Hammer." It ran more than eight minutes.

Anniston had the monitor in the restroom turned up. John Henry had just beaten the steam drill and was telling his woman – his "good woman" – to take up his hammer when he died. That meant the song was almost over. Time to do the paperwork. That's when someone pounded the door.

"Pinch it off, Stan!" It was his producer. "Breaking news! Big time."

The good people of Chicago would have to hear the rest of the story about the Steel Drivin' Man the morning after some future spaghetti-and-Italian-sausage meal. He had a bulletin to get on the air.

3

"It is a terrible thing, Mr. President. Just terrible!"

DeWitt grimaced, both at the pain in his belly and the sound of Speaker Wantner's syrupy, Southern accent on the speakerphone.

"I appreciate that, Mr. Speaker," he said as evenly as he could manage. "It is a tragedy for the whole nation."

"True, Mr. President. Oh, so very true. The former vice president was a dedicated public servant. If there is any comfort to be gained from this tragic happenstance, it is in the fact that Mr. Walters died doing the thing he loved most."

DeWitt startled. "And what, precisely, was that, Mr. Speaker?"

"Why, serving his country! Executing the art of statecraft! Trying to negotiate a trade pact with the Japanese! Why, Mr. President, whatever on earth did you think I meant?"

The president could hear suppressed snickering in the background. Probably Jimmy Langston, the speaker's aide. *The miserable toady*, he thought. DeWitt mentally slapped himself on the forehead for stumbling into that particular little trap.

"Of course," he muttered. "Then, Mr. Speaker, I can assume your sentiments of regret are an assurance that the Congress will be expedient in the confirmation of the next vice president?"

"Why of course!" It sounded like "uff cahwse" when Wantner said it. "You can rest assured, Mr. President, that the majority will give quick consideration to whomever you send up. Of course, we'll want to take a good look at the candidate's background and all, but that's just a formality."

"We'll have done that already before we send anyone up," the president responded.

"Why, I understand that, Mr. President. But a second, thorough look-see can't hurt none, now can it? You know how sometimes things get missed."

"I appreciate your concern, Mr. Speaker. Thank you for calling."

"If I can be of any assistance, Mr. President, y'all call anytime. Hear?"

I hear, you weasely little shit, the president didn't say. He hung up the speaker phone by pushing a button, eased back in his recliner, and turned on the TV by remote.

The timing of the current turn of events was troublesome, especially given the fact that the president was dying.

As far as the world knew, it was only his gall bladder that had been removed three months ago. The official story was that a blocked common bile duct and subsequent infection necessitated a more invasive operation than the three-hole-punch laparoscopy. What the public didn't know was that a good portion of DeWitt's cancerous pancreas had been removed as well.

Dr. Watterson, the White House physician, described the chances of long-term survival as slim and none; pancreatic cancer spreads like wildfire, and the president's hadn't been caught in time. The most recent CT scans had indicated new tumors in the liver and small intestines. He hoped to finish the final year-and-a-half of this term in office, but he shouldn't expect much more than that. And those estimates figured in a debilitating round of chemotherapy, which DeWitt had planned to begin upon the vice president's return from Japan.

This was why he had wanted that informal chat with a few members of the White House Press Corps. He was going to tell them – and thereby the world – the truth about his medical condition. This, he knew, would give the vice president a leg up toward a White House run of his own, if that was what he wanted. He even considered resigning, giving Walters the opportunity to run as an incumbent.

But now, with the death of the vice president, and knowing that the smarmy little asshole from South Carolina was next in line for the presidency, things were different. *Improvident timing*, DeWitt thought, as he closed his eyes and tried to relax. Walters had been making progress pushing the Japanese toward a more equitable trading stance. The public was told he had died in his sleep, but the inner circle knew the real story. DeWitt was sure that the speaker knew, for it was being whispered about among Washington insiders. And by conservative radio talk show host Clovis Plambeck, who mentioned on air that it was fitting for Walters to "die in the saddle."

As DeWitt pondered the vice presidential vacancy, it occurred to him just how alone he really was. Here in the official residential area of the White House was the only place a president could truly find solitude. Secret Service agents were poised just a few yards away in the hall. But here in the residence, with the staff dismissed for the night, a president could find seclusion. The residence was built for a president and his family. But DeWitt had no family. His wife had died ten years earlier, and they had no children.

DeWitt stared at the TV, paying no attention to the image on the screen. The Republicans would stall the confirmation process no matter who he nominated. At the very least, they would drag things out until the fall, when candidates would start tossing their hats into the ring for the presidential election the following year. Democrats were waiting on word from DeWitt about his intentions, although Congressman Montana was already raising money to challenge Vice President Walters should DeWitt decide to sit this one out. A few Republicans had already started lining up support for candidacies of their own, but the smart money was on Speaker Wantner. Faced with his impending demise, DeWitt realized that, due to the constitutional order of succession, Wanter would run as the incumbent president in the next election if a new veep wasn't appointed prior to his death. That possibility made him even more nauseous than usual.

The president clicked off the TV and walked toward the bathroom. He opened the door and flipped on the light switch. And there it was again, the cramping pain in his lower gut that caused him to double over, holding on to the counter for support.

He managed to untie his bathrobe, hang it on a hook, lower his boxers, and seat himself on the toilet. The cramping eased, but only a little, as he released his bowels. The smell was worse than usual — a heavy, oily, sick smell. It reminded him of the stench that lingered in the halls of even the cleanest nursing home. It was the reek of imminent death, and DeWitt knew it. He knew what he would find when he looked in the bowl — more of the dark, coffee-ground matter.

He wouldn't be able to conceal his condition much longer. He was already experiencing weight loss — ten pounds in the last three weeks. He was not a large man to begin with, and he knew he would soon take on the skeletal appearance of the terminal cancer patient. Others would notice. They would urge him to seek medical treatment. Then the secret would be out, and forget any hope of getting a vice president approved. He would be the lamest of lame ducks.

DeWitt needed a vice president, and he needed one quickly.

4

In the history of the United States, eight presidents died before completing their terms. Eugene Walters was the first vice president to be afforded this distinction.

Apparently, the framers of the Constitution gave little thought to this eventuality, as they neglected to include a constitutional mechanism for replacing a vice president. When one resigned or was elevated into the presidency after a president's death, the job simply went unfilled until the next election. Then came the 25th Amendment, ratified on February 10, 1967. Under the amendment, a president could nominate a new vice president subject to the approval of both houses of Congress.

Only two presidents ever had the need to apply this provision. Richard Nixon used it in 1973, when he nominated a congressman from Michigan to replace Spiro Agnew, who had resigned after being charged with income tax irregularities. Ironically, the next president to invoke the amendment was that same Michigan congressman, who became president when Nixon fled the Oval Office a year later, in the face of imminent impeachment.

On both occasions, the events leading to vacancy of the vice presidency were well foreseen, giving the president time to consider prospective candidates.

President John DeWitt had no such luxury. Thus, on the day after the state funeral of Vice President Eugene Walters, who was buried with full honors at Arlington National Cemetery, the president met with his key advisers in the Oval Office to map strategy.

"Are we limiting the search to Democrats?" The question came from Jim Englund, the president's chief of staff.

"For the time being, yes," said the president, his mouth still open, as if he were going to continue the thought. He was interrupted by his press secretary.

"Shit, if we were going to pick a Republican, we may as well just leave the job open," said Bob Hamilton.

This was followed by a moment of silence as the president slowly turned his eyes, then his scowl, toward the source of the interruption. Hamilton looked around the room for any sign of support. Seeing that none, he smiled.

"Of course, it's your call, sir."

"How soon can we have a list of prospective candidates?" The question came from Secretary of State Bill Montgomery.

"Well, off the top of my head, I can think of three or four people who would rise to the top of just about any list," said the chief of staff. "You've got Rosen, Montana, Williamson and maybe Grieves." He named the Senate Minority Leader, the House Minority Leader, the Governor of New York and the Mayor of Chicago — in that order."

The president rubbed his temples, causing his bushy gray eyebrows to jiggle up and down. "Is there anyone here besides me who thinks the Republicans are going to rake us over the coals, no matter who we send up?"

There was general murmured agreement.

It was one of the strangest elections in recent history, giving the DeWitt/Walters ticket a landslide victory while simultaneously sweeping a goodly number of their fellow Democrats out of the House and Senate. As a result, for two years the Republicans had a veto-proof majority in both houses. They took the ball and ran with it; and in the next two years the GOP neutered or weakened most of the liberal social programs left over from Roosevelt's "New Deal," Kennedy's "New Frontier" and

Johnson's "Great Society."

Soon, however, the voters decided the Republicans were moving too far, too fast, and in the following election the imbalance was modified. At the beginning of his third year in the White House, DeWitt had to deal with a House that had a no-longer-veto-proof 259-179 Republican margin and a Senate that sported a Republican advantage of 55 to 45.

Yet, instead of accepting the conventional wisdom that most Americans saw them as too inflexible and aggressive, the Republicans in Congress chose to dig in their heels and fight on practically every issue. Even the most rational-sounding, non-controversial proposal from the DeWitt Administration was met with foot-dragging by Speaker Wantner.

"Gentlemen, if we were to nominate Jesus Christ Himself, Wantner would go on the air tomorrow and say it's a bad choice because Jesus wasn't born on American soil." The sentiment – greeted with chuckles and nods – came from Don Franklin, the late vice president's chief of staff. Franklin was the kind of individual who usually became the center of attention at any gathering. He was handsome, with an athletic physique, and had a glib, sometimes acerbic sense of humor.

"He wouldn't say anything negative about Jesus Himself, mind you," Franklin continued. "But Wantner would say the president was just submitting the Savior's name to cater to the Religious Right and cover up for his endorsement of abortion on demand, financial support of the United Nations, and open practice of witchcraft in the Lincoln Bedroom."

More murmured assent. More nodding.

"So, I raise the question. What do you all think of the possibility that the Republicans won't approve anyone we send?" Franklin looked around the room.

"Wouldn't they eventually have to agree to someone?" asked the Secretary of State.

"Why?" Franklin asked. "What's in it for them?"

"Well," said Montgomery, scratching his chin. "They'd have to accept someone eventually or be seen as dragging their feet, offering opposition only for the sake of opposition."

"And that's stopped them before?" Franklin asked.

"Point taken," Montgomery said.

"Duh!" added Franklin.

The remark earned a hard stare from Montgomery who, being from Georgia, still retained an ingrained speck of the old Southern dislike for uppity Negroes.

DeWitt turned toward Franklin. "You really think they could stall it out forever?"

"Not forever, but long enough."

"And how long would 'enough' be, Don?" Montgomery asked, curtly.

"Until our esteemed president runs for re-election or drops dead."

"Actually, I haven't decided on either of those options as of yet," the president said with a smile and a shake of his head.

Franklin smiled and turned toward the chief executive.

"Sir," he said, "you are the oldest man ever to be elected president. You're going to be 78 on your next birthday. Excuse me for being blunt, but look at it from the viewpoint of an insurance actuary. You've already outdone the average life expectancy. You could live another ten, fifteen, twenty years. Or you could wake up dead tomorrow morning, and none of our friends in the media would refer to it as an untimely death. This is a fact that is not lost on our Republican colleagues. If they stall, they are rolling the dice that you might just have a convenient little heart attack and, badda-bing! Wantner is president. Then they have it all their way — Republican majorities in both houses and the White House to boot. And it sets them up very nicely for a Wantner election in the next cycle."

DeWitt smiled, his hand under his chin as he rocked in his big, padded chair.

"Well, what if we come up with a nominee that no one could possibly have anything against?" the Secretary of State asked. "Someone so pure, so incorruptible, that the voters would beat the Republicans to death with sticks if they didn't immediately confirm!"

"I thought we already established that Jesus was not in the running," said Franklin.

"Seriously, Mr. President," Montgomery said, ignoring Franklin. "If we're going to be stalled anyway, what's to stop us from taking our time, doing a thorough search, and finding the absolutely perfect man or woman for the job? Someone with no further political aspirations, willing to fill in until the next election. Like what Nelson Rockefeller did for Gerald Ford."

"Considering the similarities between the deaths of Vice Presidents Rockefeller and Walters, I think that is a comparison we'd be well served to avoid," said Chief of Staff Englund.

"And besides, Diogenes, where are we going to find this 'honest man or woman'," asked the press secretary.

After a moment, the president broke the silence.

"I want a list of prospective nominees. No career politicians. No celebrities. I want a long list. We're going to take our time and really look. But I want a tentative list by the close of business Monday. Don, you're looking for a job these days, aren't you?"

"Yes sir, I am," Franklin replied.

"Good. You're in charge."

5

Clovis Plambeck commanded the largest radio talk show audience in the country. Yet he never forgot for a moment that he owed his success to the Republican National Committee.

Tall, skinny and gawky, with straw-colored hair, a long, thin nose, and a face pockmarked from the ravages of teenage acne, he was an unlikely person to have led the new Republican Revolution. He did not have the physical characteristics for filling liberal hearts with terror, for he resembled no one more than Washington Irving's unfortunate schoolteacher, Ichabod Crane, from "The Legend of Sleepy Hollow." This fact was hammered into Plambeck's psyche during his school days when, during ninth-grade English, one of the class thugs – a cheerleader named Connie Westerson – first made the connection. For the rest of his high school years, he was plagued with the nickname "Icky."

Plambeck looked back at his childhood years with the kind of nostalgia one usually reserves for a root canal. An only child, he was raised by an alcoholic mother. His father was one of 28 men killed in an oil refinery explosion a year after Clovis was born. Talk in the town was that the senior Plambeck had been responsible for the explosion. Plambeck's adolescent life in East Butler, Pennsylvania was a period of unrelenting pain and humiliation.

College wasn't much better. In his freshman and sophomore years at Penn State, he drifted from class to class with no real plan for his future. He spent his free time reading – mostly books on American history – alone in his dorm room. He was a social outcast, the quintessential "geek" and reluctant virgin.

In his junior year, things changed. An instructor in mass communications recognized something in the ungainly student. Though he was soft-spoken and painfully introverted, Plambeck's speaking voice was clear and well-modulated. The instructor made a point of joining Plambeck for lunch at the Student Union and learned that, when someone actually made the effort to engage him, his ideas were well-conceived and clearly presented.

Finding a mentor worked like a tonic. In his association with Professor Greg Mallinger, Clovis had finally found a friend and, father figure, someone to look up to and learn from. Where Plambeck's embryonic political views tended to take a scatter-gun approach to the political spectrum, Mallinger was a career conservative. Over a period of time, he was able to inure his young disciple into a steadier, standard, right-wing point of view.

Mallinger was able to overcome Plambeck's intrinsic shyness, convincing him to accept a part-time job at the student radio station. Plambeck's "Campus Chatter" call-in show was soon a remarkable success — especially for a low-wattage college FM station. People who heard Plambeck's mellow, resonant tones and then met him in person were shocked by the contrast of reality versus the mental portrait they had created for themselves.

Plambeck parlayed his college reputation into a part-time job at the local talk station in State College, PA, where his conservative viewpoints generated lots of agitated phone calls from the local liberal academia. No matter how vituperative the caller was, no matter how angry, upset or irate, Plambeck showed an amazing ability to stay calm, cool and unruffled. He had an uncanny knack for turning a caller's arguments against him, making the caller appear foolish and uninformed.

Soon, the number of liberal callers dwindled to almost nothing, only to be replaced by an equal and then larger number of conservatives who lauded Plambeck's clear view of the issues.

When Plambeck graduated from Penn State, he was immediately hired at a 50,000-watt AM powerhouse in Philadelphia, where "The Clovis Plambeck Show" quickly became a huge sensation.

His first brush with national attention came when the Philly police set fire to a minority residential area while trying to arrest members of a militant organization. Plambeck's program was a clearinghouse for angry whites who wouldn't have been upset to see the whole ghetto set aflame. Plambeck took the more reasonable view that the conflagration could have been avoided if only: a) the criminals had surrendered as they had been ordered; b) the police hadn't been stymied by the ill-conceived search-and-seizure roadblocks set up by ill-informed civil libertarians; and c) the members of the militant group hadn't been brainwashed by the victim mentality instilled in them since birth by their leaders and the left-leaning media.

Soon Plambeck's show was picked up on a statewide network of 15 stations. And program directors in New York, Washington, Boston and Baltimore were quick to add him to their afternoon lineups. By 1987, Clovis Plambeck's "Intellectual Enlightenment Broadcasting" network was being carried on almost 500 stations from Maine to California, not to mention Alaska, Hawaii, several Canadian outlets and a few short-wave translators for worldwide distribution.

None of this would have been possible without under-the-table financing from the Republican National Committee, especially in the early days. So, when someone from high up in the GOP structure dropped by his Philadelphia office to discuss policy, Plambeck was inclined to accept any suggestions that visitor might have about how to interpret the issues.

These days, the main issue was what to do about the vice presidential vacancy. Plambeck took a sip from his coffee and regarded his visitor — Jimmy Langston, chief administrative aide to the Speaker of the House. Plambeck didn't like Langston. But then, neither did anybody else.

Langston was an obnoxious, abrasive little man, profane even in mixed company, a man with dubious business connections, and bad personal hygiene. But he kept a relatively low profile. And he was the right-hand man of Al Wantner, a man who might soon be president of the United States.

Plambeck had no idea what Wantner saw in the little dirtball, but he was a man who must be catered to.

"We're still trying to find the Jap whore," Langston said. "But the little gooners are being tight-lipped about the whole thing."

Plambeck sighed and put his cup back on the desktop.

"Well, that's to be expected, Jim," he said patiently. "They don't like being embarrassed. It's the sort of thing they commit suicide over. It would not do for them to admit to using sex to sway American influence."

Langston sat back in his chair. "Tell ya what, Clove. I've seen some of those little honeys they got over there. And they could sway me any time they wanted to, know what I mean?"

Plambeck knew what he meant. Langston's mind never seemed to drift much farther than six inches from his zipper. He managed a smile.

"Well, then, the situation remains unchanged," said Plambeck. "Without any real proof that the Walters expired *in flagrante delicto*, the best I can do is to continue making allusions, the occasional double entendre, but not much more than that."

"Actually, Clove, we're ready to move beyond that," Langston said.

Plambeck had long since tired of reminding Langston that he hated the appellation "Clove" nearly as much as he did "Icky."

"I was against the whole idea of tacking the sex thing on Walters because, let's face it, the public doesn't give a rat's ass about who's fucking who," Langston said. "The whole Clinton thing proved that!

And besides, it looks like we're kicking a guy when he's dead."

Langston picked a piece of food from between his teeth, regarded it for a moment, then wiped it on his pants leg.

"So, what we do now is concentrate on the selection of the next vice president. Or shall I say, the non-selection." Langston grinned with dirty teeth.

"Is there anything new in that regard?" Plambeck asked.

"Not so's you'd notice. Conventional wisdom is that Montana will get the nod. But we've got enough material on that bastard to keep him tied up in the Judiciary Committee for months. Every vote, every speech, every campaign promise, all of it. He'll be asked, and he'll have to answer."

Langston leaned to his left and broke wind.

"Fucking chili," he groaned. "You might want to open a window, Clove."

Windows on the 35th floor of an office building generally don't open, so he let the matter go, folding his hands, discreetly, just below his nose.

"So, we're ready to take on Montana," Plambeck said. "But suppose DeWitt chooses someone else? Rumor has it that Rosen wants the job, too."

"Same thing," Langston said. "It just don't matter. Montana, Rosen, Governor Dickie Williamson or Hizzoner the Mayor Garland Fucking Grieves. We got dirt on all of them. No matter who that fossil picks, same story. So, what we want you to do is just lay low on the veep shit for now. Go easy on the president, without going easy on him, if you know what I mean. Talk about how well he's handled the tragedy. Then keep talking about how tired he looks. Wonder out loud if the stress of the job might be getting to be too much for him. Say that there's plenty of opportunities to talk about the vice presidency, but now isn't the time. Let's just let the president have a few weeks to relax and take it easy, because, let's face it kids, he ain't getting any younger."

Plambeck jotted a few notes on a legal pad. "Sounds good. And when he does pick a candidate?"

"We hammer his ass!" Langston accentuated his point by leaning over and releasing another salvo. "Fuckin' guts are tearing me up. I've been farting like a shitmoose all damn day. Got any Maalox?"

***

Opening Monologue, Clovis Plambeck's nationally syndicated radio program, May 18.

>   Friends, in the next few days you're going to be hearing a lot of twaddle from the DeWitt White House about our current, so-called state of crisis.
>   Amid much weeping, wailing, gnashing of teeth and rending of garments, the president's hired hands will hit the Sunday morning "talking heads" circuit to tell you how vitally important it is to fill the vice presidential vacancy. "We need a vice president!" they'll shriek. "We need one right now!" Without actually coming out and saying it directly, they'll find some way to point to the president's advanced age. In some roundabout fashion, they'll get the point across — "The president ain't no spring chicken! He could topple over in his Cream of Wheat tomorrow morning. And that's why we need a new vice president. Right now! Immediately, if not sooner!"
>   Well, friends. While DeWitt's wranglers may be right on the money about their mentor's – shall we say – maturity, I submit with all my innate humility that this is all the more reason why Congress should thoroughly check out whoever the president nominates. A slow, careful, meticulous investigation into the background, character and morality of this person is made all the more necessary by the very real possibility that DeWitt could keel over before his term expires a year from next

30

January.

Not to wish anything unfortunate on the president, but one cannot quibble with the fact that he is, in fact, an old man. He was seventy-six when he took office. And, from the looks of things, the presidency has not exactly been his "fountain of youth." At recent appearances, DeWitt looks tired, weak, sometimes confused. It seems he is taking forever to recover from his recent gall bladder surgery.

Friends, there is no hurry to appoint a vice president! The framers of the Constitution were wise when they drafted the original order of succession to the presidency. If the unfortunate – but not unthinkable – should happen, the presidency would fall into the very capable hands of Speaker Wantner. And I submit that this country could do far worse than to have a president like Al Wantner.

And it usually has! Especially recently.

6

Congressman Roberto "Bob" Huerta fumbled for his car keys in the Capitol parking garage. Unlike most of his colleagues, Huerta still drove the same car he owned before taking office — a beat-up 1996 Plymouth Neon. It was the car he drove from his home town of Falfurrias, Texas after his election last November, the same car he drove back for the home visits that didn't come nearly often enough.

Huerta had never been one for visible signs of wealth, mostly because he'd never had any wealth to display. The few members of Congress who knew him thought of him as the least ostentatious person in Washington. His wife, Janelle, still lived in their modest two-bedroom home in Falfurrias, where she worked as a secretary in the Brooks County courthouse. Their son, Tommy, was a typical 16-year old — an average student, a good kid with a mouth that got just a little too smart sometimes.

Huerta had been sheriff for four years before being elected to Congress. Before that, he had been a deputy for 15 years. And before that, he had been a masked professional wrestler on the Rio Grande wrestling circuit. He had been known as "El Luchador Mysterio" — the Mysterious Wrestler. A blown knee tendon ended his grappling career, but his local fame and a high score on the civil service exam cinched the job with the sheriff's department.

When the county sheriff decided to retire, Huerta was the only candidate on the ballot to replace him. And when Zeb Collopy, the district's Democratic congressman, decided not to seek a 15th term,

Huerta was heartily endorsed by the local Democratic committee. Local folks predicted nothing but good things ahead for the unassuming, ruggedly handsome former wrestler. Yet, Huerta was beginning to doubt if he even wanted a second term.

In his former occupation, he was used to getting things done. As sheriff, he had been responsible for an anti-drug education program that relied heavily on finding counselors – "Mr. Mentors" – for many of the county's disadvantaged younger men. In just two years, the county saw a twenty percent decrease in the volume of youth-perpetrated crime. Huerta's cost-cutting management style was credited with reducing the sheriff's department budget nearly fifteen percent during his four years in office.

But this hornet's nest called Washington was different. He was amazed that anything ever got done at all. He knew it would be foolish to expect to breeze into town, six guns a-blazin', and clean out the bad guys, but the width and depth of the bureaucratic tangle baffled him.

Each initiative needed to be wrapped in a promise of political favors: I'll support you if you support me when I support him when he supports her. And even the best ideas were loudly shouted down if the other party proposed them. If you had no seniority, it was best if you didn't have all that much to say. You were to be a good follower, not a squeaky wheel.

This wasn't the way Huerta liked to conduct business. And he was too low on the totem pole to do anything about it. His opinion didn't count. He had to settle for being short-changed in speaking time on the House floor, as he had been just before the speaker announced the vice president's death. It was a fruitless experience, and he was getting tired of it.

Huerta keyed the ignition and eased his old Plymouth out of the garage. He had a small rented apartment on North Capitol Street, just a few miles away.

"Damn," Huerta said as he approached the bleak brownstone. Once again, there seemed to be no parking spaces on the street.

"That's what you get for working late," he scolded himself. "No parking. Now you gotta walk!"

"Yeah," he answered himself. "But first, I gotta find a place to park!"

He drove around the block a couple of times in the vain hope that someone, somewhere would pull out. No such luck. He headed back south on Capitol.

Three blocks later, he saw a space near the corner of Capitol and Florida Avenue. Not really a nice neighborhood, but then his apartment building wasn't exactly a Chamber of Commerce highlight. Besides, a parking space is a parking space.

He locked the car, pocketed the keys, and whispered a silent prayer that the car would still be there in the morning. He started walking north, anticipating his delicious TV dinner.

The few members of Congress who knew where he lived teased him about "slumming." No one knew the fact of the matter — this was as much as he could afford. In addition to paying the bills, maintaining a mortgage on his Texas home and paying for travel expenses out of his own pocket, much of Huerta's $154,700 annual salary was funneled into the "Mr. Mentor" program he founded in Falfurrias, a program that had been severely truncated by the budget cuts of the previous Congress.

He was a block away from his apartment when he heard a scream. He took a quick, scanning look at his surroundings. After 19 years in law enforcement, Huerta still had what they call "cop eyes" — the ability not just to see his surroundings, but to interpret them. The street was far from deserted; folks were ambling about. Others stood on corners or gathered in storefronts talking. But no one reacted to the scream, or the one that followed it seconds later. It came from a doorway in the building next to his apartment complex.

34

Huerta sprinted to the door and crouched low as he slowly pushed it open. Almost reflexively, he reached for the gun that would have been holstered at his side if he were still a sheriff.

Damn.

Then he heard the scream again. Closer. Above him. Up the stairs.

"Shut the fuck up, bitch, or I'll give you something to scream about." It was a thick, deep voice — followed by giggling as a second male voice said, "Damn, that's the same thing my daddy used to say before he'd give me a whuppin'! Except for the 'bitch' part."

There was another scream, cut off by a loud slap.

Huerta was near the top of the steps. He peered through the space at the bottom of a rickety wooden handrail. First he saw only feet. He eased up a little more and saw a man wearing an Oakland Raiders jacket and black jeans pressing a woman against a wall next to an apartment door. The man held the blade of a knife at her throat. The right side of the woman's face was starting to swell, apparently from the slap just delivered. Her eyes were wide, rolling in fear. The man's body pressed her against the wall. The hand that wasn't holding the knife was clamped over her mouth.

Another man, smaller, perhaps younger, stood about a yard away. He was also wearing a Raiders jacket. He was smiling, like he was watching something amusing on TV.

"Get her keys, man!" said the smaller one. "Get her keys, and we'll take her inside." He was almost wiggling with excitement.

"Hear that, mama?" the larger man said. "Give me the keys, and we'll all go inside. Nice and friendly. Maybe you could make us all a nice pot of coffee. After you're done sucking our dicks!"

The woman strained against the man's body, but he pressed her tighter. The younger man burst out in fresh laughter. "Coffee! She's gonna make us some motherfuckin' coffee! Man, that's some kinda shit!"

35

Huerta took stock of his surroundings. The landing was dimly lit. The trio was standing in the glow of a bare bulb next to the apartment door. He could probably get to the top unseen, if he did so slowly and quietly.

His heart was pounding. He hadn't felt this kind of adrenaline since his days as a deputy. Slowly, he eased out of his suit jacket, loosened his tie and undid the top button of his shirt. He crawled to the top of the steps and crouched in the shadows, facing the two men and their captive. They were about 20 feet away, and they hadn't seen him.

"C'mon, cunt!" The larger man pressed the tip of the knife into the soft flesh of the woman's throat, releasing a tiny stream of blood. "The fucking keys, and right fucking now!"

She fumbled in her purse and produced a keychain. A lucky rabbit's foot dangled from the fob. She held it out, her arm trembling and stiff. The younger man grabbed the keychain.

"Time for some fuckin'!" he chortled. "Some fuckin' and some coffee!" He jogged to the door and began searching for the right key.

A high-pitched scream came from the shadows, and both assailants jumped. The larger one lowered his knife in surprise. He saw a blur from the dark corner. The blur hit him at knee level, and the knife clattered to the linoleum.

"What the fuck?" said the younger one. The blur became a man who shot up from the floor and delivered a snappy kick to the older one's chin. He crumpled to the floor, unconscious. The woman remained frozen in place, her back to the wall, screaming afresh.

"Mother FUCK!" yelled the younger man, dashing for the stairway.

Huerta wheeled around just in time to see the young man reach the top of the steps. He was halfway down when Huerta got to the top. He was almost to the door when Huerta sprang from the bottom third of the stairway (feeling a long-retired hamstring in his left leg pop as he did) and delivered a drop-kick to the man's shoulder blades, sending him through the glass door.

The young man lay bleeding on the sidewalk in front of the building. Then the police arrived. One cop cuffed the bleeding thug while another raced through the shattered door, his service pistol drawn and pointed at Huerta.

"FREEZE!" the cop shouted. "DON'T YOU FUCKING MOVE!" Huerta smiled and raised his hands above his head.

Good, he thought. *Someone did call the cops.*

"Down on your knees, slowly," the cop ordered. Huerta complied. He knew the drill. "Now, flat on your stomach, arms out at your side." Huerta did as commanded. More police were arriving on the scene. The cop knelt on Huerta's neck and pulled his right arm, then his left arm behind his back, cuffing his wrists together.

"NOT HIM!" The woman screamed from the top of the steps. A policeman who had just come into the hallway pointed his weapon at her. The woman's dress was in a state of disarray. Her swollen face was starting to bruise. Her lower lip was bleeding from the corners of her mouth.

"NOT HIM!" she shouted again. "He helped me! There's one more up here!"

The cop who cuffed Huerta bolted up the steps, pushing the woman aside as he did. Huerta lay on his belly on the dirty carpet. His left leg ached and throbbed. He fought the urge to sneeze.

"Hey, up here!" the cop yelled. Two of the officers working the front of the building eased through the shattered door and ran up the steps.

Huerta could hear the upstairs thug moaning as the police cuffed him. He could also hear the woman imploring the police officers to release the man who had, in all likelihood, saved her life.

One of the cops retrieved Huerta's wallet from his back pocket and withdrew a laminated card that identified him as a Member of Congress.

The cuffs came off.

"Pretty brave thing you did, congressman," said one of the cops, though the look on his face implied "stupid" instead of "brave."

The woman was taken away by ambulance before Huerta could even find out her name. A policeman escorted Huerta to his apartment door. Before leaving, he shook Huerta's hand.

7

Don Franklin wasn't surprised by the president's decision not to offer the vice presidency to Senator Rosen or Congressman Montana. Above all virtues, DeWitt prized loyalty. During the campaign, he had offered the number-two spot to each of them. Rosen, the oily senator from Ohio, told his closest friends that he didn't think a nice old fella like John DeWitt had a fart's chance in a wind tunnel of getting elected president. He respectfully declined, saying he could be more help to the party as Senate Majority Leader (a position that, unbeknownst to him, he'd soon vacate when the Republican took over majority status the following January).

Montana turned down a face-to-face offer from DeWitt for the same reason — substitute the words "Speaker of the House" for "Senate Majority Leader" and you've got the picture.

Franklin was the only one of the president's close advisors to agree with this decision. He also had a thing about loyalty. Donald William Franklin was a risk-taker, but when he put his money on a pony, that money stayed put. He learned the importance of loyalty during the dark days of the civil rights struggle — or, conversely, how divisive a lack of loyalty can be.

His first job out of college was as an assistant to an aide of Dr. Martin Luther King, Jr. He was working in that fatal motel room in Memphis – on the phone, checking schedules – when the shot rang out. If the borders of the photo could be expanded, one would see a shocked Don Franklin standing at the sliding glass door, staring at the fallen leader while the others pointed in the direction of the shooter.

The bullet that killed Dr. King did not end "the movement," but it did have the effect of splintering the leadership. Some of King's followers took up the banner of Dr. Ralph Abernathy, while others eventually enrolled in the "Rainbow Coalition" of the Rev. Jesse Jackson. A movement that once had such a clear, directed purpose now appeared to be a fractious, unfocused gaggle of special interest groups that spent more time squabbling over minutiae and injured egos than working toward the betterment of those they professed to help.

Disgusted by it all, Franklin chose his own path, deciding to work within the system that his former mentors were striving to change from the outside. Notches on his resume included campaign work for George McGovern in 1972, coordinator of voter registration drives in Mississippi and Georgia, a staff position on the presidential campaign of Georgia Governor Jimmy Carter, then a four-year tenure as an aide to United Nations Representative Andrew Young.

During the twelve-year Reagan/Bush era, pickings were slim. He spent much of that time as a hired gun, doing odd jobs for various functionaries in the Democratic National Committee. He performed with such adeptness that he was eventually appointed chief administrative assistant to the Chairman of the Democratic National Committee. There he was instrumental in convincing Iowa Governor Eugene Walters to be John DeWitt's running mate.

Walters was so impressed by Franklin's abilities and resume that he hired the only son of a Chicago shoe repairman to be his chief of staff.

It was a job that Franklin took to with relish. It meant travel (there was always a foreign head of state dying somewhere). It meant political wheeling and dealing without the glare of the spotlight. Unless a vice president gets caught making campaign fundraising calls from the White House, occupants of that post are usually pretty free to come and go, to do as they please without having to answer a lot of questions.

He loved the job.

Now he was 54, with telling streaks of gray in his thick, closely cropped hair. And he was helping to replace a man with whom, just days before, he had been sitting, naked, drinking sake in a Japanese steam bath.

He had about 25 or so files in front of him — most of the top Democratic guns in the House and Senate, as well as a governor or two, an occasional mayor, and some career diplomats. Given the president's popularity, getting someone to say "yes" to the job didn't seem like much of a problem. But coming up with a nominee the constipated GOP assholes would approve? That was a different matter entirely. Donald Franklin didn't like his chances.

Exhaling in a long, whistling sigh, Franklin looked at his watch. Then he smiled. It was almost 11:30 p.m. No more work tonight. Time for Letterman.

8

Huerta spent the remainder of that weekend either in bed or on the couch, much of the time with a bag of ice wrapped to his left thigh. He did not read the newspaper, and he watched only sports or old movies. Saturday morning, when the phone started ringing non-stop, he unplugged it, and only plugged it back in to call his wife, Janelle. When he told her what had happened, she scolded him for being reckless. Then she praised his bravery. Even their son Tommy, who reacted to the most phenomenal events with a nonplussed "Cool," seemed marginally impressed.

On Monday morning, the congressman limped several blocks to where his car was parked. A parking ticket poked up from the windshield wiper, waving in the early morning breeze. There wasn't a parking meter on the block. But there was a sign stating that cars parked longer than 24 hours in one spot would be ticketed.

In the rush hour traffic, it took about a half-hour to get to the Capitol parking garage. Huerta limped into the Capitol and through the hallways to his dingy office.

When he opened the office door, he recoiled from a loud, booming voice.

"L...L...L...LET'S GET READY TO RUMBAAAAAALLLL!!!!"

The recorded voice of ring announcer Michael Buffer boomed from the desktop tape recorder. The entire staff was on hand, all six of them, standing and applauding.

"Way to go, champ!" said Michelle Riolas, his chief of staff. "You so baaad!" She jabbed playfully at his chin.

"What the hell are you talking about?" Huerta asked, knowing full well the answer. Riolas held up a copy of the Post's Saturday Metro section. Huerta took it and started reading.

Congressman Foils Rape/robbery Attempt

Congressman Roberto Huerta (D-TX) was credited by Washington Police with foiling an attempted rape and robbery near the congressman's North Capitol Street apartment last night.

According to police reports, Huerta was returning to his apartment when he heard a woman scream. Upon further investigation, Huerta saw a woman allegedly being assaulted by two men, identified as Jessie Cleveland, 32, and Bobby Sanders, 25, both of Washington. Both men have been charged with aggravated assault and are in the District of Columbia Jail in lieu of a $100,000 bond each.

Huerta, who served as a county sheriff before being elected to congress last year, rescued the unidentified woman by attacking her alleged assailants, rendering both unconscious, according to police reports. The intended victim suffered only superficial injuries.

Huerta has declined comment regarding the incident.

"Congressman foils rape/robbery attempt!" Riolas trumpeted. "You so damn baaad!"

"Cut the crap, Michelle." Huerta put the paper back on the reception desk. He limped from the cramped outer office into his cramped inner office. Riolas followed.

"Mess up a wheel, did ya?"

"Yeah," he said. "Pulled a hamstring. Not as young as I used to be."

As usual, Riolas was dressed to the nines: red wool dress (attractive, but all business), her dark hair streaked with silver over the right temple. Her face looked younger than her 52 years, and this morning, it shone with pride.

"Hey," she said. "In all seriousness. That was a really great thing you did, Bob. That woman is alive today, thanks to you."

Huerta grimaced as he eased himself into his chair. "C'mon, Michelle. It's no big deal."

"My sweet ass, it's no big deal," she said. "This is gonna get you some notice around here, tough guy!"

Huerta flipped open his appointment book. "What kind of notice, Michelle? You think some of the bigger, tougher congressmen are gonna call me out? Try to pick a fight? Or even worse... a senator?"

Riolas rolled her dark eyes in exasperation. She rose from the chair and stalked to the outer office. Huerta turned his attention to the appointment book. Then Riolas breezed back in and set a stack of "While You Were Out" messages on his desk.

"This kind of notice, smart-ass."

She rifled through the phone messages. "'Meet the Press' wants you for next Sunday. So does 'Face the Nation'. Let's see what else — Larry King, 'Firing Line,' and, oh! Letterman wants you!"

"Fine," Huerta said, not quite believing it. "I can go on and do 'Stupid Congressman Tricks'!"

Riolas sat on the corner chair. "Bob, I worked for Zeb Collopy for the last ten years of his career. I know this place. I know the people who work here. And I know that this is big! Like it or not, Bubba, you're gonna be a star!"

***

In the end, Huerta opted for the Letterman show. Since the whole damn thing was more or less a joke, why not go on a comedy show?

The acerbic Letterman was unusually kind and deferential.

"So let me get this straight," he said. "You're walking to your apartment. May I ask, isn't that a rather crappy part of town for a congressman to call home?"

"Well, Dave," Huerta said, "I don't call it home. Home is in Falfurrias, Texas. I just live in Washington because it's close to where I work. And yes, it is a rather run-down neighborhood. But maybe more people in government should live in areas like this. Give them a little perspective."

The audience gave Huerta a rousing ovation. Letterman beamed.

"So, what was going through your mind when you saw these two thugs?"

"Well, just that someone had to do something, and I was the only one there."

"So you reverted to your old pro wrestling days and kicked ass?"

"Not quite," Huerta said. "Back then, I was in better shape."

"Well, we had to do some digging to find this clip," Letterman said. Knowing what was coming next, Huerta grimaced. "But we found some film of you back in your wrestling days." He motioned to the director. "Roll it!"

The clip showed Huerta in his black and red "El Luchador Mysterio" costume, complete with mask and cape. He stood on the top turnbuckle and leaped, landing with the point of his elbow on the ribs of a fat, hairy wrestler known as "El Oso del Diablo" ("The Devil's Bear").

When the clip ended, Letterman turned to Huerta. "Is that the kind of stuff you dished out to these punks?"

"A little less theatrical, but yeah, basically the same." He could feel himself blushing. "Except for the costume."

"This is what we need in Washington," Letterman shouted to the audience. "A congressman who kicks ass and takes names!"

"No, Dave," Huerta said. "If I can be serious for a moment, what we need are more people who are willing to take some sort of responsibility for the well-being of their fellow citizens. We need to study the root causes of crime, not just punish the criminals. We need a government that is less concerned about making sure the fat cats can squeeze an extra dollar of profit out of the bottom line and is more concerned about eliminating the causes of crime: poverty, social injustice and substandard education. Excuse me for preaching, but it just seems to me that we're more interested in punishing the bad guys today than we are in making sure they don't become bad guys in the first place. If those kids had been raised to think that there was any hope for them, if someone had taken a serious, positive interest in them when they were younger, then I would probably have been shaking their hands instead of having to, well, kick their asses."

There was an unsettling moment of silence. Huerta mentally chided himself for being so damn preachy. Suddenly the audience erupted into a standing ovation. During the uproar, Letterman leaned over and whispered, "What did you say was the name of the town your from?"

For the next two years, Letterman's mythical "Home Office" was located in Falfurrias, Texas.

***

At the end of the Huerta segment, Don Franklin clicked off the television and sat alone in his darkened living room, his ebony face illuminated by the glowing red tip of a fine (albeit contraband) Cuban cigar.

"Helloooooo, Mr. Vice President," he whispered, to no one in particular.

***

Over the next several days, Huerta turned down dozens of requests for interviews. But that didn't stop the media from running with the story, embellishing with opinion and conjecture whatever they couldn't confirm with facts.

The TV tabloid shows jumped on the story like a duck on a June bug. Since there were no video cameras at the scene of the crime, most utilized graphic "re-creations," with actors portraying the congressman, the victim, and the two hoodlums. One of the sleazier shows incurred the wrath of the African-American community by portraying both assailants as young black men when, in fact, only one of the youths was black.

"Extra" called Huerta "the feisty Hero on the Hill." "American Journal" said the congressman was "a shy lawmaker by day, a bold jawbreaker by night." All utilized the same pro wrestling footage as Letterman.

Although Huerta refused to appear on any further talk shows, Amber Nicholson – the woman he rescued – was more than happy to comply. She appeared over and over on television touting, Bob Huerta as her hero, describing in graphic detail her rescue in that dark hallway.

In the span of several days, a new pop culture icon was born.

9

Huerta's chief of staff was going over the day's scant appointment schedule when Franklin breezed into the office. He paid little heed to the office staff, other than a smile, a wave and a wink to Riolas, and headed right for the inner office door. Riolas jumped from her chair, positioning herself in front of the door.

"May I help you?" she asked with a cold smile.

"Yes," Franklin said. "I'm here to see Congressman Huerta."

"Do you have an appointment?"

"I sure do. It's with my dentist, in about an hour. So you'd better let me in to see the congressman or I'm going to be late."

He made an effort to get around her, but she wouldn't budge.

"Ma'am, I have to get in to see the congressman. If I'm late for the dentist, he gets grumpy and skimps on the Novocain..."

"Sir, unless you have an appointment, with the congressman..."

Huerta stepped from his office. Franklin brushed past Riolas, walked over and extended his right hand. Huerta did not take it.

"Hi there, Congressman! Got a minute?" He kept his hand extended.

"Do I know you?" Huerta asked. He reluctantly took his hand. "Are you a reporter?"

Franklin reached into his coat pocket and pulled out a business card. "That's what you get when you work for the vice president," he said over his shoulder to Riolas. "Nobody knows who the hell you are."

Riolas grunted as if to indicate she couldn't care less.

Huerta studied the card then looked at its owner.

"I'm sorry, Mr. Franklin. And I'm very sorry for what happened to him." This time, Huerta extended his hand. Franklin shook it heartily.

"We're all sorry," Franklin said. "But like I said, got a minute?"

Huerta looked at his watch. "Just a few. I'm due at a committee meeting. It's one of those meetings where I sit there and do nothing and keep my mouth shut because it's only my first term. So I'd better not be late."

He smiled. Franklin was impressed by the warmth that radiated from that smile.

"You know, I don't think we pay you boys enough," Franklin said, following Huerta into his office.

When both men were seated, Franklin didn't waste any time. "I know you're tired of hearing this, but that was a helluva thing you did Friday night."

"That's what they say," Huerta replied. "I'm starting to wish that there had been an open parking space in front of my apartment building."

"You don't mean that," Franklin said. "Because if there had been an open parking space in front of your apartment building, then that woman would have been raped and killed."

"Someone else might have helped her."

"You don't know that."

"No, but I hope so," Huerta said.

"Hope is a wonderful thing, but it don't feed the bulldog. But hope can motivate. Isn't that basically what you said on Letterman the other night?"

"I don't think I expressed it quite that colorfully, but you got the gist of it."

"Do you think there's enough hope out there, Mr. Huerta?"

"Can there ever be enough?"

"Hmm..." Franklin grinned. "Everything in your bio sheet – the wrestling, the law enforcement – all true?"

"Of course," Huerta said.

"Married — wife's name, Janelle. One child, a sixteen-year old named Tommy?"

"Also true."

"Anything bad out there? Anything that would be embarrassing if someone really went looking?"

"Not that I can think of."

"Finally, you are forty-six years old and were born a citizen on U.S. soil?"

Huerta stood and began walking to the door. He put out an arm as if to escort his visitor to the outer office.

"Yes. And yes. And I have to be going. If you'd like more time, please talk to my chief of staff. Set up an appointment, and I'll be able to devote my full attention..."

"Gladly," Franklin said, smiling at Huerta's aide. She did not return the smile. "Actually, I don't need another appointment. But I will call again in a few days, if that's all right?"

Huerta was already limping down the hallway, his strained hamstring still smarting.

"Fine. Whatever."

"Whatever, indeed," Franklin said, under his breath. Then he turned to Riolas, who stood in the doorway, hands on hips.

***

A half-hour later, Franklin was ushered into the Oval Office.

President DeWitt reclined in his office chair, eyes closed. He was breathing deeply and slowly. Franklin thought he might be sleeping.

"Sir?"

"Yes?" The president's eyes stayed closed.

"Mr. President, is this a good time?"

"It never is." He sat up and focused on Franklin. "What?"

"Are you ready to discuss a potential vice presidential nominee?"

"What do you mean 'a' nominee? I thought I ordered a long list."

Franklin sat across from the president's desk. "Honestly, sir, I could give you a list from here to Philadelphia and no name on that list would have as much of a chance for confirmation as the one name I have."

DeWitt stared at Franklin. Then he smiled.

"And am I supposed to guess who it is we're talking about?"

Franklin returned the smile. "Sir, do you watch Letterman?"

"Nope. Always been a Leno man. Before him, Carson. Before him, Paar. Didn't much care for Steve Allen, though. Too much of a smart-aleck. Why?"

"Then, did you see a blurb in the Post last weekend about a congressman who foiled a rape attempt?"

"I think I heard something about it. Is that your man?"

"Yes sir, and I'll tell you why." Franklin eased a portfolio containing facts about Huerta's background onto the desktop. "The man's made to order. For one thing, he's squeaky clean. I've already run two separate background examinations on him, and he doesn't have so much as a jaywalking ticket. Married to the same woman for 26 years. One kid, a sixteen-year-old named Tommy. No evidence of philandering. A long history of public service. Four years as a county sheriff, fifteen years as a deputy. And before that, about five years on the Mexican pro wrestling circuit as a 'good guy' wrestler."

"And that makes him your top choice — your only choice? Frankly, my dear Donald, I'm skeptical."

Franklin was ready for just such a response.

"Everybody's skeptical, Mr. President. And that's part of the problem. That's why the GOP thinks they'll be able to pull off this little delay gambit. They know that you can pick whoever you want, they can delay it for as long as they want, and the American public will probably not give two farts in a hurricane one way or the other. The GOP leadership is likely expecting you to nominate someone like Montana or Rosen. Hell, they're probably salivating at the prospect. There's nothing they'd like better than to get either one of those wonks in front of an unfriendly committee. What a great opportunity, on live TV, to tie one of our top Democratic legislators to the public pillory for a good old-fashioned horse-whipping. If you send someone like Governor Williamson, then the committee will focus on crime in New York, the governor's liberal policies, all the while painting an unflattering portrait of your own legacy. Pick Mayor Grieves, same deal, substitute Chicago."

DeWitt exhaled slowly. "And how does this," he looked at the name on the portfolio, "this Roberto Huerta measure up any differently?"

Again, Franklin was ready with an answer.

"Mr. President, by this time next week, Bob Huerta will be a household name in the great American hinterlands. I've gotten wind that Time Magazine is going to do a cover piece on him. The other news weeklies will follow suit. He's already been plastered all over the networks. He looks good on TV. He comes across like a regular guy. And he has a good message. What's more, he's a hero! He saved a woman's life! And he did it by kicking the shit out of two guys who were going to rape and kill her. America will eat that up with a big old wooden spoon! And if we put the right kind of pressure where it belongs, the Republicans will look like Grade-A assholes if they fight to keep him out of office!"

"What about his lack of government experience?"

"Hey, the guy's a congressman," Franklin protested.

"Yeah, but not even for a year. He's still a rookie."

"So, we turn that around. We say that this country already has a lot of politicians with a lot of political experience, and look what a mess we're in! We say that this county needs a new perspective, someone who isn't part of the problem, someone who might still be so unspoiled by the taint of power that he could come up with solutions."

Franklin smiled.

"No offense to your former profession, Mr. President, but if I had a kid and he said 'Dad, I wanna be a lawyer when I grow up,' I'd be thinking of a way to end his life as painlessly as possible while his immortal soul could still get into heaven."

DeWitt eased back in his chair. A wave of pain rolled through his abdomen. Franklin noticed the change in the president's expression.

"Sir, are you all right?"

"It's just gas," DeWitt said. "Too much spicy food."

The president waited for the cramping to subside and hoped he wasn't going to foul his pants. A few moments later, the worst of it passed.

"The man's name is Huerta? Hispanic?"

"Yes."

"Won't that cause some trouble with the racists in our midst?"

"Racists tend to shut up when you call them racists," Franklin said. "They're the least of our problems. Even racists want to be reelected."

"This Huerta. Does he know what you're up to?"

"Not a clue. And I think that if he did know, he might've punched me in the mouth when I barged into his office."

DeWitt picked up the portfolio.

"I'll look through this. Go see him. Tell him to be here tomorrow morning at eleven. I'll bring the Secretary of State and my chief of staff in on this." DeWitt leaned back in his chair and folded his hands under his chin."

"Yes, sir, Mr. President." Franklin smiled. "In fact, if you're interested in doing something tomorrow afternoon, I saw a brief item in the Post this morning saying that the District's CrimeStoppers League is throwing a little award presentation for the congressman in his office at 2. Maybe you and Englund could swing by and say some nice things about what a brave guy he is and all that. Should be some cameras there."

"Fine," DeWitt said, tiredly. "On your way out, tell Gina to set it up with the Secret Service."

Franklin got up to leave. "Thank you, Mr. President."

When Franklin was out of the office, DeWitt paged his secretary. "Gina, call Secretary Montgomery and Jim Englund. Tell Englund to come here as soon as he can. Tell Montgomery to be here tomorrow morning at ten. Thank you."

Another wave of pain crossed his belly. He got out of his chair and walked as quickly as he could toward his private bathroom.

10

"You're gonna love this, hero." Michelle Riolas leaned in through the office door. "Remember that crime fighters group that wants to give you a certificate?"

Huerta looked up from his desk. Things were just beginning to return to normal in his little corner of the Capitol, when a group of local citizens decided to give him their annual "Hero of the Streets" award.

"Yes, Michelle. I remember," he said curtly.

"Ooooh! Aren't we the Grumpy Gus?" Riolas said, smiling. "Well, this should improve your mood. I just got a call from the White House. The president is gonna drop by and shake your muscular, heroic hand."

Huerta stared at his assistant for a moment, then looked down at his desktop and slowly shook his head.

"This thing ain't ever going away," he muttered.

"The world loves a hero," said Riolas. "And everyone loves having their picture taken with one. Even the president."

***

Huerta couldn't shake the feeling of surreality. The little group of community crime fighters couldn't take their eyes off the president. Their leader – a tiny, withered, black lady – shook noticeably as she handed a gilded, framed certificate to Huerta. The group of citizens, none of whom seemed to be under the age of 70, were completely awestruck in the presence of President DeWitt.

The president grasped Huerta's hand and turned toward the cameras.

"I would like to thank the District of Columbia's Crimestoppers League for honoring Congressman Huerta," he said, smiling. "And I hope that the congressman's actions, at the risk of his own life, will prove to be an example for all of us. If we will all fight crime, one person at a time, then we will find ourselves living in a safer world."

The president smiled and waved. The community members stood and stared. Huerta didn't know what to do with his hands, so he smiled and waved too.

DeWitt turned to Huerta and spoke quietly. "Congressman, why don't we duck into your office a moment and chat?"

"Of course, Mr. President," said Huerta, somewhat flummoxed. He pointed to the door. "This way."

Huerta held the door open while DeWitt, Franklin, Englund and two Secret Service agents entered his inner sanctum. The cameras continued clicking and flashing as Riolas announced that the party was over.

Huerta closed the door and surveyed the situation. The president was seated on the couch across from the desk, with Englund standing to his left. One Secret Service agent stood at the end of the couch, the other near the door. Franklin sat on the coffee table. The president motioned toward Huerta's desk.

"Please, Congressman. Have a seat. Relax."

Huerta went to his desk and sat. But he couldn't relax.

"Mr. President, I can't begin to tell you what a distinct honor it is to have you in my office," Huerta said.

"You are most kind, Congressman Huerta. And it is an honor to meet someone in Washington who has actually done something for the people. Your constituents are lucky to have you."

Huerta didn't know how to respond, so he just smiled and blushed.

"I hope you'll forgive my intrusion," said the president. "But it isn't very often these days that I get a chance to direct the nation's attention to

56

something so positive. I wanted to use your heroism to demonstrate to the public that there are still people who place a high value on honor."

Huerta shook his head. "Sir, I thank you for your kindness, but I just did what every former law enforcement officer would have done.

"Or former pro wrestler," Franklin added, smiling. Huerta winced.

"I believe you are the first professional wrestler I've ever met," the president said. "Did you ever wrestle Jesse Ventura?"

"Uh, no sir. I never got beyond the minor leagues. Just the high school gyms and little civic auditoriums along the Rio Grande."

The president regarded his host with a smile.

"Mr. Franklin told me what happened in that apartment house hallway. He also told me you have been consistently trying to downplay it. Now I've seen it for myself. Mind if I ask why?"

Huerta shifted in his seat. "Well, Mr. President, maybe it's because the whole thing was just so sudden, so spur-of-the-moment. Again, I just did what most people would have done. It shouldn't become extraordinary just because I'm a member of Congress.'"

"It is extraordinary, regardless," said the president's chief of staff. "And I think you know that, Mr. Huerta. You've been in Congress for several months now. How many congressmen have you met who would do what you did last Friday?"

"I don't know, Mr. Englund," Huerta replied. "I'd like to think that most people would…"

"Congressmen aren't most people," Franklin butted in. "And most congressmen wouldn't piss on their own grandmothers if they were on fire — unless the cameras were rolling. And first they'd check their polling data to see how the voters felt about using urine to extinguish a burning relative."

"That's a very cynical view, Mr. Franklin," said Huerta.

"Washington makes one cynical, Mr. Huerta," Englund said. "Maybe you haven't been here long enough to notice, but, at the risk of sounding pontifical..."

"Oh, risk! Risk!" Franklin said.

"Thank you, Donald. I believe I shall. At any rate, I think a lot of folks enter government service with the thought of doing good. But they get so worn down by the process that every day they care just a little less than the day before. You've seen 'Mr. Smith Goes to Washington'?"

"I've never been much of a Capra fan," Huerta said.

"Nevertheless, the point is valid," the president said. "Too many of us are only concerned with covering our own keisters. Doing right falls second to getting re-elected. And that cynicism is contagious. Fewer and fewer folks bother going to the polls because they don't think it matters who they vote for. They think we're all crooks."

"And for the most part, they're right," said Franklin. After a moment's silence, he added, "Present company excepted, of course."

"Of course," the president allowed, with a wry smile.

"But you, Mr. Huerta, are something special," said Englund. "And the fact that you choose to deny it makes you even more special."

"You are a rare commodity indeed," added Franklin. "A publicity-shy politician."

"Mr. Huerta, most people in your position would chew off the foot of their choice, right at the ankle, if it would get them the kind of positive publicity your single act of selfless citizenship has garnered," said the president. "Time calls you the 'Crime Fighting Congressman.' US News and World Report says you are 'a throwback to the days when the words public service were taken seriously.' And it goes on and on."

"And don't think the rest of the denizens of Capitol Hill aren't taking note," Englund said. "You've started a trend, Congressman Huerta! As the next congressional election approaches, no doubt we'll be seeing congressmen and senators walking little old ladies across the street and heading up neighborhood watch patrols."

"The publicity is there, whether you like it or not," Franklin said, leaning toward Huerta. "The question is – what are you going to do with it?"

All eyes in the room were on the first-term congressman from Falfurrias, Texas. The pressure was on. He was being worked and he knew it. He just didn't know why.

"What can I do with it?" he asked. "I'm a junior member on an irrelevant congressional committee. And I don't even think I'm going to run again next year."

"Why not?" asked the president.

"Because nothing ever gets done!" Huerta was startled by the force of his reply. He tried to tone it down a little.

"When I was in law enforcement, I saw results — every day! Almost everything I did had a direct effect on someone. But this, this Congress! This Government!"

He gestured around the office.

"With all due respect, Mr. President, the process of government in this country is so constipated it would take a truckload of Ex-lax and a ton of dynamite to bust it loose! A good idea can't survive, can't make its way to the floor for consideration, unless it gets the support of someone senior, and then that someone wants to get his back scratched by someone else whose back you have to scratch before he'll scratch the other guy's back, and if you belong to the minority party, well, then you should just forget having any kind of good idea in the first place. To put it plainly, Mr. President, and please forgive my language, but it's a clusterfuck of the highest magnitude!"

The president leaned back in his chair and laughed out loud. "Mr. Franklin, your Boy Scout swears like a whiskey peddler!"

Huerta felt his cheeks redden with embarrassment — and a touch of something like anger. DeWitt seemed to sense Huerta's discomfort. He put on a serious expression and leaned toward the congressman.

"Well, thank you for letting us share some of your afternoon," he said. "We'll let you get back to your work." He stood – somewhat shakily, Huerta noticed – and started toward the office door. "Just keep something in the back of your mind, Mr. Huerta. You might be a junior congressman. But don't let that stop you. Don't let it hold you back. Say what you have to say. Do what you have to do. You've been noticed. And if you play your cards right, you'll never be anonymous again."

He smiled, winked, and turned toward the door. The Secret Service agent held it open, and the presidential entourage departed while the media people Riolas had failed to flush from the outer office shouted questions and flashed cameras.

When everyone was gone and the area had returned to a state of quiet, Riolas entered Huerta's office. She found the congressman sitting at his desk, staring at the wall.

"So?" she asked. "What happened?"

Huerta shrugged. "Damned if I know. Just sort of a 'rah-rah' talk, I guess. I shot off my mouth a little more than I should have. But I don't think I did any real damage. Ya know, this may sound crazy, but I really think they might appoint me to something big."

"Like what?" Riolas asked.

"Not sure," Huerta conceded. "They asked me a lot about wrestling. Maybe the Presidential Council on Fitness? It's hard to say."

"This is the Nation's Capital, Congressman. Anything's possible," Riolas said, smiling.

***

The limo ride back to 1600 Pennsylvania Avenue only took a few minutes. In that time, DeWitt sat with his hands folded under his chin, smiling. Englund was on the phone with the House Librarian, ordering transcripts of Huerta's voting record and speeches.

11

Excerpt from a May 24th *Time Magazine* article:

It's one of the oldest one-liners in the world: "I'm from the government. I'm here to help you." Yet when Congressman Roberto Huerta (D-TX) came to the aid of a young woman being assaulted, he wasn't acting in his official capacity as a member of Congress.

He was acting as a human being.

The 46-year old Huerta (who repeatedly refused *Time*'s request for an interview) was credited with possibly saving the life of Amber Nicholson, 26. She was being mugged by two assailants outside her Washington, DC apartment, when Huerta heard her screams and came to her rescue, disabling both of her attackers.

This came as no surprise to folks in Huerta's hometown, Falfurrias, Texas — a sleepy, depressed city in the southern section of the state.

"That's the sort of thing you'd expect from our boy Bobby," said Milton Anderson, owner of Anderson's Tack and Saddle. "He never was much of one to sit around and let things happen. He's always been sort of a 'take-charge' kind of guy."

Huerta was born in Falfurrias to Oscar and Maria Huerta. The father was killed in a ranch accident when young Huerta was only 3. The same fate befell a younger brother, Octavio, when Huerta was 25. A younger sister, Julia, died of pneumonia at the age of six months. Maria raised the children on her earnings as a laundromat worker and part-time waitress. She died in

1989 at the age of 60.

When Huerta graduated (with honors) from Falfurrias High School, there were no scholarships available for the young Hispanic man. He worked his way through four years at South Texas State as a professional wrestler on the Rio Grande circuit.

It was while working the high school gymnasiums and local civic centers that Huerta met his wife, the former Janelle Swenson. She was a waitress in a Corpus Christi restaurant that Huerta frequented during his visits to that city. They were married on the six-month anniversary of the day they met. Their only child, Tommy, didn't come along for nearly ten years.

No wonder, considering how busy the young Huerta was — then and now.

"We used to love it when the wrestlers came to town," said Rodrigo Sanchez, a local ranch hand. "If 'El Luchador Mysterio' (Huerta's wrestling persona) was on the bill, you could always count on filling up the high school gym. He was a skilled performer, one of those high-flyer types."

It was that high-flying style that cost Huerta any hopes of a career in pro wrestling. A torn anterior cruciate ligament ended his pursuit of championship gold.

Following reconstructive surgery, Huerta was hired as a deputy in the county sheriff's department. After 15 years on the force, he was elected sheriff.

"He had a knack for law enforcement," said Rick Engleman, 76, whose retirement from the department created the vacancy Huerta filled. "A real community policeman is what he was. He took no guff, but he wasn't a tin dictator, either, like so many small-town cops can be. He had a real skill for dealing with people, getting to the roots of their problems, helping them reach solutions."

During his four years as sheriff, Huerta instituted several programs to deal with the county's burgeoning gang problem. One – the "Mr. Mentor" program – was acknowledged by the governor as "a progressive solution to the scourge of criminal gangs." Huerta's program enlisted the help of area businessmen and workers. They identified high school aged boys who seemed ready to take part in gang activities and paired them off on a voluntary basis with gainfully employed adults.

"It really helped me see that the gang wasn't the only place I could go to get some acceptance," said Luis Gonzales, a 22-year old factory worker. "It showed me that hard work has rewards. He made me feel good about myself."

Duty called again when Congressman Zeb Collopy announced he would not seek another term in office after more than 30 years in Congress. The local Democratic Committee drafted a reluctant Huerta as its candidate, and he ran unopposed.

"He wanted no part of it at first," said Isabella Ruiz, the county's Democratic chairperson. "He just wanted to continue on as sheriff. But we eventually convinced him that Congress needed a man of honor like Roberto Huerta, and he reluctantly agreed to run."

Since a recent appearance on the David Letterman show, Huerta has refused to discuss the events that occurred in that dark Washington apartment building hallway. But Michelle Riolas, the congressman's chief of staff, did issue this statement:

> "What the congressman did was what any responsible citizen would have done, no more and no less. The congressman is glad that the young woman wasn't severely injured and that her alleged assailants are in custody. Other than that, he is concentrating on his duties in the House of Representatives and will have no further comment."

12

Riolas looked up from her stack of correspondence and saw the man standing in the doorway. She was immediately annoyed beyond description.

"Hi there. Me again!"

Don Franklin smiled broadly, waved a cheerful "howdy," and extended a bouquet of flowers.

The annoyed look melted from her face. "Such lovely flowers," Riolas purred, smiling, as she walked to the doorway.

She took the flowers, smiled warmly, took a deep whiff and sighed, rolling her eyes. Then she dropped the bouquet into a wastebasket near the office door.

Franklin's smile didn't waver. "Is that any way to accept a gift? Those were perfectly beautiful flowers. And I won't even mention how much they cost."

"Where did you steal them from?" Riolas asked, arms folded.

"Such an impolite question," Franklin replied, pretending offense.

"As nice as it is to see you again, does your visit have a purpose?"

"You mean it's not enough that I should just drop by and exchange pleasantries with the most beautiful woman on the southwest side of the third floor of the congressional office complex?"

"Are you going to tell me why you're here, or am I going to have to put you in the basket with the flowers?" She couldn't help but smile — just a little.

"Fair enough," said Franklin.

He eased past Riolas, who was nearly – but not quite – blocking the door, and sat on one of the office chairs. "I'm here to talk to your boss. I bear an invitation. Well, that's not quite accurate. One has the option to decline your regular, garden-variety invitation. This is nothing so mundane." He reached into his jacket and produced a white envelope bearing a prominent emblem. Riolas had been a Washington functionary long enough to recognize a presidential seal. She stepped forward to take it, but Franklin drew it back and held it in the air.

"Uh-uh, sorry. It's for the congressman."

"I'll tell him you're here," Riolas grunted. "Stay where you are." She turned away and added, almost as an afterthought, "And don't touch anything."

She walked to Huerta's door, opened it, and stepped inside. Franklin was right behind her.

"Afternoon, Congressman!" Franklin said.

"Mr. Franklin, is it?" Huerta asked, visibly irritated. He cast a stern glance at Riolas, who shrugged her shoulders and retreated to her desk. "I'm rather busy here, Mr. Franklin. If you'd have the courtesy to call and make an appointment..."

"So, I should tell the president that you're too busy to see him?" Franklin asked. He flipped the envelope onto the desk.

The congressman picked up the envelope and studied it for a moment. He looked up at Franklin.

"So, you gonna read it?" Franklin asked. "Or are you going to do like 'Karnack' on the old Johnny Carson show and tell us what's on the inside by using your mystical mental powers?" He plunked down on a seat, crossed his legs and smiled.

Huerta paused a moment. Then he carefully opened the envelope and withdrew the piece of White House stationery inside. He studied the handwritten note silently.

Dear Congressman Huerta:

First of all, please allow me to apologize for Mr. Franklin's behavior. He is without a doubt one of the most brash, obnoxious, and insufferable individuals I have ever encountered in all my years of public service. But, as is the case for all God's creatures, he serves a purpose. And right now, that purpose is to convey an invitation for you to accompany him to the Oval Office.

I look forward to seeing you again.

Sincerely,

President John W. DeWitt

Huerta looked up from the letter. His eyes found Riolas'. He winked at her.

"Well! Glad I remembered to shave this morning."

He rose from his desk, gestured to the door, and followed Franklin. As they walked out, Huerta turned to Riolas. "Michelle, in as much as I am being kidnapped, would you please cancel my afternoon appointments? I'll be at the White House."

"Well," she said, eyeing Franklin. "There's gonna be some less-than-happy people around here, but I'll tell them it couldn't be helped." In fact, the congressman had no afternoon appointments, but damned if she was going to admit that fact in front of this glad-handing buffoon.

"Oh," Franklin said before exiting, "almost forgot. This is for you."

He pulled another envelope out of his jacket pocket and plopped it onto Riolas's desktop. As she studied the envelope, she heard Franklin's voice echoing in the hallway.

"If you're thinking about putting that envelope the same place as the flowers, please reconsider. It's not from me. It's from the president."

13

The president rose to greet Huerta as he entered the office.

"So, this is the ass-kicking congressman's first visit to the Oval Office?"

"If you care to use that characterization, yes sir," Huerta said.

Huerta felt horribly out of his element. He had seen pictures of the Oval Office, but he never expected to be inside it, making small talk with the president of the United States.

The president was seated at his desk. Franklin sat on the arm of the office's couch. Chief of Staff Englund stood behind and to the right of the president. Secretary of State Montgomery sat on a chair near the office door.

Franklin patted the cushion next to his on the couch. "Have a seat, Congressman. We have things to discuss."

Huerta did as asked. "Mr. President, thank you for the invitation. I've always wondered what it would be like to sit in this office."

"It's a peculiar place, isn't it?" the president asked, looking around. "One time, when I first came here, I told an aide to put a chair 'over there in the corner.' He looked at me like I had broccoli coming out of my nose. I repeated the order, and the poor slob just walked around the room with the chair for a few minutes while I pretended not to notice. I finally told him it was a joke, that I knew an Oval Office had no corners, and that I was just having a little fun. He looked at me again, this time like I was a jerk with broccoli in my nose, and went away frowning. No sense of humor, I guess."

"I guess," Huerta said.

The president shifted in his chair. "The last time we spoke, Mr. Huerta, you had a lot to say about how government works — or doesn't work. Is my memory serving me correctly?"

"Yes sir."

"Has anything happened in the last several days to change your mind about that?"

"No sir," Huerta said.

"So, you don't much cotton to the way government works? Well how would you like to do something about it, Mr. Huerta? Take all your newfound and unwanted celebrity, the fact that you are quickly becoming a household name in the hinterlands – as Mr. Franklin would say, and do something with it. You haven't said anything that most Americans wouldn't agree with. Take that message to them, tell them you are going to try to do something about it."

Huerta stared at the president. *Here it comes*, he thought. *I really am going to be on the President's Council for Fitness.* He looked at the others in the room. Franklin was studying his fingernails. Montgomery was looking at his well-polished wingtips. Englund was gazing at a picture on the wall.

Huerta's focus returned to the president, who was rocking in his chair and smiling. It was obvious no one in the room was going to say another word unless it was him.

"Mr. President, I just finished explaining why I'm probably not going to seek reelection. There's little – if anything – that a junior congressman can do..."

"That's true, for a junior congressman," said the president. "That's a piss-poor platform! A junior congressman calls a press conference, only the weekly newspapers and shoppers show up. But the vice presidency! Now there's a platform! When a vice president has something to say, microphones and cameras come popping out of the wall."

Huerta blinked. Again, his gaze swept the room. Franklin was still sitting on the arm of the couch. Montgomery was seated on a chair next to the wall, parallel to the desk. Englund was standing just behind and to the left of the president, who was rocking in his chair, both hands folded under his chin. All of them were looking at him. All were smiling. And suddenly, in his mind, it all fell together.

Huerta could hear blood pounding in his ears. His face felt hot. His fingertips tingled as if both hands had fallen asleep.

"Vice president? Me?"

The president smiled and nodded.

"You, Mr. Huerta."

There was another moment of silence, broken by Don Franklin.

"Hey, just think! You'll always have a parking space!"

14

During her two decades in government service, Michelle Riolas had seen many things.

She had been a legislative assistant to a formidable Texas congresswoman who once voted for the impeachment of a president. She was first an office assistant, then the good right arm of another Texas congressman who rose from obscurity to become chairman of the House Ways and Means Committee. In the scope of her duties she had seen many, many things that left her shaking her head.

But nothing had ever left her speechless. Until the letter from the president.

> Dear Ms. Riolas,
>
> Please excuse Mr. Franklin for dragging your boss away so unceremoniously. If what Don tells me about you is even a quarter true, then you are a fiercely loyal assistant, a no-nonsense administrator, and (these are Don's words) "a solitary light of beauty in an otherwise dismal and dingy backwater congressional office."
>
> Please be assured that Mr. Franklin has been acting on my behalf all along. And because I am going to ask for your assistance in this endeavor, it is only fair that I let you know what's going on.
>
> I am going to ask Congressman Huerta to serve out the rest of this term as vice president of the United

States. If what I've been reading about Mr. Huerta is correct, he will be inclined to refuse this offer. Ms. Riolas, I am not asking Mr. Huerta to assume this responsibility solely on the basis of his heroic actions in that apartment building the other Friday night. That is, of course, what brought the congressman to my attention. But it, of itself, is not the reason why he is uniquely qualified to take on the job. I'm sure I'm only telling you something you already know when I report that our investigation into his background has shown a Roberto Huerta that is possessed of a genuine desire to serve the public. He seems to be bereft of corruption, unfazed by the lure of big money and the lust for power.

If you would do me the favor, I would ask that you bring whatever influence you can to bear on Mr. Huerta. Call his wife, Janelle, and fill her in on what's happening. If we can get her behind this effort, then it may be easier to convince Mr. Huerta that this is the right thing at the right time for our country. If she is against the idea, maybe you can help convince her.

I look forward to working with you and Mr. Huerta. Please call my office without hesitation if there is any assistance we can provide.

Sincerely,

John DeWitt
President of the United States

She refolded the letter and replaced it in the envelope with the Presidential Seal emblazoned over the upper left corner. Placing the envelope on her desktop, she removed her glasses and rubbed her eyes. Then she picked up the phone and dialed a number.

Moments later, she asked the switchboard operator at the Brooks County Texas courthouse to connect her to Janelle Huerta. The congressman's wife answered on the third ring.

"Janelle? This is Michelle. Honey, you're not going to believe what's going on. Do you have a minute?"

"Yeah, why?"

"Janny, your husband is on his way to the Oval Office right now," Michelle said. "The president of the United States is going to ask Bob to serve out the rest of this term as vice president."

At first, Janelle thought it was a joke. It wasn't above Michelle Riolas to pull someone's leg. Janelle remembered the Christmas party the year before, when a slightly tipsy Ms. Riolas had her believing that she was considering a somewhat-more-than-professional relationship with Roberto. Janelle was just about to convey this bit of information to her husband when Michelle let the cat out of the bag by planting a somewhat-more-than-friendly kiss on the lips of the actor hired to portray Santa Claus, and then swore to all in the room that Santa was the only man she would ever allow to come down her chimney.

But this time, Michelle made it clear that this was serious business. She read DeWitt's letter to Janelle. That made it very real.

"Is he going to take it?" Janelle asked.

"Honey, when he left the office, he thought he was going to be offered some blue-ribbon commission."

"Do you think he'll take the job, Michelle?"

Michelle paused. "I don't know. To a large degree, I think it depends on you. Do you want him to?"

"God, I have no idea! I mean, this is so surreal! It's like finding out my husband is actually Godzilla or something. I don't know what to think!"

"But you know your husband," Riolas said calmly. "Do you think he'll be able to turn down an offer like this?"

Janelle thought about it.

"Again, Michelle, I just don't know. He had to be pushed into running for sheriff. The first year was tough, with that terrible thing that happened to his nephew, but after a while he really seemed to enjoy the job. And you remember how he was dead set against running for Congress until you and your friends practically twisted his arm…"

"Look. I have to believe there's a reason the president is asking Bob to take the job. And I think it's up to us to stand by him and support him no matter what decision he makes. I just wanted you to know so you'll be ready when he calls."

Janelle thanked her and hung up.

As she replayed the phone call in her mind, she didn't notice that she had parked her car half on and half off the driveway. The two left tires sank into the lawn, made soft by a rare May rainstorm.

She walked like a zombie to the front door, heard the stereo booming out some alternative rock CD. The high notes made the fillings in her teeth tingle, and she could feel the bass reverberating in her chest. It was a welcome sound. It meant Tommy was home. And that was a rarity these days.

More often than not, Tommy was out with his friends. He would come home from school, eat a quick bite – if he ate at all – and then he was gone. He was always home by curfew, his grades were as good as they ever were (which wasn't that great) and the same could be said about his general attitude. Tommy was at the age where most teenagers dwell in a narrow band of emotions ranging from bored distraction to outright resentment. But it was better to have him home sulking or smart-mouthing than it was to have him out God-knows-where doing God-knows-what.

At least she wouldn't have to worry about that this evening.

"Hi, Sweetie," she said as she walked into the living room.

Tommy was draped over the couch, head on the floor, feet over the back. He was reading a hot rod magazine. Three earrings glistened in his left ear. His hair was parted down the middle – long on the sides, short in the back, dyed black to match the clothes he always wore – black jeans, black T-shirts bearing the satanic emblem of one rock band or another, black leather boots and a black wrist band with a pewter skull on it.

Janelle could remember when her little Tommy had been a fastidious youth. He preferred the stiff feel of new blue jeans to the more casual stone-washed variety then in style. He wore his shirts buttoned all the way to the top. He was fussy about his haircuts and kept a neat room. He used to like hugs from his mother.

Then something happened. Janelle was certain it had something to do with his cousin's death. Almost overnight, Janelle's sweet, fussy little angel turned into a surly teenager who seemed to care about nothing in particular.

And tonight that teenager was going to get the shock of his life.

"Yo, Momster," he said, without looking up.

Janelle sat on the plush chair next to her husband's all-too-vacant recliner.

"Well, I got a phone call about your Dad today," she said.

"What did he do now?" Tommy asked. "Get his picture taken helping a little old lady cross the street?" He said it without a trace of humor.

"No, nothing like that."

"Good," Tommy said. "It's getting a little old, seeing his face on the news all the time."

"Oh, do you watch the news to see your Dad?"

Janelle could tell by his expression that Tommy could see the trap she had set. Saying yes would mean that he actually gave a damn.

"No, but some of my friends' parents do," he said. "And they're always talking about how proud they are of Dad and how wonderful he is, then I catch a ration of shit about it all night."

"Don't say 'shit' to your mother," Janelle said, admiring how deftly her son had avoided the snare. "Well," she said, shifting in her seat, "I hate to tell you this, then, knowing how you feel. But things are just about to get a little bit, actually, a whole lot more interesting around here."

"Why?" Tommy asked. "Is Dad going to be on a box of Wheaties now?" He allowed himself a chuckle.

"Nothing quite so grand," she said. "He's going to be asked to be vice president of the United States."

She paused to watch her son's reaction as her words registered. He looked up from his magazine. For the first time in what she believed to be several days, he actually looked directly at her.

"He's... what?"

"President DeWitt is going to ask your father to take over for the vice president who died a couple weeks ago."

Tommy stared at his mother.

"Is he going to take the job?"

"I have no idea. I think he will, actually. You know your father. He'll resist, he'll say he's not the man for the job, he'll say they should pick someone..."

She stopped when Tommy jumped to his feet and stalked to his bedroom.

"Great! Just fucking great!" he shouted.

"Watch your language, mister," was the best she could manage. The bedroom door slammed shut.

Janelle looked down the hallway. A different alternative rock CD blared from her son's room, the noise doing battle with the CD that was still playing on the living room stereo. She rose from her chair, walked over and turned it off.

Then she sat back down to await the phone call she both anticipated and dreaded.

***

He had the rest of the night to think about it.

The rest of the night.

It took him and his wife nearly a decade to decide to have a child. It took him six months to decide whether or not he wanted to run for Congress. Now he had fewer than 14 hours to decide whether or not he wanted to be the next vice president of the United States.

The president understood his desire to discuss the situation with his wife, but he was clear that he wanted an answer by morning.

As the limo rolled north along Capitol Street, he was inclined to say "no." After all, the whole idea was simply ludicrous. He was a junior congressman — a "nobody" on the Hill. And it seemed somehow dishonest to parlay his accidental fame into a fast one like this.

However, on the ride back to his apartment building – in a presidential limo, no less – Franklin made it sound, if not probable, at least plausible.

"We need a vice president," Franklin said as the sleek, black limo wound through downtown construction. "The Republicans don't want a vice president — not right now. The president's an old man. If he should die in his sleep tonight, Wantner is in the White House. Now there's a thought that should keep you awake at night. The bastards are willing to roll the dice in the hopes that the Grim Reaper comes a-calling at the White House before the next election cycle. Then Wantner can run as an incumbent."

"That part I understand," Huerta said. "But I still can't understand why it has to be me!"

"Bob, fate has cast you in the role. You are simply in the right place at the right time. Or the wrong place, depending on how you look at it. You are a public figure — a congressman. You did something incredibly heroic, no matter what you may think about it. The average

Joe and Jane at home read about you and they wonder why more people in government can't be like you. So, the president announces that your extreme gallantry – along with a distinguished record of public service that shows you to be a capable and honest administrator of the public trust – qualifies you for a caretaker role as veep for the next year or so, just to finish out the term. Come reelection time, we'll take another look at the situation. But for now, you're the man!"

"Nobody will buy it," Huerta protested.

"Ah, but that's where you are wrong, sir. You may not be much for Frank Capra films, but the masses just love that stuff. You are possibly the only person drawing breath on American soil who is so politically pure as to make the Republicans look like partisan political dickheads should they drag their feet at confirming you. I'd do it myself, but then the media would discover my thirty-two illegitimate children."

"Fuck," Huerta whispered. Several reporters and photographers were milling about the lobby of his apartment complex. As luck would have it, there was a parking space right in front of the door. As the limo pulled to a stop, the media descended. He hurried to the door as they shouted questions.

"Congressman, how did your meeting with the president go today? Do you think the president is too soft on crime? Is the prison system unfairly slanted against minorities? Do you favor capital punishment?"

He said nothing as he punched the security code into the keypad and let himself in. As soon as he got to his apartment, it dawned upon him that none of the reporters had asked anything about the vice presidency. So the secret was still a secret. And that meant he could still say no.

He called his wife; she picked up on the first ring.

"Before you go into any longwinded explanations," Janelle said, "I already know."

"How the hell did you find out?"

"Michelle called me about an hour ago."

"How did she find out? I haven't said anything to anyone."

"The fellow who spirited you off to the White House left her a note," Janelle said. "The note asked her to call anyone who might have any influence over you."

"Isn't this the sort of news a wife should hear from her husband, not from her husband's staff?"

"Oh, relax. She was doing her job, which includes looking out for your best interests. And besides, I'm glad she called. It gave me some time to think about it."

"Well, you can stop thinking about it. I'm not going to do it."

"Yes, you are," said Janelle. "You will because you know it's right."

"I know nothing of the sort," Huerta replied. "How the hell can it be? I've only been a congressman for five months. I still get lost between the parking garage and my office. And now I'm supposed to be vice president?"

"You know it's right because the president wouldn't have asked you if he didn't think you were the person for the job. And you've never said no to duty when it calls."

Huerta said nothing.

"Look," Janelle said softly. "I know you wanted to keep things simple. Hence the simple apartment in the bad part of town instead of some condo like the others. You wanted to be a public servant instead of some feudal lord. Your motives remain pure, Mr. Huerta. And that's why you have to take this job. Every time you call, you complain about how useless you feel, how you can't get anything done. Well, this is your chance to get something done. Set an example for others to follow. Show the public that not all politicians are in it to fill their pockets. You can do more good in a few months as vice president than you could in ten terms as a congressman from Falfurrias."

"It means you and Tommy would have to move out here with me."

"Good. I'm tired of only seeing you on TV."

"Have you talked about this with Tommy?" Huerta asked.

"I mentioned it to him, after swearing him to secrecy, of course."

"And what did he say?"

"The usual. 'Cool'," she lied. "He's in his room listening to music. And that, or course, means I'm listening to it, too."

Huerta frowned.

"Next time I'm home, that lad and I are going to have a little chat," he said. "I think it's about time he was reminded who are the parents and who is the teenager."

Huerta started as the security buzzer went off. Someone had pushed the button for his apartment.

"Fucking reporters," he hissed.

"My darling, such language. It's so not vice presidential."

"I'm sorry, Janny. I'll call back soon."

"I'll be waiting right by the phone, love."

He hung up and hurried to the speaker by his door.

"Who is it? And if this is a reporter, how many times do I have to tell you..."

"Hey, cool your jets, *jefe*. It's Michelle. I come bearing gifts. And don't worry. I told these media idiots down here that I work for you, not on you. I even displayed my congressional ID, so your reputation as Captain Pure is safe. Now let me in, or else I may be forced to use one of these fools as a battering ram."

Huerta pressed the button unlocking the lobby door. He heard Riolas fending off the reporters.

"Back off or walk with a permanent limp, dirtbags."

Huerta smiled, walked to his door to await her knock, then opened the door to find her holding a brown paper bag. She was wearing a black sweatshirt and blue jeans. And no makeup. She looked nice.

"You just gonna stand there, or are we gonna drink this cheap wine?"

"Forgive my shabby manners." Huerta stood aside to admit his visitor. She stepped into the apartment and looked around the living room.

"Jesu Christo! What a dump! Who's your decorator, Zippy the Pinhead?"

"Please, save the comments about my personal space," Huerta said, chuckling.

Riolas moved toward the kitchenette. "I haven't seen anything like this since college." She set two bottles of wine on the table. "You got any glasses that don't have pictures of the Flintstones?"

"Yeah, but they're plastic. Green Bay Packers, 1997 Super Bowl Champions. Good enough for my lady?"

"I never figured out how a good ole Texas boy like you ended up as a cheesehead." She took a bottle out of the bag and unscrewed the top. "I never trust wine that comes with a cork. Give me a good, fresh wine every time. Vintage — last week!"

She poured the wine into the glasses and offered a toast.

"To the next vice president of the United States."

Huerta set his glass on the table.

"I can't drink to that, Michelle."

"Why not? You're gonna take the job, aren't you?"

"No. I don't know. I don't think so."

Riolas folded her arms on the table and rested her forehead on them. She shook her head slowly back and forth. "Please, Lord," she groaned in mock prayer. "Protect your humble daughter from fools, idiots, monsters, and jackasses like the one across the table from me."

She looked up. "Are you stupid? Or are you just pretending to be stupid? Please say you're just pretending, or baby's gonna cry."

Huerta stood and walked to the living room. Riolas followed.

"You want to talk about stupid? How's this whole situation for stupid?" He plopped down on a dusty easy chair, and waved Riolas toward the couch.

Riolas eyed the couch suspiciously, looking for a not-particularly-stained cushion.

"How in the hell am I supposed to take this seriously? A week ago today, I was just another congressional rookie, ignored by the muckety-mucks, a junior member of the minority party. I have a crappy office, crappy furnishings, a crappy parking spot."

"But a top-notch staff, right?" Riolas asked, raising an eyebrow.

Huerta smiled. "Of course. Best anywhere."

He raised his plastic glass in salute. Riolas returned the gesture.

"But look at all of this, Michelle. I do something on the spur of the moment and all of a sudden I'm Captain Fucking America! I'm on all the talking head shows. I can't walk past a magazine rack without seeing my face glaring back at me. Every day someone from some press service is calling to get my opinion about something — crime, punishment, race relations. All of a sudden, I'm Bob Huerta, Superstar! And not because of anything I've ever done in Congress – which is nothing, mind you. I came to the rescue of some woman. And now they want me to be vice president. How in the hell does anything I've done in life qualify me to be a heartbeat away from the presidency?" He took a deep slug from his glass and grimaced at the taste.

Riolas set her glass on the coffee table and applauded.

"Helluva speech, Mr. H.," she said. "But you can cut the humility act with me. I know you. I've known you since you were wearing that itchy wool-wrestling mask. My nephew Billy was one of the kids who benefited from your 'Mr. Mentor' program when you were sheriff. And I know the real reason you started the program in the first place, in case you forgot! It was me who put the bug in Zeb Collopy's ear to endorse your bid to replace him when he retired. I know you, Bob Huerta. And I know you'd be a fine vice president. And I know you've never run from a challenge. And I know you're not going to this time."

She took a sip of her wine and frowned as she regarded the glass — a picture of Brett Favre unleashing a touchdown pass.

"Packers. Feh!" She set the glass back on the coffee table.

Huerta stared at his shoetips. Riolas stood and walked to where her boss sat. She eased down on the arm of the chair and put an arm around Huerta's shoulders.

"Listen to mama," she said softly. "If you say no to this opportunity, it's gonna eat at you for the rest of your life. You're always going to wonder 'what if?' I don't have to tell you the good you could do as vice president. Maybe not so much directly, like in getting legislation passed, stuff like that. But just think of the example you could set. Kids could have someone other than a sports hero to look up to. Regular folks would see that regular folks still count for something." She ran her fingers through his hair. "You'd be standing up for the men and women in this country who go to work every day to make their lives better, for themselves and their kids."

Then she opened her hand and smacked him – hard – on the back of the head.

"Besides, it's you or nobody."

She walked back to the couch and plunked down on it.

"Have I ever told you how much I despise you?" Huerta said, smiling and rubbing his head.

"This is no time to start telling fibs," Riolas replied, smiling sweetly.

15

The security buzzer went off at eight a.m. "Morning, Bob. Ready to go?" It was Franklin. He and the limo were right on time.

Huerta walked down the three flights of stairs and found the limo double-parked in front of the building. Franklin was standing near the open back door.

"Hop in," he said. "The Boss is waiting."

To Huerta's surprise – and to Franklin's credit, the congressman decided – Franklin did not ask him if he had made up his mind, or what his response would be. If he had, Huerta wouldn't have told him. Franklin probably understood that.

It took 20 minutes for the limo to arrive at the White House. The driver flashed an ID to the guard, who smiled and waved the vehicle through the gate. Five minutes later, Huerta found himself in the Oval Office for the second time in as many days.

The president was at his desk. Unlike the day before, the president did not rise to shake Huerta's hand. Instead he merely motioned to the same chair Huerta sat in the previous afternoon. DeWitt's chief of staff stood just behind the president, to his right. Huerta was offered coffee, but declined.

"So, shall we cut to the chase?" the president asked.

"Yes sir, Mr. President. I'm almost prepared to respond to your kind but bewildering offer."

A presidential eyebrow went up.

"Almost?"

Huerta cleared his throat nervously.

"With all due respect, sir, I still have a few questions."

DeWitt leaned back in his seat. "Oh, by all means."

"First off, I want to be clear that I don't agree with all of the stances this administration has taken. For instance, for the sake of a balanced budget I think we've been cutting too much out of social welfare programs. I think the administration didn't raise enough of a ruckus when the Republicans made those huge cuts in the WIC program earlier this year. That's just an example. I don't expect to have much to do in the way of setting policy, sir. But if I were to accept your offer, I want it known here and now, that I'm still my own man. If someone asks me how I feel about something, I want to be able to answer truthfully, even if I'm at odds with the administration's stance. Is that a problem?"

"Of course it is," DeWitt replied without hesitating. "But I would expect nothing less from you. Just do me a favor. If you're going to say something contrary to the administration's viewpoint, let me know ahead of time so I don't have to learn about it in the morning paper."

The president leaned forward, placing his elbows on the desktop.

"And you're wrong about something, young man. If you accept the job you will have a lot to do with setting policy. In my administration, vice president is a cabinet-level position. You won't just be window dressing. Walters had a knack for trade diplomacy and foreign relations. He was a hell of a spokesman for the administration. You will be asked to identify several areas of expertise and then work in those areas. This isn't just a title that needs to be filled, Mr. Huerta. It's a job."

"Uh, thank you."

Huerta hadn't expected the president's response. He expected (perhaps hoped?) to hear that a vice president had to stand by the official party line come hell or high water. (How long did it take George Bush to lose the phrase "voodoo economics" when Ronald Reagan picked him for the number two slot?) DeWitt's answer set him aback.

"You said you had a few questions," asked Englund, smiling amiably. "That was one. Are there more?"

"Well, sir, yes there are," Huerta tried not to stammer as he struggled to remember his other questions. At length, he came up with just one.

"You and Mr. Franklin both indicated that this will just be for the remainder of this term. Do I have your assurances that there will be no pressure to sign up for another term if you decide to seek reelection?"

"That will not be a problem, Mr. Huerta," the president responded. "I won't announce this officially for some time, but there's no harm in your knowing that I will not be seeking a second term. That will make you the front-runner for the nomination, should you decide you want it. If you don't, then don't run. As simple as that. Anything else?"

Huerta searched his brain for another question. He had lain awake the better part of the night, his mind swimming with questions. Now he couldn't come up with one.

Englund broke the silence.

"Bob, you should know that this is by no means a done deal. We need to get confirmation by both houses of Congress. And, as you know, the GOPs on the Hill are not in the mood to do us any favors."

Franklin added, "You are going to be as welcome as the first skid mark in a brand new pair of white cotton undies."

Englund grimaced. "In a manner of speaking, that is correct. At any rate, it's going to be a long, nasty process. First, an appearance before the House Judiciary Committee, followed by debate on the House floor and a vote — if it gets that far. Ed Gilbertson, as you know, is the chairman of that committee. He's in Wantner's back pocket, so there's a chance he might refuse to consider your nomination. With some pressure applied in the right places, however, we might be able to jump that hurdle."

Franklin interrupted. "That'll be my job, to apply pressure where pressure will do the most good."

Englund continued. "If we can get you through the House, then the Senate shouldn't be that much of a problem. But getting you through the House is going to be a world class, grade A, dyed-in-the-wool pain in the rumpus room."

"But one thing we know about Bob Huerta," said the president. "He ain't scared of a fight."

Again the room was silent.

"What about staff?" Huerta asked.

"Like Mr. Englund said," Franklin replied, "I'll handle the rough, tough, dirty stuff for you — if you want. Used to do the same for Walters, bless his departed, fornicating soul. Once you're in, you pick whoever you want to head your staff. Use your congressional staff for the day-to-day stuff. You don't resign your post until you're confirmed."

Again, silence.

"Mr. Huerta," the president said. "I need an answer."

Huerta met the president's gaze. He looked at Franklin, who smiled and nodded. Englund was his usual dark, impassive self.

"Well, I think you are all out of your minds, but if this is what you want, what you really want, then I guess I have to say yes."

Franklin slapped him on the back, knocking a gust of air from his lungs.

"Hot damn doggies," Franklin exulted. "We got us a veep."

The president merely smiled and punched the intercom button on his phone. "Sheila, put in a call to the Hill. Ask Speaker Wantner, Minority Leader Montana, Senate Majority Leader Bilson and Minority Leader Rosen to come to the Oval Office for a one p.m. conference. Thank you."

He rose from his chair (quite shakily, Huerta noticed) and walked to where Huerta was seated. Englund stayed behind the president. Huerta rose to shake the president's hand.

"Welcome aboard, Bob. I'm looking forward to working with you." DeWitt smiled slyly. "In the interest of honesty, though, I must tell you that I'm most looking forward to making football bets with you. This year, the Redskins are going to kick the hell out of the Cowboys."

Huerta smiled. "I certainly hope so, Mr. President. In the interest of honesty, I must tell you that I'm a Green Bay fan."

DeWitt's eyes widened. "You're shitting me. A Packers fan from Texas?" His gaze shifted to Franklin. "Will wonders never cease?"

16

It took the president's secretary 45 minutes to line up the requested congressmen and senators. At one point, she buzzed DeWitt with the news that Speaker Wantner's office had to respectfully decline the president's kind invitation, due to pressing congressional business.

"Tell Wantner's people that if he isn't here, in my office," said DeWitt, "smiling at me with his pearly white, store-bought teeth at precisely one p.m. this afternoon, then the esteemed Speaker of the House of Representatives will be the only person in the congressional leadership who will be taken by surprise by an announcement I'm going to make in time for the network newscasts this evening. I'll bet you a cup of coffee that'll change his mind."

He was correct. In fact, Wantner was the first to arrive — 15 minutes early.

"Tell the speaker to have a seat and make himself comfortable," DeWitt instructed his secretary.

Moments later, when the other members of the leadership arrived, they were immediately escorted into the office — save for Wantner, who was the last to be invited in.

The silver-haired South Carolinian took stock of the room. He recognized everyone, except for the muscular, black-haired, mustachioed Hispanic standing between the president and his chief of staff. DeWitt rose to greet the speaker.

"Mr. Speaker," DeWitt purred. "So glad you could find a moment in your busy schedule to cater to the whims of an old man."

"Why, Mr. President," Wantner said in a voice that would *not* melt butter, "I can always find time to pop over for a little chat." He looked around the room again, nodding and smiling as he made eye contact with each person. He turned to the president and asked, "And, if I may ask, to what do we owe the honor?"

"Please have a seat, Mr. Speaker," said the president, gesturing toward the only unoccupied seat in the room. It also happened to be the one most distant from the president's desk. The insult was not lost on Wantner.

"You are most kind, sir," Wantner said, with only the slightest hint of irritation.

Assured he had the attention of everyone in the room, the president spoke.

"Gentlemen, and Honored Lady," (Grace Bilson, the first female to hold the post of Senate Majority Leader, smiled at the recognition) "The gentleman standing next to me is Congressman Roberto Huerta, a first-term congressman from Falfurrias, Texas."

"Huerta!" Wantner interrupted. "I thought you looked familiar, sir. You're that former wrestler who rescued a lady in distress recently. How gallant of you, sir."

"Once again, the speaker impresses us with his knowledge of current affairs," the president said, smiling. Wantner bristled at the sarcasm.

"Like all of you, especially the speaker, I was impressed by the lifesaving action taken by the congressman. After meeting him and talking with him, learning more about him, his stand on the issues, and his history of public service, and after considering the advice of my chief of staff, the former vice president's chief of staff, and several others whose opinions I trust and value, I have asked Mr. Huerta to serve out the rest of this term as your new vice president. And he has most graciously accepted my offer."

The room was stock-still. DeWitt surveyed the room and smiled, pleased by the effect of his bombshell.

"I will conduct a live press conference at three this afternoon announcing that I have asked Mr. Huerta to accept this weighty challenge. And I look forward to working closely with both houses of Congress toward Mr. Huerta's speedy confirmation."

"Well, I never," Wantner stammered. "Mr. President, we all salute the congressman's heroism and all that, but to make him vice president? I'm sure there are more suitable candidates."

"Suitable as in how, Mr. Speaker?" DeWitt asked. "People with more government experience? People with political baggage, favors to repay, backs to scratch? Yes, Mr. Speaker. There are a lot of people with more government experience. And I wouldn't trust most of them to watch over my laundry bag while I went to the bathroom. Mr. Huerta is a rare commodity in Washington. He's an honest man who knows what it's like to work eight hours a day for eight hours' pay. As far as learning the duties of the vice presidency, my staff will work with him as we go."

"But Mr. President," Senator Bilson said, "we all understand your desire to work with the person of your choosing. But we don't know Mr. Huerta. The American people don't know him either, except for what they've been reading in the past week. It's going to take some time to learn more about him."

"Our full FBI and NCIC investigative reports will be made available to your staffs as soon as we officially make the announcement," DeWitt said.

Senator Rosen crossed his legs and leaned back in his seat. "Mr. President, I'm just wondering. Was Congressman Huerta your first choice?"

"He was my only choice, Senator." The message was clear to all. Rosen and Montana had their chances three years ago. This time, they weren't even considered.

All eyes were on Congressman Montana, the only member of the leadership who hadn't asked a question. He shrugged his shoulders.

"What can I say? If that's the way you want to go, Mr. President, then I think you can count on the Democratic leadership in the House for full support."

"Likewise for the Senate," Rosen added quickly.

"Well, let's not be too hasty here," Wantner said. "I have some questions here and now for the congressman, if I may."

Huerta opened his mouth to reply but he didn't get the chance.

"No, you may not," the president interjected. "There will be plenty of time for questions and answers. Mr. Huerta will appear with me at a press conference this afternoon. I'd tune in and watch if I were you, Mr. Speaker."

Wantner stood and walked to the door. "Mr. President, I can assure you that the House of Representatives will take a close look at this nomination. A good and thorough look. Now, with your leave sir, I have work to do." He turned to leave.

"Mr. Speaker, just a moment," the president barked. The tone of his voice startled everyone. Wantner froze in his tracks and turned, slowly, to face the president.

"Have a nice afternoon, Mr. Speaker," the president said. He turned away, giving the speaker his backside.

Wantner stormed out of the Oval Office. The sound of muted chuckling could be heard in the office.

"Mr. President," Bilson said. "Is it wise to tweak the monkey's tail when you're going to need that monkey's cooperation?" (Bilson's dislike for the Speaker of the House was legendary.)

"I'm sorry, Senator." DeWitt smiled sheepishly. "He just makes it so easy."

"Believe me, I understand," the senator replied. "I would just advise some restraint. If the nomination clears the House, then I think you can count on the Senate to fall in line very quickly."

The matronly senator from New Jersey stood and walked to the vice president-designate, reaching for his hand. "Personally, sir, I think you are a fine choice. Though I'm not going to say that in public until the House is done with you, of course. I'm sure you can understand that."

Huerta said he could. The majority leader was an up-and-comer, widely touted as one of the few women in government to have a legitimate chance at becoming president. She would not risk political capital on a nomination that might be doomed, nor would she be expected to. Rosen and Montana also rose to shake hands with Huerta.

Only Englund noticed the president's pained expression as he groped for the armrest of his chair, one hand over his cramping abdomen. "Mr. President?" he whispered.

"I'm fine," said DeWitt, with a slight groan.

17

When the remaining members of the congressional leadership had departed, Franklin and Englund took Huerta into an adjacent office, where they were joined by Press Secretary Hamilton. It was time to prepare the nominee for the upcoming press conference.

"Look for a gaggle of reporters in the briefing room," Hamilton said. "Word has already been leaked to the press, I'm sure."

Franklin laughed. "Hell, I'll bet Wantner called CNN himself. Off the record, of course."

"The point is, Bob, the media will have about an hour to prepare," said Englund. "Have you ever done a press conference?"

"Just locally, in Texas," Huerta replied.

"Well, just forget that experience. This will be nothing like it. These sharks won't be asking questions to get answers. More than anything, they want you to look like a babbling idiot."

"The media has been sweet as sugar pie to you up to this point because, until now, you were just a public hero," Hamilton added. "But as soon as we enter that briefing room, you are the vice president-designate. And every smart Johnny and Jane with a tape recorder or notepad wants to be the one who takes you down. They're all a bunch of fucking Woodwards and Bernsteins and Michael Fucking Isikoffs. And, they're all looking for a break. If you understand that and consider each answer carefully before you open your mouth, you should do just fine."

Huerta felt beads of sweat rolling between his chest and T-shirt. He smiled. "Is it too late to change my mind?" he asked, only half-kidding.

"Of course not," Franklin said, placing an arm around Huerta's shoulders. "You can back out any time you want to. Of course, that means I'll have to kill you with my bare hands."

Franklin leaned closer to Huerta and whispered loudly.

"Have I ever told you about my ten years with the CIA? Covert actions, mostly. Strictly 'Black Ops' kinda stuff."

Huerta grinned, betting that Franklin was kidding.

***

Twenty minutes after leaving the White House, Al Wantner, stormed into his office at the Capitol.

"Where the hell is Langston?" he demanded, to no one in particular.

"Right here, Mr. Speaker." The speaker's chief aide replied through a mouthful of donut.

"In my office, now!" He marched inside, slamming the door behind him. Langston brushed donut crumbs from his shirt, opened the door, and entered the office.

"This will not stand! This will not stand!" Wantner shouted, thumping his fist on his desktop. "That doddering, senile son-of-a-bitch thinks he's going to put one over on me? On ME?! Well, I'll be damned straight to hell, that's what I'll be! STRAIGHT to hell!" He noticed Langston.

"Get Plambeck on the phone."

"Mr. Speaker, it's two o'clock. He's in the middle of his show right now."

Wantner's steely blue eyes fixed on his subordinate. "Did I ask you what fucking time it is?" he hissed. "No, I don't think I did. Get Plambeck on the phone, right now! Tell him to get his bony ass on a plane to Washington as soon as he's off the air. Then make dinner reservations for three — eight o'clock tonight at the usual spot. You,

Plambeck and I are going to have a little skull session."

"Mr. Speaker, may I ask what's going on?"

"Oh," Wantner said, staring at Langston. "There's a LOT going on, Jimmy! A whole FUCKING lot! And tonight, we're going to decide just what the hell we're going to do about it."

18

"Ladies and gentlemen, the president of the United States."

Press Secretary Hamilton stood back from the podium as President DeWitt, Englund, Franklin and Huerta entered the room. DeWitt walked to the podium. The others stood behind him.

The president took stock of the number of reporters in the room, nodded, smiled, and spoke without the benefit of notes.

"Good afternoon. It has been two weeks since the tragic death of Vice President Walters. He was my friend, my partner. His loss continues to be keenly felt, but the business of government goes on. As you all know, the twenty-fifth Amendment to the Constitution of the United States gives the president the power to appoint a new vice president when death or resignation creates a vacancy in that office. I'm here this afternoon to tell you that, this afternoon, I will officially submit the name of Congressman Roberto Huerta as my nominee for that office. You all know what Congressman Huerta did a week ago Friday. And truthfully, it was that act which brought the congressman to my attention. But it is not just that act of bravery that qualifies him for this appointment. Bob Huerta has a long history of public service, as a law enforcement officer and county sheriff, as well as his brief time in Congress. His views are generally compatible with mine. But mostly, he is a rare commodity in government today. He is a man who owes no political favors. He is an honest man. The people of his hometown, Falfurrias, Texas, knew this when they trusted him to protect their lives and property as a law enforcement officer. They knew this when they sent him to Congress. And now, the rest of America will know this as well. I introduced Mr. Huerta to the congressional leadership earlier this afternoon, and was assured that his nomination will receive expeditious consideration. Now, Mr. Huerta has a thing or two to say, and then you may ask a few questions. Mr. Huerta?"

The president stood aside. Huerta moved to the podium. He looked at the hundreds of reporters jammed into the room and fought the urge to faint. He cleared his throat as cameras clicked.

"If I might borrow a line from W.C. Fields, 'On the whole, I'd rather be in Falfurrias.'"

Huerta waited for laughter that didn't materialize.

"I'd like to first of all thank the president for his kind remarks. I'm honored by his trust in me, and I look forward to justifying that trust in the months ahead. As surprised as many of you might be about this announcement, just imagine how I felt. It came as a total shock. But when the president explained his reasons for asking me to fill the post of vice president, just for the remainder of this term, I felt I had no choice but to put my personal preferences aside. I guess it just came down to this — when the president of the United States asks you to do something, you do it. I really don't have all that much to add at this point, so I'd be happy to answer a few questions."

The cacophony was deafening as reporters tried to out-shout each other. Hamilton stepped to the podium. "Let me handle this," he shouted into Huerta's ear.

"ALL RIGHT! QUIET! ONE AT A TIME!" the press secretary screamed into the microphone. "The vice president-designate doesn't have the advantage of knowing you each individually, so I will point to each reporter, who will then ask his or her question. Understood?"

The reporters gave a murmured assent.

"Very nice," Hamilton said. He pointed to a reporter from CNN.

"Mr. Huerta, are you qualified to be vice president?"

"Well, I must be or the president wouldn't have asked me."

"But your lack of government experience..."

"I believe that's one of the reasons I was chosen. As for qualifications, I believe they're the same as those the Constitution sets down for the president. I'm over thirty-five, was born a United States citizen on American soil. As for the rest of it, I guess it's a matter of interpretation."

Hamilton pointed to a news service reporter.

"Mr. Huerta, forgive me for asking, but a former pro wrestler as vice president? Isn't that sort of an insult to the nation's dignity?"

Huerta paused a moment.

"Sorry, but I have to remark at the silliness of that question. 'An insult to the nation's dignity?' Why would that be? We had a former actor as president. He was in a movie where he co-starred with a monkey. Yet he was a pretty popular president, as I recall. Also, if memory serves, a young man named Abraham Lincoln used to get paid to wrestle. Then there's a former professional wrestler who, I believe, did a capable job as governor of Minnesota a while back. And be that as it may, it's been twenty years since I was in the ring, earning money to pay for my education and to put food on the table for my family. After that, I had fifteen years as a deputy sheriff, four years as a sheriff, and just under a year as a United States Congressman. Let me ask you something, if I might. If you worked at a convenience store to earn money for college, would it be reasonable for me to ask you if it assaulted the dignity of your news organization to allow a former checkout boy to ask questions at a presidential news conference?"

The reporter's face turned red. "Well, I think there's a difference, sir."

"Oh? And how's that?"

The reporter was obviously flustered. He was used to asking the questions, not answering them. "For one thing," he stammered, "being vice president means you're a heartbeat away from the presidency."

"That's true. And as a White House correspondent, you are supposed to be serving as a surrogate of the people, asking the questions they would ask if they were here instead of you. That means that there is a huge amount of public trust placed in your judgment, that you'll ask the right questions. Now, do you think the dock workers out there will be insulted by the president's choice? How about the single mothers? The truck drivers — how insulted do you suppose they'll be? I imagine there are a few lawyers and professional politicians who will have their noses out of joint, but I don't think the average American is as elitist as you make him out to be. Next question."

Behind the podium, Franklin took a notepad and pen out of his coat pocket, scribbled a note and handed it to Englund.

I think I'm in love, the note read.

19

From the intimate corner table of a darkened restaurant, Wantner and Plambeck could see the TV. A news anchor was giving his report of Huerta's news conference. They watched and listened while Langston devoured fried mozzarella sticks.

"A former pro wrestler, Huerta came out swinging at the news conference, where his selection as vice president-designate was announced."

The screen was filled with the image of Bob Huerta as he answered the question about the so-called insult to the national dignity.

"Well, this proves it," Plambeck said, shaking his head. "DeWitt is senile."

Without taking his eyes from the screen, Wantner corrected him.

"That's where you are wrong, Clovis. It was a well-calculated move. A political master stroke. Choose someone with no skeletons, no paper trails, no history. Someone who the public knows – or thinks it knows – only on the basis of a single, heroic deed. The public will clamor for his confirmation. Unless we stop it."

Plambeck dipped his spoon through the melted cheese skin covering his French onion soup.

"And that's where I come in," he said.

"Precisely," Wantner replied. "On Monday's program, begin the counter-education program. I will be on 'Meet the Press' Sunday morning. Chairman Gilbertson will be on 'Face the Nation.' We will have other friends on other talking-head programs throughout the weekend. We will all congratulate Huerta for his fine, heroic deed. But we will hammer the point home that it takes more than rescuing a woman in a dark hallway to qualify a person to be vice president. We will be above-board and friendly. You, on the other hand, will not be."

Plambeck raised an eyebrow.

"You will not ridicule Huerta. Many of your listeners respect what he did. We will not alienate them. But you will say a single act of heroism does not qualify a man for high office. You will say that the man has no business even being considered for such a post. You will say that his behavior at the press conference proves he doesn't have the temperament for it. You will say that the nomination of Roberto Huerta was a crass political move by the president, a cynical ploy to capitalize on the congressman's newfound popularity. You will encourage Chairman Gilbertson of the House Judiciary Committee to let the nomination die on the vine. Then, on Tuesday's program, Gilbertson will call you on the air to tell you that he has heard the cries of the people, for which he will give you credit. He will state that it is his informed opinion that DeWitt's choice of Huerta was a slick, cynical, political move designed to embarrass the Republican leadership. You will agree with Gilbertson that the status of the United States of America in the court of world opinion should not be jeopardized just because the president wishes to engage in a pissing contest with his political foes. He will say that by refusing to act on the Huerta nomination, he is encouraging the president to get serious and nominate a qualified candidate. Time is of the essence. Right now, especially with the way Huerta handled the press corps today, he has public opinion on his side. But if you do what I know you can do, we can turn things around."

Wantner turned toward Langston, who was slathering a ridiculous amount of butter on a large chunk of bread.

"Your job, Jimmy, is to call people you know in Texas. I want everyone who ever had a bone to pick with Huerta. I want addresses and phone numbers. If there is any dirt on Huerta, I want it. A guy doesn't move up so fast in the South without having enemies. Your job is to find them, pay them, and make them talk."

"Should I apply the usual standards of verification to their statements?" Langston asked.

Wantner sneered and folded his hands under his chin. "Jimmy, one thing I really appreciate about our working relationship: if I don't know about things like that, then I sleep very well at night."

***

From the opening monologue of the May 27th Clovis Plambeck Show:

> Like most Americans, I was shocked when the networks broke into their regular programming to broadcast unconfirmed reports that President DeWitt had selected an unknown congressman from Texas to fill the unexpired term of deceased Vice President Eugene Walters. I, like most of you, assumed it was either a joke, a hoax, or someone was hopelessly mistaken.
>
> Well, as we all saw later that afternoon, it turned out to be true. The president of the United States stood in front of the assembled White House press corps and introduced Roberto Huerta as his choice to be your next vice president. And throughout the Great Republic the cry went up — "What in the name of all that is holy is this man thinking?"
>
> Friends, I will be the first to say that what Roberto Huerta did in that apartment complex, risking his life to save a woman in distress — that was a noble act. A bit foolhardy, perhaps. The act of a man who acts before thinking, perhaps. A bit hotheaded, perhaps. Yet noble. But does it qualify the man to be vice president? The answer is so obvious I dare not insult you by stating it.
>
> In fact, the very act that brought Congressman Huerta to national attention could be seen as a very good

reason not to confirm the president's ill-advised choice. In the arena of politics, just as in the physical world so aptly described to us by fabled physicist Robert Newton, every action has an equal and opposite reaction. Therefore, in the world of politics especially, all actions must be carefully considered, all options fully weighed and examined. If the unthinkable – but not impossible – should happen, should President DeWitt not survive his term in office, Roberto Huerta would become president, leader of the free world.

In the world of professional wrestling, we expect to see people losing their tempers, rushing to the center of the ring, blasting their opponents with a straight-arm to the chest, then finishing them off with a leg drop across the neck. But is that what we want in a president?

You all saw how Huerta acted during the press conference Friday afternoon. A reporter asked a simple question. But it was a question Huerta didn't like. So Huerta launched into a personal attack on the reporter's character and qualifications. It was hardly a statesmanlike performance.

Now, before Huerta can take the oath of office, he must be confirmed by both houses of Congress. The process begins with confirmation hearings in the House Judiciary Committee. Congressman Ed Gilbertson heads up that committee. And I hope Congressman Gilbertson is listening to this program. Maybe some of his Michigan constituents could call him and tell him what I'm saying right now — not that he hasn't probably already thought about this.

The president has done his job. He has submitted a name for nomination as vice president. But nowhere in the Constitution does it say that the House has to consider that nomination. This would not be the first time an inappropriate nomination was allowed to die on the vine without benefit of congressional consideration. In fact, it happens all the time. Congressman Gilbertson could rightly say that DeWitt's nomination of Huerta was nothing more than a cynical political ploy. That based on Huerta's lack of any real governmental experience, the president had to believe that Huerta stood two chances of being confirmed — slim and none. That the only reason DeWitt made this unbelievable nomination was to embarrass the Republican leadership in the House and Senate.

My friends, the president is playing games with the prestige and security of the United States of America. And it's up to us to make sure he doesn't get away with it. You all know my toll free number: 800-555-2712. But that's not the number I want you to call right now. I want you instead to light up the switchboard at the Capitol. Call Congressman Gilbertson's office right now at 800-555-2349. That's 800-555-2349. Leave a message with whomever answers. Tell the head of the House Judiciary Committee that you will stand by him should he decide it is in the best interest of the nation to refuse to consider this unfortunate nomination.

My switchboard is lit up like a Christmas tree. Thanks for holding on. We'll get to your calls, but first we have to take a break.

For the remainder of the afternoon, Plambeck took calls from folks around the country who shared his outrage at the president's ill-advised choice. At least, those were the calls that made the airwaves, thanks to Plambeck's adept call-screeners. The next afternoon, ten minutes into the first hour of the program, Congressman Gilbertson called on a special number reserved for congressional Republicans. He told Plambeck, and therefore the nation, that he had decided – after much thought and prayer – that the nomination of Roberto Huerta was not to be taken seriously, and that, his committee would not consider it.

Therefore, as far as the House of Representatives was concerned, Roberto Huerta would never become vice president.

20

"It is always so nice to be surrounded by friends," Wantner said. He settled into his large, overstuffed office chair.

"Yes, I'm sure it is," said Senator Bilson, with a sarcastic smile. Of the assembled Republican leadership, the senator was the only one who felt comfortable insulting Wantner to his face. She was a rarity — a Republican who owed no favors to the Speaker. It was well-known in party circles that she and Wantner would likely be opponents in the GOP presidential primaries.

If Wanter were successful in his presidential aspirations, House Majority Leader Eddie O'Hara had designs on the speakership. He wouldn't take unnecessary chances by alienating the current holder of that office. Senator Harold McGee was in line to take over the Majority Leader spot when Bilson left the Senate, so he wasn't looking for enemies, either. Congressman Eddie Gilbertson knew that he owed his position as chairman of a powerful House committee to the speaker's largess. Clovis Plambeck sat in the corner with his hands laced over his bony chest. Although not an elected official, he enjoyed the direct access he had with the speaker and would say nothing to jeopardize it.

"Yes sir," Wantner purred. "This is going to be a fine little sit-down among chums."

Bilson grimaced.

"So, what are you folks hearing from home about DeWitt's foolhardy choice?" Wantner asked. He gestured to Gilbertson.

"My calls, quite frankly, are running about even," he said. "That surprises me a little. My district is conservative in nature. But a lot of the people who are calling seem to think that Huerta would be a good choice. For some reason, they identify with him."

"Well, that's where your stellar leadership skills come in handy, Eddie," Wantner said. "You are no doubt explaining that while Huerta is a fine human being, he just does not have what it takes to succeed as vice president. I'm sure your people will come around eventually."

"I'm hearing pretty much the same thing," O'Hara said. "The polling shows that Huerta is being seen as a new American 'Everyman.' Are you sure we're doing the right thing by not even holding hearings?"

"I've never been more sure of anything in my life. If Congress were forced to consider every harebrained idea to come out of the White House, we wouldn't have time to take up the important business of the country. I'm sure, by working together and saying the right things, we can make people see that."

"But doesn't the president have the right to choose the person he wants?" Bilson asked. "Does our legislative role of 'advise and consent' extend so far as refusing to even consider his choice?"

"It's a foolish choice, Grace," Wantner said. "It has no merit whatsoever. He picked a junior congressman with no political record for one reason and one reason alone — to embarrass the Republican leadership. If we let DeWitt get away with this one, we're going to have to deal with scads of other harebrained ideas."

"Still, what's the harm of holding hearings?" O'Hara asked. "Agreed, Huerta is unqualified. Why not make that painfully obvious by holding hearings?"

"Because it would be a waste of time," Wantner hissed. His patience was beginning to fray. "Because it would not be productive."

"Will it be productive to have the American people think you're waging a personal war against DeWitt?" Bilson asked, smiling. "Will it be productive if people start thinking that you're gumming up the works because you're hoping DeWitt will just do you the favor of dropping dead without having a vice president in place?"

"Grace, I don't think it's necessary to..." Gilbertson started. Wantner interrupted him.

"Is that how you see it, Grace? You think I'm rolling the dice here, hoping that DeWitt will keel over in his scrambled eggs?" He smiled a cold shark smile.

"Are you saying no one else will see it that way?" Bilson asked.

Wantner tapped his desktop with a pen.

"Oh, I'm sure there are some narrow-minded people with their own agendas who will think whatever they want," he said finally. "But my job is to consider what's good for America, not to placate idiots."

He turned to Plambeck.

"Clovis, how are your calls coming in on this issue?"

Plambeck leaned back in his chair, scratching his cheek thoughtfully. His call screeners kept him informed, and the calls were running about 50/50. So Plambeck decided to tell the Speaker what he wanted to hear.

"Solidly against the Huerta nomination," he said. "They see it the same way you do, Mr. Speaker. The nomination is a cynical political ploy by a desperate politician. Nothing more, nothing less. They want you to stay the course and force the president to get serious and select someone with the proper qualifications."

Wantner smiled.

"No matter how long it takes?" he asked.

"Precisely."

Wantner stood and walked toward his office door.

"Well, once again I am impressed by the wisdom of the American people," he said as he opened the door. "We'll do things their way. Thank you, everyone."

He gestured toward the door, indicating that the meeting was over.

21

Michelle Riolas had heard about these political meetings in smoke-filled rooms, but this was the first time she had ever been in attendance. The smoke came from three cigars, burning her eyes and nose.

"For crying out loud, boys." She fanned the air around her face. "Are those things necessary?"

"A good cigar clears the mind, it helps you think," Franklin said.

Riolas frowned. "You know what Freud said about cigars," she growled.

"Yes, I do," Franklin said. "But I'd like to hear you say it, if you don't mind." Riolas swatted in his general direction, as if he were a troublesome fly.

The cigars, however, were serving their purpose. For one thing, they made the long periods of silence seem less awkward.

It had been almost a month since the nomination, and the House Judiciary Committee remained steadfast in its refusal to hold confirmation hearings. Most of the major newspapers had published editorials in favor of hearings. However, most also blamed President DeWitt for precipitating the crisis by choosing someone with Huerta's lack of experience.

For his own part, DeWitt hadn't been able to do much in the way of promoting his choice. He had been laying low since his follow-up for gall bladder surgery in early June. The doctor said he was doing too much too soon, which accounted for his weight loss and weakness.

Huerta and Franklin had been on most of the Sunday morning interview programs to push their side of the story. But Chairman

Gilbertson continued to stand firm that DeWitt was playing games with the American people. Clovis Plambeck's daily radio program served as a sounding board for all those opposed to the Huerta nomination. Eventually, the story moved from the front pages to the inside. Then there was only the occasional story about how the gridlock was continuing, with no apparent end in sight.

Conventional wisdom said there would be no hearings, and Huerta would not be vice president.

Riolas was angry with the cigar-smoking men gathered in her boss's office. They seemed to be at a loss for what to do next.

"You guys are such geniuses," she said. "All along, you knew the House would probably refuse to hold confirmation hearings. Now you don't know what to do about it? What's that thing they say about 'prior planning?'"

"Yes, Michelle," Huerta responded. "It prevents 'piss-poor performance.' I've heard it a million times, mainly from you."

More silence. The smoke cloud was beginning to spawn its own weather system.

"I guess I'm just an old optimist," Englund said. "Part of me hoped that we'd at least be able to get you into hearings." He took a draw from a fine Honduran and puffed out a sizable smoke ring, which he quickly penetrated with a smaller ring.

"You could go on Letterman with that trick," Riolas smirked.

"Nah, I'm the only trick pony in this room," Huerta grumped.

Franklin eased back in his chair, slowly blowing out a prodigious stream of thick, blue smoke. "You know what really sucks? When they do the TV movie about all this, and they get to this part of the story, they won't let the actors smoke cigars. Bad influence on the kids. Very P.C."

"You'll probably be played by James Earl Jones," Huerta smirked.

"Oh, Christ!" Don said, slapping his thigh. "I can see it now..."

He stood and walked to where Huerta sat, leaned over and placed a hand on his shoulder. In a passable James Earl Jones, he said, "You must become vice president, young Asskicker! It is your destiny! Feel the dark side of the force, Roberto. I am your father! This is CNN."

Huerta shrugged Don's hand from his shoulder. "On second thought, maybe you'll be played by Jimmy Walker."

"Dy-no-MITE!" Don said, resuming his seat. "And you'll be played by Cheech Marin."

"Hey, mon. The vice president's not here," said Huerta, aping Cheech and Chong's Chicano druggie routine.

Riolas sat near the window, opened just a crack to let some air in. "I want to be played by a twenty-five-year-old Rita Moreno."

"I think I'll insist on playing myself," Englund mused. "I don't think there's an actor out there who can adequately capture the subtle nuances that are such a big part of my rich, full character."

"Hey, I'm with you," Huerta said. "I'll play myself, too. God knows, I'll need a job."

That sentiment drew a rousing round of silence. Huerta took stock of his surroundings. Riolas was looking at her shoes. Englund seemed to be fascinated by one of the cheap oil paintings on the wall. Only Franklin was looking at Huerta.

"See something green?" Huerta asked.

"I see something, all right. And I don't like it much."

"And pray tell, good Mr. Franklin, what would that be?"

"I see a man who is ready to throw in the towel prematurely," Franklin said, as a cloud of smoke encircled his head.

"Who said I was ready to quit?" Huerta asked.

Franklin rose from his seat and sat on the corner of Huerta's desk. "You did. Not with words, but with your expression. With your attitude. You reek of death, man."

Riolas continued fanning the air around her face. "You sure that ain't just the cigars?"

Franklin smiled. Then he turned to Huerta.

"Where's the fire that used to be in your belly, man? Where's the spirit you showed at the press conference? Where's the gumption? How come you're not out there, right now, holding another press conference, rallying the public to stand by you? How come you're just sitting here wearing a hang-dog expression, smoking cigars?"

Huerta stroked his chin, then considered his cigar.

"If I'm walking through the pasture and I see a withered-up old cow carcass on the ground, I don't need a doctor to tell me the critter's dead," he said.

More silence, more smoking. Huerta rose from his chair and wandered to the single office window.

"I don't mind losing a fight, fellas. I just wish there had actually been a fight to lose. This one was called on account of lack of interest."

"Sort of like they threw a wrestling match and nobody showed up?" Franklin asked.

"That's part of the problem," Huerta snapped. "Everyone wants to focus on the fucking wrestling. All the editorial cartoons show me wearing wrestling tights. Every news story makes at least one reference to 'the former professional wrestler.' Christ. I was a wrestler for six years. It paid for college, and kept meat on the table for the first couple years of my marriage. I never intended it to be a career."

"Sorry about that, Bob. But you know the media," Franklin said. "They grab onto what they can. They set the tone of the story, we have to live with it. It ain't nice, but it's the way it is."

Huerta grumbled something unintelligible and sat back down.

"Maybe part of the problem is that we're telling the wrong part of the story," Englund said. "Maybe we should be focusing more on what you've accomplished in the past and less on the fact that you're an alleged incorruptible non-insider."

Huerta raised a bushy eyebrow.

"Alleged?"

"I'm reserving judgment," Englund replied.

"Smart boy," Riolas said, with a smirk. "Hedging his bets."

"Be that as it may, I believe my point is valid. Why aren't we talking more about your record as a sheriff? That 'Mr. Mentor' program of yours, for instance. Why aren't we hitting on that?"

"Because it has nothing to do with where I am now or what we're trying to do," Huerta said sharply.

"The hell it doesn't," Englund responded. "It has everything to do with it. It speaks of trust and courage and commitment to the public welfare..."

"And we're not going to use it as an issue," Huerta barked. "End of story!"

"Look, Huerta," Englund said, rising to his feet. "This isn't just your political bacon in the fire. It's mine, it's Franklin's, and it's even President DeWitt's. Do you think anyone is ever going to take anything he says seriously ever again if Wantner and his allies are permitted to stonewall your nomination? DeWitt will be politically crippled for the rest of his term. And, if I may be selfish for a moment, I am a relatively young man. I hope to have a life after the DeWitt Administration. And I'm sure I speak for Don as well."

Franklin nodded slightly.

"So, if there's some huge, unshakable principle that forbids you from using the great and wonderful things you've done in the past as political fodder, then perhaps you would be good enough to share it with me!"

Englund plopped back on the sofa. Huerta looked at him, then turned toward Riolas. She smiled and nodded.

He leaned back in his chair and put his arms behind his head.

"Jim, Don, there's a reason I started that program, and it has nothing to do with trying to do something nice for my fellow man. It was a program born of a guilty conscience."

Huerta took a deep breath and continued.

"I had a younger brother. His name was Octavio. He died when he was twenty-two in a farm accident, leaving a wife and a little boy named Julio. It was the same kind of accident that killed my father. Stupid, really. A tractor rolled over on him. He was in the field, alone, and his legs were crushed. He lived about three hours, probably conscious the whole time. His wife, Martina, was a good woman, but she was just a little flighty. And she didn't really give Julio the attention he deserved or the discipline he needed. So, as you might expect, the kid grew up kind of wild. Martina didn't have any brothers living nearby and I was busy — first on the road doing the wrestling thing, then as a deputy. So I didn't have much time to spend with him, either.

"Well, Julio wound up running with some other wild kids. And he started getting into trouble. Small stuff at first — breaking windows, vandalism. Then, about the time he turned sixteen, the trouble started getting more serious. Stealing cars, snatching purses. He got caught in a stolen car with an ounce of grass, and did a turn in a juvenile home for a year. There, he learned how to commit bigger, better crimes.

"It happened the same year I was elected sheriff. Now, you understand that in a backwater little spot like Falfurrias, the sheriff isn't a person who just sits in his office drinking coffee and issuing press releases. Being sheriff where I come from is a real, live, law enforcement position. That means that sometimes you find yourself out on a job with your troops. That particular day, I had two guys out on vacation and we got a call about a breaking and entering at a local feed store.

"I happened to be in the office along with Deputy Martinez. Together we jumped into a squad and headed to the store. There was a pickup truck parked in the front and a broken window in the back. We could hear voices and stuff being moved around inside the store.

"I hollered out the traditional 'This Is The Police' bullshit and ordered them to come out with their hands raised. That's when someone inside the building fired a shot.

"Martinez and I took cover and I radioed for backup. Then we kicked in a door and entered the store with our weapons drawn.

"It was dark, of course, and we couldn't see that well. But I could make out two kids trying to climb out one of the windows at the front of the store. A third kid stood on the floor, and I could see he was holding something in his hand.

"I identified myself and ordered him to drop it. But he just stood there. I told him again to drop what he had in his hand, and he swiveled around and pointed the thing toward Martinez.

"I had no choice. I fired my weapon twice, hitting him in the chest with both bullets. I flipped on the lights and walked, weapon still drawn, toward the kid I shot. There, lying on the floor, eyes open wide, was my nephew Julio. He had a twenty-two caliber pistol in his hand. I kicked it away from him. He was wide-awake. The holes in his chest were making snotty, bubbling sounds."

"He looked right at me and said, 'Hi, Uncle Bob.' Then he died.

"His eyes... It was like someone hit a light switch. One second they were alive and aware. The next, they looked like glass doll-eyes. They rolled back in his head, and he was gone.

"I had to drive to my sister-in-law's house to tell her that I had just killed her son. She spit in my face and tried to claw my eyes out. She called me a murderer. And for a while, I guess I sort of believed her. She moved away shortly after the funeral. I heard about a year later that she hanged herself in her laundry room.

"Well, after a few months of talking to psychologists, I decided the best way to deal with this thing was to do whatever I could to make sure it didn't happen to any other fatherless kids — at least not in my county."

Huerta's eyes were dry and clear as he told the story. Then he turned toward Englund.

"And I am not going to repeat that story to the press. I will not use my dead nephew to attain the vice presidency."

Englund smiled sadly and nodded.

"Remember when I said I was reserving judgment? Consider that reservation canceled."

Franklin regarded his cigar as he rolled it between his thumb and forefinger. "Whenever I smoke these things, I feel somewhat Churchillian," he mused. "Now there was a guy. Bombs falling all around his big, bald head. And what does he do? He goes on the radio and tells his people to be brave, to be stalwart, to believe in the righteousness of their cause. How did he put it?"

He closed his eyes and did his best impression of Churchill's thick, deep British accent.

"If the empiah should last a thousand yeahs, historians will look back at us and say, 'This was their finest houah!'"

"Bravo, Sir Winston," Huerta said, clapping. "Now do General Eisenhower."

"I'll do better than that," Franklin said, setting his cigar down to smolder in the ashtray on the coffee table. "I'll do Chuck Colson."

He looked around the room. To their credit, no one said "Who?" at the reference to Richard Nixon's chief dirty-tricks contriver. Yet they were all puzzled.

"The great Chuck Colson once said, 'If you've got them by the balls, their hearts and minds will soon follow.'"

"I think, perhaps, that somebody has somebody's balls in a vice grip," Englund muttered. "They are the squeezers and we seem to be the squeezees."

"Another quote, if I may," Franklin said, leaning back with his hands behind his head. "The only constant in life is change. Everything changes."

"Who said that?" Riolas asked.

"I did, just now. Weren't you paying attention?" He grinned as she picked up a pad of *While You Were Out* message blanks and pegged it at him.

"Fine, so everything changes," Huerta said, stubbing out his cigar (which he didn't really enjoy and only lit to be polite). "Are we coming up with nice little sayings to embroider on pillows or are we planning what we're going to do next?"

"Never been much for artsy, craftsy stuff like embroidery," Franklin said. "But I love a good fight. Avoid 'em when I can. But when someone gets in my face, I can give better than I get."

"Fine," said Huerta. "When this whole mess is over, you can join me when I go back to wrestling. We can be tag-team partners."

"Oh-ho! So I bring up the wrestling angle and you get pissed," Franklin said. "OK, champ. You want to use the wrestling analogy now, let's use the wrestling analogy. Assume for a moment that professional wrestling is real."

"I used to love it when reporters asked if it was real," Huerta interrupted. "I'd put them in a nice, tight headlock and say, 'You tell me, hotshot. Does this feel real to you?'"

Franklin smiled. "Yeah, we all saw a streak of that at the press conference the other day. But let's say you and I were going up against the tag-team champions of the world. What would our strategy be?"

"To follow the script or else get our asses fired," Huerta said.

"Remember, for now, just for the sake of argument, it's real."

Huerta thought for a moment. "Well, for the sake of argument, I'd say that before the match you and I would agree on which of our two opponents was the strongest and the toughest. Then we'd concentrate on bringing him down, getting him out of the way. Then we'd go after the weak link and win the belts."

Englund, who had been smoking in silence, perked up at that

116

remark.

"So, Don, what you're saying is that if we go after someone in the GOP hierarchy..."

"Not necessarily in the GOP itself," Franklin said. He appraised the expressions of all in the room.

Riolas was the first to get it.

"But someone the GOP listens to," she said.

"Bingo!" Franklin shouted, reaching into his vest pocket.

"You're thinking about Plambeck, aren't you?" Englund asked. "How would you do it?"

"Suppose for a moment old Clove could be made to see things our way," Franklin pondered. He could be a powerful force for good in this wicked and mean old universe."

"And what are the chances of that?" Huerta asked. "He's the asshole leading the charge against me."

"Maybe he just hasn't seen the light yet," Franklin said. "Maybe he just doesn't know all the facts. Even the most resolute soul can change his mind once he knows all the facts. All it takes is for someone who knows the facts to approach Mr. Plambeck and explain them to him in a calm, clear, pleasant voice. And I nominate me. Do I have a second?"

"I second the nomination," said Riolas.

Franklin stared in surprise. "Does this mean we're going steady?"

"Take a cold shower, my boy. It's just that a job like the one you described will take a bullshit artist of the highest degree. And you, my dear, have more of that particular commodity than my Uncle Raoul had on his whole cattle ranch."

Huerta regarded Franklin closely. He was getting fonder and fonder of the old conniver. "Quite the scrapper, aren't you Don? Are you sure you ain't from Texas?"

"Nope, Chicago born and bred, that's me. I did spend some time in Texas, though. Back in my voter registration days, all that 'Freedom

Rider' stuff, remember? I think it was somewhere around your neck of the woods. I wouldn't say it was hell, but it was close enough that you could send a 'Howdy from Hell' postcard if you wanted to."

He rose from his chair and walked to the coffee pot. Riolas followed. The others continued in quiet conversation.

"You've got a plan," she whispered. "I know you've got a plan. You are a devious, underhanded, slick, slimy, political, creepy piece of shit and I know you've got a plan."

"The lady is astute," Franklin replied. "I'll fill you in if you'd like. But you have to promise not to tell the boss. I'm sure I don't have to explain the term 'Plausible Deniability.'"

"Spare me the details. It's better I don't know. But you do have a plan, don't you?"

"Yes, ma'am. I do have a plan."

Riolas smiled at him, and Franklin felt the temperature in the room climb a couple degrees.

22

As the rental car threaded the worn-down hills of eastern Pennsylvania, Don Franklin had time to let his mind wander.

This is good, he thought. *Good to remember that people live in places like this.*

The turnpike skirted the hills, taking the long-time Washington denizen through towns with names like Aroma Heights, Donegal and Sommerset. He got off the Pennsylvania Turnpike at McCandless and drove north along State Highway 8.

The Pittsburgh area was definitely blue-collar, with a respectable dose of agriculture. Old farmsteads mingled easily with the nearby steel factories and oil refineries. The air smelled of hay and petroleum.

The car handled the sharp curves and steep grades with ease, and soon he found himself on the outskirts of East Butler. The sign at the city limits proclaimed, *Hometown of Clovis Plambeck!* Franklin extended a middle finger in tribute. He smiled at his petty little act of vengeance. He had bigger things in store for the hometown hero.

His first stop: the local library.

He guessed at Plambeck's age and asked for all of the high school yearbooks between 1967 and 1975. He hit pay dirt with 1971.

And there he was — Clovis Plambeck, Senior, no sports recognition, no clubs, none of those numbers by his name to show on what pages he would be seen in other pictures. The black-and-white picture showed a misfit — unkempt hair, black horn-rimmed glasses, a near-terminal case of acne.

He must have gone through hell, Franklin thought. And for a moment he had to force himself to concentrate on the task at hand. "The predator does not pity the prey," he mumbled. That was the law in every jungle, especially the one known as Washington.

He paged through the rest of the senior class and jotted down names. David Sproul, class president. Steve Hammer, valedictorian. Connie Westerson, homecoming queen.

In all, Franklin jotted down 15 names. All would probably swear on a stack of Gideons that Clovis Plambeck had been one of their best friends. They took hay rides together. They spun 45 rpm records at the sock hop. They all gathered at the Plambeck house for cocoa after going on sleigh rides. Funny how memories can change when a classmate gets famous. But that was not the sort of information he was looking for. He wanted to find someone with a grudge — a long-standing enemy bearing the kind of spite that grows and festers and turns downright venomous when the object of that hatred reaches the top of the ladder.

Franklin reached for the East Butler phone book. Three of the names on his list had local numbers. He jotted them down on his pad.

An hour later, Franklin sat down in a dingy little motel room on Highway 422 to make some calls.

David Sproul was a bank president now, but he was away on a business trip, according to his wife. Steve Hammer now ran a chain of local hardware stores, but he was never so busy that he couldn't take a few minutes to talk about his good friend Clovis Plambeck, especially to a reporter from *New Republic* magazine.

"I always liked Clovis," Hammer said. "But he didn't always get the best of treatment by a lot of the kids here."

Hammer explained it as a result of Plambeck's shy nature, awkward looks and the fact that his father was widely blamed for an industrial accident that took the lives of several area workers.

Franklin asked if Plambeck's celebrity had changed the attitudes of any of the locals who had once detested him.

"Oh, you'd have to look far and wide to find anyone who would ever admit now that they used to call him 'Icky.'"

"Icky?" Franklin asked. He jotted the word on his notepad.

"Yeah, after Ichabod Crane, 'The Legend of Sleepy Hollow,' remember that story? One of the girls in our class pinned that moniker on him in the ninth grade, I think. As I recall, this particular girl was the worst. She was always on his a... his case. It was as if tormenting Plambeck was her hobby."

Franklin asked if Hammer remembered the girl's name. He did. He also knew her married name. And, yes, she still lived in town.

Franklin thanked Hammer for talking to him, promised to send him a copy of the article, and hung up the phone with a smile.

"Connie Westerson Pronchinske," he muttered as he flipped through the phone book. There was only one Pronchinske listed, and they answered on the third ring.

"Hello?"

"Yes, is this Connie Pronchinske?"

"Yes?"

Franklin cranked up the charm.

"Hi there, my name is Stuart Graves. I'm a reporter for the *New Republic* magazine, and I'm doing a story about one of your local hometown celebrities..."

"Clovis Plambeck," she said curtly. "I know. I just got a call from David Sproul's wife. She said you might call."

She sounded like she'd rather eat arsenic than talk about Plambeck.

He asked if he could meet her for a face-to-face interview. She let out a long sigh.

"I don't know what for," she said. "If this is going to be another one of those feel-good things about what a wonderful man Plambeck is and how proud we all are to have known the asshole in his youth, then you're wasting your time."

Franklin assured the woman that this wasn't going to be that kind of article.

"Quite the opposite," he said. "We're trying to find out why a working-class child would grow up to be such an elitist."

She took the bait and said she would need an hour to get ready. She suggested a local restaurant where they could meet for coffee.

Franklin hung up the phone, quite pleased with himself.

He recalled Connie's high school picture. If she had aged well at all, she would likely be a beauty. And if she really hated her old high school classmate and was willing to cooperate, his plan just might work.

He took a quick shower, put on a journalistic-looking shirt-and-sweater combo, and departed for the cafe.

An hour and 15 minutes later, Franklin stood from his booth in the corner and shook hands with his new helpmeet. His heart sank at what he saw. The face still bore a basic similarity to the perky but mean-eyed high school honey. But time had not been friendly. Her face bore the brunt of the years, and after seven children and years of hard factory work she no longer had anything resembling a "girlish figure."

Plambeck would giggle like a schoolgirl if he could see you now, Franklin thought.

The haggard-looking woman was all too happy to talk about her association with Plambeck. She still hated his guts. She refused to let her husband listen to his show in the house. (It turns out, her father was one of the men killed in the industrial accident Hammer had referred to.) If she saw him today, she would spit in his eye, give him a wedgie, and then kick him right in his scrawny ass, she said.

Franklin saw his original plan flying away on wings of spite. Still, he went through the motions of a magazine interview as his mind concocted a new plan.

23

Donald Franklin was not the only man on an information-gathering mission.

Jimmy Langston couldn't remember feeling so crowded and uncomfortable. The second-rate airline took him only as close as Kingsville, Texas. The rest of the way was on a rattletrap bus down the four-lane highway to Riviera — a misnamed place if ever there was one. How the town's only rental car company could be entirely out of stock is something he mumbled he'd never understand.

After disgorging its passengers, the bus sat idle for three hours. Langston had little choice but to wait at the broken-down bus station. There was only one place to get something to eat, an enchilada stand across the street. But it was closed. Langston dined on mints from the bus station candy machine.

The bus was once again packed to capacity for its journey west to Falfurrias. It was the longest 23 miles in Langston's years of international travel. For one thing, the air conditioning was either broken or intentionally left off. He complained earlier to the bus driver, who told him it was only 92 degrees, so using the air conditioner would be a waste of the company's money.

For another thing, the seats on the bus seemed to be built for skinny midgets, not for overfed Washington functionaries. The old woman in the seat next to him was almost, in fact, in his lap. And she kept staring at him! She stared at him the whole way, with an open, empty expression. Langston returned the stare, but only once. The woman's face wrinkled into a toothless smile.

The bus pulled to a stop in front of a slightly less ramshackle bus station in downtown Falfurrias. Langston had to wait for the old woman to exit the bus before he could dismount. He gathered his baggage and asked the driver where he could hail a cab.

"In New York, probably," the driver said with a sneer. "Here, in Falfurrias, you want a cab, you have to call for one on the phone."

An hour later, Langston was in his room at the Stay Awhile Motel on Highway 281, the four-lane that runs north and south through the town. It was not quite what he was used to. The rug crackled when he walked on it. In the bathroom, crickets moved lazily across the floor when he turned on the light. A lizard watched warily from the shower curtain. Given the condition of the shower cubicle, he wondered if he would be even filthier after using it.

For not the first time in recent years, Jimmy Langston cursed the name of Al Wantner.

He had been Wantner's "go-to" guy for ten years. All during the climb from obscurity to fame, Langston had been there. And still the tight son-of-a-bitch wouldn't legitimize Langston's efforts with the title "chief of staff." As far as the Congressional Budget Office knew, Langston was nothing more than Wantner's "Special Administrative Aide."

It was the "Special Administrative Aide" who was responsible for doing the things that needed to be done, but that the congressman himself would not be caught dead doing. If a fellow member needed convincing, and that convincing came tied to a bundle of twenties, it was Langston who delivered the goods. For the rare individual who would not be financially enticed, it was Langston's job to come up with something incriminating — real or created, it didn't matter.

Wantner had a special way of asking Langston to do the tasks that would land them both in jail should anything go wrong. He would direct

Langston *not* to commit the act, and that was as good as an order.

"Now, Jimmy," he would simper in his sugary sweet Carolina accent. "I want you to make absolutely certain that Congressman So-and-So has every opportunity to see the error of his ways on his own accord. I do not want to hear that he has been pressured in any way. It would be a terrible thing if someone were to go digging around in his past and find or fabricate some sort of dirty, scandalous secret that would embarrass the congressman and his family. So let's keep it all above-board, hear?"

Wantner did not know, however, that Langston always carried a microcassette recorder in his inner jacket pocket, and that the recorder was always switched on when he was summoned before the speaker.

Langston slept well in the knowledge that he'd make sure the feds would found out about them if Wantner ever decided to sacrifice his special administrative aide.

After re-examining the grime-caked shower, Langston opted to splash himself with some Aqua Velva and get to work.

His previous phone calls to folks who knew folks who "did business" in this area were fruitless. Nothing unseemly had been discovered about the spic asshole who wanted to be vice president. Frankly, Langston doubted that this little in-person Texas Trek would dig up any more dirt than his calls.

But, as the saying goes, his was not to reason why.

24

She was an exquisite beauty, and vaguely familiar.

Even as a celebrity, Clovis Plambeck did not regularly enjoy the company of such women — unless they had been paid for, discreetly, by the organizers of speaking engagements like tonight's. But this one had come up to him unbidden.

"You don't remember me, do you?" she asked, batting her long eyelashes.

Plambeck found himself being drawn into her dark brown eyes. He searched his memory. She was definitely familiar. But he'd never known anyone who looked like... like this! Long jet-black hair that cascaded to just below her tanned shoulders. A black, low-cut dress that revealed bare shoulders and a bounteous valley of cleavage.

He forced his gaze back to her eyes.

"Have we met before?" he asked, working hard to keep his voice steady.

She laughed a merry laugh, nothing harsh or ridiculing in its nature.

"Have we MET? You really don't recognize me, do you!?"

Plambeck smiled and shrugged.

Since his show went national, people were always approaching him like this. People he had never met claiming past associations. He would generally smile and nod and feign recognition. It came with celebrity. But this was the first time he had been approached by one so delectable.

And she did look familiar.

She extended her right hand and took his. "Connie Westerson," she said. "Ring a bell?"

It wasn't just a bell — it was a sledgehammer blow to his stomach. He almost dropped her hand in shock.

Everyone in the Class of 1971 at East Butler High School knew Connie Westerson. She was a cheerleader, the homecoming queen. A vicious little bitch who once drove a gawky boy named Clovis to the point of considering suicide with her relentless, mean-spirited teasing. The one who started calling him "Icky."

"Ah," he said. "Now I remember."

Ever since he began to realize years ago that he was becoming a famous person, he wondered how he would react if faced by one of his former tormentors. He told himself he would smile with all the dignity he could muster, toss a cutting insult, turn and walk away.

But this was Connie Westerson. She held a special position in his Hall of Hate.

He had hoped that she had grown old and miserable and fat and lonely, with an abusive, alcoholic husband and droves of unkempt children. But here she was, beautiful, radiant, the same age as he but not showing it at all.

"Long time, no see," she said. "You've certainly done well for yourself."

You too, you malevolent bitch, Plambeck thought but didn't say.

"I've been lucky," he did say. "Being in the right place at the right time, you know how it goes."

"More than luck, Clovis," she said (this was the first time he could recall her speaking his given name). "You did what it took to get you where you are. You've made folks see things the way they are, not the way they think they'd like them to be. You are a hero, Clovis Plambeck. A hero and a patriot."

Her eyes dropped. "And when I think about what a – you know – I was to you back in high school, it makes me ashamed."

She made eye contact again and Plambeck felt electricity running through his body. "Maybe it's too late to apologize?" she said with a touch of pleading.

"A sincere apology is never too late," Plambeck said. "But it would probably sound better over dinner. Do you have any plans for later?"

His heart sank as she bit her lower lip and looked away. "Ooooh, I'm afraid I do," she said.

"Well, maybe some other time."

He was bitterly disappointed. For just a moment there, he was beginning to believe he might have a chance at bedding Miss East Butler Bitch, and that would set a lot of things right in his mind. An evening of rough sex would be expiation for a multitude of sins.

Ah well, he thought. Then he asked, "But you are staying for the speech?"

"Oh, of course! That's what I'm here for" she said, her dark eyes brightening.

***

Transcript of Clovis Plambeck's June 24th speech to the National Federation of Republican Women:

> I don't want anyone to think that my opposition to the president's unfortunate nomination of a vice presidential candidate reflects unfavorably on the character of the person so chosen. I have nothing against Roberto Huerta. And many of you ladies have no doubt been impressed by the gallantry of his actions in that dark hallway. Surely, he is responsible for saving that woman's life.
>
> So, and I want to be very clear about this, nothing I'm about to say should be taken as an assault on the integrity of the great congressman from Texas. I have no doubt about the purity of his motivations, as naive as

they may be. I am convinced that he is possessed of a genuine desire to serve his country.

It's just that if the congressman had a little more government experience under his belt, he would recognize a cynical political ploy for what it is. He would have realized that the only reason President DeWitt proposed making him vice president was for the "good will" DeWitt envisioned reaping for his administration.

My friends, let there be no mistake. John DeWitt's liberal policies are facing a tough go in Congress. In the last two elections, the American people have opted for a conservative Congress. There's nothing DeWitt would like better than to shove his liberal agenda down your throats.

In the past several years, the Congress has been doing the will of the people — paring down the size of government, cutting back on wasteful spending, putting deadbeats to work and beefing up the national defense. All of these things fly in the face of liberal John DeWitt.

But one thing you can say about John DeWitt. He is not stupid. He is out of touch with reality, behind the times politically, a walking, talking, breathing political anachronism, if you will. But he is not stupid.

By nominating Roberto Huerta to be his new vice president, DeWitt is rolling the political dice, maybe the last gamble of his long career. He is betting the farm that you will all get the "warm fuzzies" because of Huerta's courageous, headstrong actions. He's hoping against hope that you won't look any further than Huerta's well-chiseled Hispanic features, that you won't examine Huerta's brief political career and come to the realization that the Texas congressman is even more liberal than DeWitt.

My friends, as usual, the president has underestimated the political savvy and common sense of the American people. In the days and weeks to come, there will be considerable pressure brought to bear on Congressman Gilbertson, chairman of the House

Judiciary Committee.

The liberal media, which has taken the lead in lionizing Huerta, will whine and wheedle and gripe and moan. They will say Congressman Gilbertson doesn't have the right to oppose this nomination. And in so doing, they will demonstrate their lack of knowledge about how things are done in Washington.

The chairman does indeed have the right to refuse to hold hearings. By doing so, Chairman Gilbertson is forcing the DeWitt Administration to quit playing games with the American people. It forces the president to take a little time to find a nominee who is qualified for the job, not because he happened to thrash a couple hoodlums in a tenement hallway, but because he – or she – has a record of government service that qualifies him – or her – to occupy that office, to be the person a heartbeat away from the presidency.

25

Stan Anniston believed that a local radio talk show should focus on local issues. But these days, most callers wanted to talk about the raw deal Roberto Huerta was getting from the Republican congress.

At first, Anniston tried to brush off calls of this nature. "Hey, let the idiots like Plambeck talk about the national stuff," he'd say. "Here in Chicago we have troubles of our own. We have a whole sector of the population that's disenfranchised from the recent economic boom. We live in a city that is, by some accounts, the most segregated large city in America. We're losing jobs to industries south of the border."

But as hard as he tried to stay local, the callers still wanted to talk about developments in DC.

"They don't listen to what we want!" one lady said. "They don't care what we want! All they can do is bicker and fight."

"So, who did you vote for in the last election?" Anniston asked.

"Nobody. And don't give me that stuff about how I don't have a right to complain, either," she said. "You are smart enough to know that my vote doesn't matter, your vote doesn't matter, nobody's vote matters. All that matters is who can get the most money to go on TV and call the other candidate a crook — and that money doesn't come from folks like you and me, Stan. It comes from the tobacco companies, the lawyers, the health care industry, the NRA, the AARP, and the labor unions. So why should we bother?"

It was Friday afternoon as he sat in his office making notes for Monday's show. The woman's call was running through Anniston's mind. She really made a point, he decided. Here was this perfectly inoffensive guy from Texas who apparently didn't have any skeletons in his closet. If he had some, anyway, no one had found them yet. The president had the right to choose whoever he wanted to be his vice president. The polls had been running in favor of Huerta's nomination. Yet the House Judiciary Committee wasn't even going to hold hearings. It reeked of unfairness.

The newspaper on his desk was open to the local news section. On the page was a picture of Stuart Kleskowicz — one of the Chicago area's rare Republican congressmen. He would be in town for the remainder of the summer recess, and planned on holding a series of "town meetings" to discuss local issues.

Anniston had an idea. He picked up the phone on his desk, called the engineering department and asked what it would take to do a spur-of-the-moment remote broadcast on Monday.

26

With the nomination stalled, seemingly for good, Huerta found himself with more time for his congressional duties. One such duty confronted him at the moment. It was one he actually enjoyed, one where his input actually meant something — going through service academy nomination applications.

"Billy Molina," Riolas said, handing a folder across the desk. "Going into his senior year at Falfurrias High, GPA 3.4. One of the kids who looked like gang-bait before he signed up in the Mr. Mentor program. Three letters of recommendation from teachers, one from the principal. He wants to go to the Naval Academy."

Huerta sat back in his chair. "Billy Molina? Is his mother a waitress at the El Camino Diner?"

"Gabriella Molina, one and the same."

"Damn. It was only yesterday that I was pulling that kid's wiggling ass out of a back alley store window that he just broke. He wasn't more than eleven years old. Put up a hell of a fight for such a squirt. Called me all kinds of names, none of which was 'Mr. Deputy.' Shit, where does the time go?"

"Out the window, never to return," Riolas said. "Is Tommy giving any thought to what he's going to do after high school?"

Huerta shrugged. "To tell you the truth, Michelle, I don't know if the kid has given any thought to what he's going to do after dinner tonight."

"Sorry about that, Bob. Sore subject, I know."

Huerta smiled sadly. "Don't worry about Tommy. That's my job."

He paused, looking down at the applications.

"For the life of me, Michelle, I can't figure the kid out. He's never wanted for anything in his life, yet he seems to go out of his way to find things to be upset about. Janelle only seems to be able to get through to him about half the time. And Tommy and I haven't had much to say to each other since..."

"He took it pretty hard, didn't he?" Riolas said, sitting on the corner of Huerta's desk.

Huerta sighed. "They were almost like brothers," he said. "Tommy really looked up to Julio. Thought he was cool. Admired the way he rebelled against authority. He's never talked to me about what happened, but it doesn't take a psychology degree to sense the resentment. I don't think he'll ever forgive me for taking his cousin away. It's almost like I lost them both that day."

Riolas rubbed Huerta's shoulders as he sat. "Give it some time. Time is the great healer."

Then someone else spoke. "To every thing there is a season, and a time for every purpose under heaven."

Huerta and Riolas looked up to find Al Wantner, standing alone in the doorway. Riolas hopped down from the desk, and Huerta rose to his feet.

"Mr. Speaker," he said, crossing the office to greet him. "It's an honor to have you in my humble office. Please come in, have a seat."

"Why thank you, Congressman Huerta. I believe I shall."

"Would you like a cup of coffee?" Huerta asked.

Riolas immediately shot him a look that said, *You want coffee for this asshole? Get it yourself!*

"Well, thank you, but no. Mrs. Wantner is always on my backside about cutting down on caffeine. But thank you just the same."

Huerta reassumed his seat behind the desk, folded his hands on the desktop, and gave his visitor his full attention.

"So, Mr. Speaker, to what do I owe the honor?"

"Well, Mr. Huerta, Roberto. May I call you Roberto?"

"Call me Bob if you like," Huerta said.

"Fine. Well, Bob (the word had two syllables when Wantner said it), there are some issues I'd like to discuss with you. If you have the time, that is."

"I always have time for the Speaker of the House," Huerta said.

Riolas rolled her eyes.

"Well that's just fine," Wantner said, clapping his hands together. "But given the sensitive nature of the issues I'd like to discuss, is there any chance I could bend your ear in private?" He looked at Riolas with a smirk.

Riolas looked at her boss, shrugged her shoulders, then looked at her watch.

"Goodness, would you look at that," she gushed. "Almost two o'clock! My novela will be on in a minute! Gracious! I'd best skeedaddle." She rose and fairly stomped toward the door, doing her best not to slam it behind her.

Both men watched her go.

"She's a handsome, solid woman," said Wantner.

"She's a fine assistant," Huerta said. He noticed the Speaker had been watching her ass.

"No doubt, sir." Wantner cast his gaze around the congressman's dingy inner office. "My goodness," he said. "It's been a hound's age since I've been in this part of the building. I had forgotten how, well, lived-in this area was."

"It's not the Ritz Carlton, that's for sure. But we're able to get the job done here."

"It just doesn't seem right," Wantner said. "A smart young fellow like you, and this is the best we can do for you? A cubbyhole in a closet?

Land's sakes! Someone oughta whup me for a hoss! First thing I'm going to do when I get back to my office is see if I can find some better accommodations for you and your staff. Speaking of which, how large is your staff, Bob?"

"Six, including Ms. Riolas."

"Is that all?" Wantner seemed genuinely shocked. "Well, that just won't do at all!"

He pulled a microcassette recorder out of his jacket pocket and punched the record button. "LuAnn, let's see about increasing Congressman Huerta's staff. And let's get him into a more spacious office."

He paused for effect.

"As soon as all this vice presidential nonsense is over with, that is."

He clicked off the recorder and replaced it in his pocket. What had just happened was clear to Huerta: there was a bribe in the works.

"And when will all this vice presidential nonsense be over with, Mr. Speaker?"

"Why, as soon as you want it to be, Roberto!" Wantner spoke slowly, as if addressing a brighter-than-average cocker spaniel. "I'm sure I'm not telling tales out of school when I tell you that your nomination is dead in the water. I suppose that silly old man in the Oval Office can drag things out as long as he wants to. But he's just wasting time!"

Wantner leaned toward Huerta, as if he were about to share a great confidence.

"You want to help the president, don't you Roberto?"

"Call me Bob," Huerta replied.

"Congressman Huerta, this is not a time to be flip," Wantner said, his voice stern. "The media is crucifying the Congress, saying that we're stonewalling the vice presidential nomination. But the truth of the matter is that the president is the one who is doing the stonewalling. And if he's so damn stubborn that he can't see the futility of this effort, then it is up to his supporters, his colleagues, and his friends to tell him otherwise. You are his friend, Huerta. You can help him in a way nobody else can."

"And how might I do that, Mr. Speaker?"

"You can call a press conference. The sooner the better. This afternoon. Say how much you appreciate the president's confidence in you, but that you understand the political certainty that you will never be vice president. You will urge the president to withdraw your name from consideration and to choose someone with more experience." He paused a moment. "You will be doing your president – and your country – a great service."

Huerta leaned back in his seat.

"And when I do, that's when I get the nice new office and a larger staff?"

"It would only be the thing to do," Wantner said, brightening. "After all, you are no longer an invisible, anonymous legislator from a poor district in south Texas. You are a celebrity, sir. Given a few years, you could be a force to be reckoned with. Especially if you have friends in Congress. And I'd like to be your friend, Roberto."

"Please, call me Bob," Huerta said.

"Bob, then. Whatever. Being able to read the handwriting on the wall is a valuable political skill, Bob. Not everyone gets the hang of it. It would be helpful to know that you have that ability, at least."

Huerta leaned back even further. A broad smile crossed his face. Wantner leaned forward, anxious for an answer. The silence was thick and heavy. Finally, Wantner could wait no longer.

"So, do I call that press conference?"

Huerta sat upright.

"Oh, goodness, no!" he exclaimed. "Your offer is a kind one, Al, but the president has placed a lot of faith in me, and I'm not about to back out on him when I've given my word. But thanks for asking!"

Wantner stood and wheeled toward the door. He stopped and turned to face Huerta.

"This is not the worst office in the complex. I hope you know that. There are far worse offices than this. Some are in the basement. I hear there are rats down there!"

Huerta crossed his arms over his chest and smiled.

"Mr. Speaker, the work of the people can be done anywhere, even in the basement. There are worse things in this building than rats. And as soon as you come up with the order to move, I'll issue a press release letting the media know all about my new address — as well as the reasons for the relocation."

Wantner stomped toward Huerta and thrust a shaking index finger under his nose.

"You're a smart little bastard, aren't you? Smart little bastards like you tend to get ground up in the machinery. If I were you, I'd watch my ass. You're not going to be vice president. You're going to be nothing more than a lowly little congressman from a pissant district in Texas. I can make it hell for you, Huerta! Don't doubt it for a minute." He turned and marched to the door.

"Mr. Speaker." Wantner turned around.

"Please," said Huerta. "Call me Bob."

Wantner slammed the door behind him.

Riolas rushed into the office.

27

After 20 minutes of hand shaking, Plambeck walked out the front door of the hotel to his waiting limo. The speech seemed to have gone well, and Plambeck was happy. The doorman opened the limo door, and Plambeck slid inside.

"Hi there."

Plambeck felt the little hairs on the back of his neck standing up. His eyes were not yet accustomed to the dark interior. But his nose recognized the perfume.

"I thought you said you had plans," he said, trying to force his heart down from his throat.

"I do," Connie Westerson purred. "Just wait and see."

She motioned to the driver, who pulled the limo away from the curb.

"Am I being kidnapped?" Plambeck asked, only half-kidding.

"I don't know," she replied. "Do you want to be?"

She was all the way across the back seat from him, her back propped against the corner, her long legs draped over the velour seat.

"Where are we going?" he started to ask, before being cut off by a deep, probing kiss.

She attacked him, her lithe body pressing him against the door. One hand caressed his face. The other rubbed his right thigh. His arms found their way around her slim waist and pulled her closer. She moaned into his open mouth.

Plambeck worked his right hand down to her tight buttocks, then to her bare thigh — smooth and hard as marble. His hand found its way under her dress. The nerve endings in his fingers reported that she wasn't wearing panties. This bulletin was interrupted by a message from his crotch. Her hand found his zipper.

I'm the luckiest boy in the world, Plambeck thought as she freed his eager member from its white cotton confinement.

Her touch was light but firm. His often-ignored libido came rushing to the surface and overthrew whatever reasonable thoughts still lingered in his brain. He felt the sweet moment of release getting closer, still closer as she stroked. Her tongue teased and flicked at his lips, then thrust itself between his teeth, probing the top of his mouth, then his throat.

Plambeck was within moments of soiling his tuxedo pants when he felt the limo pulling to a stop. Connie suddenly released her grip and sat upright. She adjusted her dress, smoothed down the skirt, and scooted across the seat away from him. Plambeck's unsatisfied urgency jutted from his pants like an accusation.

She smiled as she took a brush from her purse.

"Best holster that weapon, soldier. For now."

She brushed her silky black hair as Plambeck fought to package himself.

"You ready to walk?" she asked.

He found himself unable to speak. He gestured with a thumb as if to say, "Out there?"

She folded her arms under her breasts. "We can't go up to my suite unless you open the door," she said patiently.

***

Five minutes later, Clovis Plambeck was on his back on the king size bed in Connie Westerson's hotel suite. He was fully clothed. So was Connie. But she was laying on top of him, her body pressing him into the mattress.

Her legs parted, and he could feel the pressure of her sex against his. After being so close to orgasm in the back seat of the limo, he knew he wouldn't be able to endure much more without ruining his pants. He grabbed her hips and rolled her over on her side, facing him.

"God," he moaned. "This is so fucking intense. I used to fantasize about this very thing, you know. In high school, I used to dream at night about doing this to you — with you, I mean."

Of course, in these particular dreams, I would wind up bashing in your head with a brick or a baseball bat, he didn't say.

"I was a problem child back then, as well you know," she said. "I suffered from PLT Syndrome — 'Pretty Little Twat.' I got over it in college."

Plambeck rolled to the side of the bed, stood, and began removing his clothes. "May I ask how?

"Getting gang-raped will square away the attitude of even the snootiest bitch," Connie said. "While you were applying yourself in college, I was just there for the party. I was going out with a guy on the football team. I won't say who he is, except that he's now making a lot of money in the NFL. I played him like a violin, but I really wasn't any nicer to him than I was to you, if you can believe that. Then, one night after his team won a bowl game, he got drunk and came to my apartment with a bunch of his buddies. They were drunk, too. He said something about me thinking my vagina was made of solid gold, and that he was now a big NFL prospect who'd go in the first round and he could find women who would make me look like a bag lady. He said he didn't need to put up with my crap anymore. I told him that was just fine with me because I was getting tired of wasting my time with a pickled gherkin dick like him when the world was full of fine, ripe cucumbers. Well, he slapped me – beat the shit out of me, actually – ripped off my jeans and fucked me. Then he drank beer out of my refrigerator as his friends fucked me on the floor of my living room. After I got out of the hospital, I found a cashier's check for $25,000 in my mailbox. I suspect a thorough investigation of the athletic department's budget for the year would find that $25,000 was expended for miscellaneous purchases."

Serves you right, Plambeck thought. But his facial expression was one of utter concern.

"And you didn't press charges?" he asked, as he eased back onto the bed.

"No. I figured I pretty much had it coming. And the money helped me get my real estate agency started. I told the police some thugs had attacked me. No one was ever arrested."

"And somehow you survived, and if you don't mind my saying so, you don't look particularly worse for the wear," Plambeck said.

"Yeah," she said, a hint of weariness in her voice. "My nose and cheeks were broken, so — voila! A new nose, cheekbones slightly higher, a new look for the little princess. Did they do a good job?"

"Exquisite." *And soon we shall see how those new cheekbones of yours look with my cum all over them*, he didn't say.

He pulled her close, but she pushed him away.

"Hang on there a second, tiger," she said. "The lady must prepare herself. Be right back."

She got off the bed, grabbed her purse and walked to the bathroom. She blew him a kiss from the door. "Don't start without me," she said.

Fuck you, he thought as he rubbed his swollen manhood absent-mindedly.

As she busied herself in the bathroom, Plambeck took stock of his surroundings. The hotel suite looked like something out of pornographer's dream. The centerpiece of the room was the big four-poster bed, complete with a canopy. The bedspread was dark blue velvet, making the whiteness of his skin seem downright stark. The door to the main sitting area was big, wide, ornate and closed. Another door, presumably a closet, occupied the far wall.

He folded his arms behind his head and let himself sink into the mattress. He felt oddly mixed emotions. The story she told about being sexually abused evoked feelings of sympathy. And sympathy was the last thing he wanted to feel toward the chief tormentor of his childhood.

He decided to dredge up one of the most unpleasant memories of all to fight back this unwelcome tinge of compassion.

He let his mind drift back to his senior year in high school. Physical Education, or "Hell on Earth," as he used to regard it.

A group of football players grabbed him while he was drying off after a shower, and carried him out the door leading to the gymnasium. At the same time, the cheerleaders were practicing, going over their routines for the game that night.

The young athletes carried their wriggling victim to the center circle on the basketball court, deposited him unceremoniously on the hardwood floor, and dashed back to the locker room, locking the door behind them before Plambeck could reach it.

The sight of skinny, naked Clovis Plambeck, screaming and crying and banging his fists on the locker room door, stopped the cheerleaders in mid-cheer. Most stood and watched in shocked silence.

Only Connie Westerson spoke. Bitch Queen Cuntsie Westerson.

"Hey, Icky," she sneered. "Is it that cold out here, or is your pee-pee always that tiny? Yikes!"

It took almost five minutes before one of the cheerleaders returned with the physical education teacher, who ordered the boys to open the door. The students who participated in the prank each got two days' suspension and a letter to their parents.

He would never be able to get even with them. But God had delivered his chief tormentor to him. Sympathy, empathy, compassion, or whatever soft feeling had attempted to corrupt his revenge had been banished.

Retribution was at hand.

She was in the bathroom for almost ten minutes. When she came out, he decided it had been worth the wait. She was wearing something lacy, revealing, exciting. She was also holding a small canvas bag.

"My toys," she said. "It's just no fun to play unless you have toys." She reached into the bag and produced two pairs of fur-lined handcuffs.

Plambeck sat up on the bed. "Uh, I'm not really into the paraphernalia," he said. "Is that stuff really necessary?"

"Oh, I'm afraid it is," she said in a near-whisper. "Call it a result of my college trauma, if you will. But the only way I can get up for this sort of activity any more is to take a dominant role. Of course, if you have a problem with that, I can call a cab for you."

Plambeck certainly didn't want to leave. At least not until he had a chance to unload the burning cargo in his loins.

"It's not that I'm a prude or anything like that," he explained, lying back on the velour bedspread.

"Of course not," she said, in a voice as soft as silk. "It's just that you've never played this game before. I think you'll like it. In fact, if I know you at all, I think you're going to have the most intense climax you've ever experienced. But you have to trust. Can you trust? Just for a little while?"

Plambeck decided he could. More accurately, his eager protuberance decided for him.

"Hey, whatever it takes," he said. "What do you want me to do?"

She twirled the fur-lined cuffs. "Hands above your head," she ordered. Plambeck did as he was told. She crawled over him, wriggling her hips as she went. Plambeck strained and wriggled beneath her as she cuffed his wrists to the bedposts.

That's fine, bitch, he thought. *We'll play your fun, fun little game. And as soon as I'm free again, I'm going to roll you over and shove myself up your ass.*

Plambeck tugged at the cuffs. Both arms were fastened securely to the bedposts.

"Now what, the cat of nine tails?"

"Why Clovis, I thought I told you my days of bitchery are behind me."

And suddenly he was in her mouth, all the way to the hilt. His eyes rolled back in his head and he automatically tried to bring his hands down, to play with her hair, to shove himself even further down her throat. The cuffs restrained and frustrated him. *Part of the game*, he decided.

He wasn't far from climax. In the same zip code, and getting closer. Now on the same block, then within sight of the front porch.

And then she stopped.

"More toys," she said thickly. She reached into the bag and pulled out a pair of black nylon stockings and a garter belt.

"I don't fucking think so," Plambeck protested.

"Then I guess I'll have to call that cab," Connie said. She started putting them back in the bag.

"Fuck!" Plambeck hissed. "If I have to wear the stockings, then I guess I have to wear the stockings." *And you're going to be wearing a black eye as soon as I'm out of these cuffs*, he thought.

"You're so reasonable," she said. She unrolled the stockings onto his legs, first the left, then the right. "So reasonable and accommodating of a lady's foibles. Now lift your butt."

Plambeck complied, and she wiggled the garter belt over his hips, snapping the stockings onto the belt. No sooner was she finished with this operation than he found himself back in her mouth.

This time he was determined to blast his seed down the bitch's throat before she could stop again, before she could interrupt again, before she could frustrate him again, before she could...

"More toys," she said as she wiped away a string of saliva.

"Come on!" he pleaded, sounding a little too whiny for his own liking. "Finish me first, and then we can play with all the toys you want!"

"Mr. Plambeck, we mustn't be so hasty," she pouted. "I've promised you the most intense climax of your life. And I'm going to deliver. But you have to cooperate."

She reached into the canvas bag and pulled out a feather boa and a mask like the ones worn by women during Mardi Gras, covering just the eyes, narrowing to a point at the temples. The boa was a thick rope of day-glo yellow feathers. She put on the mask, snapping the elastic string around the back of her head, bunching up her thick black hair, and straddled his hips (his manhood straining against her lacy panties, trying to determine on its own if they were of the crotchless variety). Then she placed the boa around his neck.

She rocked back and forth slowly, rubbing herself against him, sending him nearer and nearer to that point of no return. Her eyes were wide open and sparkling. His were narrowed into slits. His breath hissed in and out through clenched teeth.

"And now, the moment we've all been waiting for," she proclaimed as she dismounted, kneeling by his side, taking him firmly in her right hand as his hips rose and fell keeping time with her strokes massaging ever so gently (but firmly!) up and down and up and down and up and down and up and...

"Methinks the gentleman is about to go a gusher," she said (a little too loudly, Clovis thought, but he was too close to the brink to care).

The pressure grew and grew. His hips took on a life of their own, pumping up and up, reaching higher and higher as the hot essence of his lust began to surge forth. The door to the sitting room burst open, a flashbulb flashed, a camera clicked, and Clovis Plambeck had the most intense and powerful climax of his life.

"My, oh my, oh MY!" Donald Franklin exclaimed as he stepped

into the bedroom.

The photographer whizzed around the room, taking pictures from different angles. The masked face of the prostitute who was pretending to be Connie Westerson smiled as she continued stroking the only part of Clovis Plambeck that wasn't frozen by a state of panic.

"Just look at this mess!" Franklin said, shaking his head sadly. "All over your belly and chest, and even on the headboard! No wonder you're such a repressed asshole. You've been saving this up for a long time, haven't you?"

Plambeck wanted to scream. All he could do was gobble.

Franklin moved to the edge of the bed as pseudo-Connie sashayed to the bathroom.

"Don't try to talk now, Clovis. You've been through a lot." He clucked his tongue. "Man, what a mess. In more ways than one."

Plambeck struggled against the handcuffs that held him to the headboard.

"This just doesn't look good, Clove! Not good at all! Somehow, a professional lady tricks you into thinking that she's an old high school nemesis of yours, and you fall for it like a big old hungry catfish chasing after a stinky old doughball on a hook. Mmmm. Not a pretty sight. And not a good thing for your reputation and career — especially if these photos should wind up in the hands of some tabloid newspaper editor. Know the kind I'm talking about, Clove? The kind of editor with the ethics of a sea slug? Oh, sure — they'll black out your naughty parts and all, but your face, your unmistakable Clovis Plambeck face, will be there for your admiring public to see."

Plambeck opened his mouth to speak. Instead, overcome by impotent rage, he started to sob.

Franklin sat on the bedside, taking care not to sit anywhere near the stream of passion that was beginning to dry to a crust on the bedspread.

"Take it easy, big boy. We'll get you out of these cuffs, clean you up, and then we'll talk. There'll be plenty of time to talk. And I'll be the one who tells you what to say. And after you say what it is you're going to say on Washington Cloak Room tomorrow, and then after you say the same thing on your little radio show on Monday, you can take a nice little vacation. Maybe a month. How does that sound? A big media hotshot like you probably gets as much vacation time as he wants, now doesn't he?"

Plambeck just moaned.

"Nothing for you to worry about now, Clove," Franklin purred. "I'll do the worrying for you. Now, isn't that a comforting thought? Hmmm?"

"See you later, Icky!" faux-Connie said with a smile as she closed the bathroom door.

28

Blair House had about as much in common with Huerta's former apartment as an I-20 truck stop had with the Ritz Carlton. The furnishings were opulent, to say the least. It was only a "house" in the loosest sense of the word — actually, it was a complex of four buildings, used by the president as his official guest house.

Huerta had been the chief resident of Blair House since the nomination a month before. In its ultimate wisdom, the Secret Service decided that it would not do to have the vice president-designate living in a seedy apartment in a rough section of town. Huerta knew these restrictions on his movements were a necessary evil, but he bristled nonetheless. He was quickly coming to think of the ornate 19-century mansion as a finely upholstered prison.

He clicked the TV remote, abandoning "The McLaughlin Group" and its cerebral discussion for "Firing Line," where the puffy pundit with the perplexing phraseology pontificated on a plethora of prevalent problems with a perspective perilously proximate to prejudicial and pernicious pomposity.

Tonight he, like most official observers of the American political scene, was sounding the death knell over the failed Huerta nomination.

"Personally, I should have enjoyed watching the young solon's reaction to the withering interrogation of the committee chairman, the redoubtable Congressman Gilbertson," the host opined. "Sadly, such entertaining sport is not to be, thereby denying professional political wags, such as your amicable master of ceremonies, the opportunity to wax humorous at the expense of that master political harlequin, the patriarchal President John DeWitt."

"It would be nice if he'd speak English once in a while," Huerta said to Jim Reigel, Huerta's primary Secret Service agent, who sat in a recliner across the room.

"He's been talking bullshit so long, I think he's lost the knack," Huerta said.

He liked Reigel. He was the kind of guy he'd be comfortable hanging out with, the kind of guy you could knock back a few beers with while watching a game on TV. It helped not to think about his true relationship with the man, that his primary function was to use his athletic bulk to stop a bullet headed in Huerta's direction.

"Everyone seems to have an opinion these days," Reigel said. "And most of the time, they're full of shit."

Huerta was about to agree wholeheartedly when there was a knock at the door. Reigel walked to the door, looked through the peephole, then smiled at Huerta.

"You've got company."

He opened the door, and Michelle Riolas walked in. She was followed by the wife and son he hadn't seen in nearly four months.

"Howdy, toots!" Janelle said. Tommy just looked at his shoes.

"Howdy, yourself," Huerta answered. He leapt to his feet, took his wife in his arms and hugged her tight. Then he turned to his son.

"So, Mom managed to drag you away from the stereo, huh?"

Tommy avoided eye contact. "Yeah," he said. "But I guess it's only for a little while, if what they're saying on the news is right."

Riolas elbowed Reigel in the ribs.

"C'mon, Pilgrim. There's donuts and coffee in the Ready Room. Want some donuts, Tommy?"

"Yeah," he said with as surly a tone as he could muster. "The food on the airplane was crap."

Tommy and the agent followed her out the door.

After a hug that seemed to go on for hours, Huerta led his wife to the couch along the far wall.

"How tough was it to get Tommy to come along without strapping him into one of those 'Hannibal Lecter' devices?" he asked.

"Not as tough as you might think," she said. "For one thing, it gets him out of school for the summer ahead of the other kids, and he's never been to Washington. He was a more-or-less willing co-traveler."

She looked around the room, taking in the furnishings.

"Some joint you have here," she said as she sat on the center cushion. "Has someone gone and made you King or something?"

"If you think this is nice, wait till you see the official vice presidential residence down at the Washington Navy Yard. I'm told it's a friggin' palace!" Then he added, "If you ever get to see it, that is."

He held her hand over his chest. "Hon, Tommy was right. It's not looking like this is ever going to happen."

She freed her hand from his and slapped his shoulder.

"That's you all over, always ready to throw in the towel just because things are looking a little tough. No wonder you never won a championship belt."

She smiled and leaned toward her husband, burying her face in his chest. He wrapped his arms around her, pulling her close.

"If it was a fair fight, I think I could win," he said softly. "But there's nothing fair about it. I don't even get to tell my side of the story, except on the interview shows and such. I'm on Washington Cloak Room Sunday. Guess who's gonna be there with me?"

"I have no idea, and it's probably someone I've never heard of anyway," she said.

"None other than Clovis Plambeck — his own bad self." He ran his fingers through her long, black hair. "The grand poohbah. The Lord High Executioner. We're going face-to-face."

Janelle looked at her husband. "You gonna kick his butt? Spit in his eyes?"

Huerta laughed. It felt good.

"Something like that," he said. "I figure this is going to be my last national TV appearance. I'll make my case one last time, let Plambeck make his, let the public decide for themselves. Then, I'm figuring the president will realize this is a lost cause. In a few days, I'll bow out gracefully."

"Then what?" She rubbed his thigh through his black dress pants.

"Then I'm going to serve out the rest of this term in Congress and come home. Maybe I can run for county commissioner or something." He was rubbing her back through her satin shirt.

Janelle swiveled around, laying back on his lap, wrapping her arms around his neck.

"But then, maybe it isn't over yet," she said. "Who knows? You're a good talker. Always have been. Maybe when you meet this Clambake guy and get him to change his mind." One hand rubbed through his hair while the other worked the buttons on his white cotton shirt.

"Never know," Huerta said, loosening the buttons on his wife's blouse. "Anything is possible."

"Yeah. There's always hope," Janelle said. "You can always hold on to that. And while you're at it, you can hold onto this for awhile." She took her husband's hand and slipped it under her blouse.

For the next hour, while Michelle Riolas, Tommy and several Secret Service agents ate donuts in the Ready Room, Roberto Huerta got to know his wife again.

29

Partial Transcript from the June 30th "Washington Cloak Room" broadcast:

BERNARD: Good morning and welcome to "Washington Cloak Room." I'm your host, Sean Bernard. This week should be a pivotal one as the showdown continues between President John DeWitt and Congressman Ed Gilbertson, chairman of the House Judiciary Committee. Gilbertson is refusing to hold confirmation hearings for vice president-designate Roberto Huerta. Most political observers have begun to question how long the president can hold out hope for the viability of that nomination, which to those of us familiar with the way things are done in Washington, now seems to be dead in the water. With us this morning are two of the key players in this political drama. Here in our Washington studio we have vice president-designate Roberto Huerta. From our affiliate in Philadelphia, we're joined by nationally syndicated conservative radio talk-show host Clovis Plambeck. Mr. Plambeck has been a leading voice of opposition to Mr. Huerta's nomination. Good morning, gentlemen.

PLAMBECK AND HUERTA: Good morning.

BERNARD: Mr. Huerta, let's start with you. Are you still holding on to any sort of hope that your nomination will be considered, let alone be approved by the House?

HUERTA: Well, Sean, where there's life, there's hope. I'm not ready to throw in the towel just yet. I

realize that Chairman Gilbertson has the constitutional
right to refuse to hold hearings. I guess I just can't
understand the reason. Why not let the committee hear
the president's reasons for appointing me? Then let
them vote. What's the harm in that? But I am a realist.
And I understand the fact that the ball is entirely in
Congressman Gilbertson's court right now.

BERNARD: As you know, sir, Congressman
Gilbertson says that taking the time to consider your
nomination would be a waste of effort. He says you
don't stand a chance of approval, and that the president
should get busy appointing someone who can pass
congressional muster.

HUERTA: So why not give the individual
members of his committee the opportunity to decide that
for themselves? Unless they intend to drag it out, they
could hold a meeting in one day, ask all the questions
they want to ask, vote me up or down one way or the
other, and then we could get on with the business of the
country.

BERNARD: Mr. Plambeck, we all know your
stand on committee hearings. You were the first to call
on Congressman Gilbertson to, as you put it then, "let
this nomination die on the vine."

PLAMBECK: That is absolutely correct. When
President DeWitt announced his selection of
Congressman Huerta as his choice to fill the vice
presidential vacancy, I felt that he was being less than
genuine. I thought he was just playing games with the
American people. But I've been thinking about that
stance lately. And I'm starting to think that I have been
a bit hasty.

BERNARD: Excuse me?

HUERTA: Yeah! Excuse me?

PLAMBECK: I am an opinionated man. But I am
also a reasonable man. After hearing all sides of the
discussion over the past several weeks, all the arguments
for and against, I've come to the conclusion that I may
have been in error by calling on my good friend Ed

Gilbertson to stonewall the nomination. I've spent a considerable amount of time looking into Congressman Huerta's background. He's a tad more liberal that I would like, but I have come to the determination that the president should have the right to pick whomsoever he chooses to serve in this very important position. Actually, on the whole, it is my considered opinion that Congressman Huerta is a far better choice than any of the others originally considered as front-runners for the position. And I will begin conveying that viewpoint to my millions of listeners beginning with tomorrow's broadcast.

BERNARD: Well! There, as we say, you have it. Congressman Huerta?

HUERTA: I'm somewhat flabbergasted myself, Sean. This comes as a complete, but happy surprise.

***

Franklin and Riolas sat side-by-side on a couch in the Green Room, watching the live broadcast on a monitor.

"Jumpin' Jehosaphat!" Riolas exhaled. "Did I just see what I think I just saw?"

Franklin leaned back on the couch and smiled, his face a picture of composure.

"Yes, ma'am. It's a whole new ball game. The bottom of the ninth, the bases are loaded, their pitcher is getting shaky, and our power hitter is coming to the plate."

His left arm extended over the back of the couch until it was almost, but not quite, draped over Riolas's shoulders.

She turned toward Franklin, her face set with a grim expression. "So, what did you do to Plambeck? Brainwash him?"

Franklin placed his right hand over his heart, as if such an accusation went to the very core of his being.

"Me? Do something? To him? Perish the thought, gentle lady.

We met, we talked, we discussed. But brainwash? Never!"

He turned to her and flashed a big, toothy smile.

"And besides, you said you didn't want to know the details."

Riolas leaned back on the couch. Her head nodded ever so slightly to her right, toward Franklin's shoulder. His left hand inched over the edge of the backrest until his fingers barely touched her left shoulder.

Together they watched the drama unfolding on the screen. Plambeck was now actually apologizing to Huerta for leading the drive to hold off the hearings. Huerta, to his credit, didn't appear nearly as baffled as he must have felt inside.

"Does this change anything, really?" Riolas asked.

"Oh my goodness, yes it does," Franklin said. "Plambeck has been the GOP's conduit to the people! A large number of his listeners tune in every day just to hear Clovis tell them what they should think. Tomorrow, he'll will hit the airwaves and make it sound like this has been his stance all along. And by the end of the day, he will have convinced himself – and most of his listeners – that he actually advised the president to choose our boy Bobby. And then the chain reaction begins. The phone calls start coming in. And Gilbertson starts to see the support for his position crumble."

"I must be losing my mind," Riolas said. "I don't hate your guts nearly as much as I did when I first met you." She leaned a little closer.

"Yup. Sounds like a crazy woman, all right." He lowered his hand until it rested on her shoulder. Riolas responded by laying her head on Franklin's shoulder.

"Don't get a swelled head over this, Franklin. And don't ever take me for granted, either. I know sixteen ways to cripple a man with my right thumb."

"Somehow, I'm not surprised."

***

Speaker of the House Al Wantner was watching the same program as Franklin and Riolas. He hurled a full coffee cup at the TV screen and cursed when the screen refused to implode.

The phone on his bedside table rang. The caller ID indicated it was Ed Gilbertson, Chairman of the House Judiciary Committee.

"Al, we're going to have to rethink our position on this one," said Gilbertson. "If we've lost Plambeck, we're going to lose our base of support."

Wantner was silent.

"Al, are you there?"

"Oh, I'm here all right," Wantner hissed. "You just go ahead, Eddie my lad. Go ahead and crumble, and announce that you're listening to the voice of the public. Announce that you're holding hearings. But they don't start for at least a week. Better, two weeks. That will be plenty of time to get the information we need."

He slammed down the phone, picked it up again, and dialed a cellular phone number. Jimmy Langston had been in south Texas for nearly a week. He must certainly have some information by now.

A female voice answered on the third ring.

"Is this the right button to push?" the voice asked. "I've never used one of these things before."

"Just gimme the phone, babe," said Langston. "Hello?"

Wantner smiled coldly.

"Hello, Jimmy. Sounds like things are going well for you down there. Meeting some of the locals? Some deep, probing insights? That's nice. That's very nice."

"Well, you gotta break a few eggs to make an omelet," Langston stammered.

"I didn't send you to Texas to break eggs, Jimmy. Or to fertilize them. Now I want you to listen to me and listen to me well. The situation has changed. There's going to be congressional hearings for

Huerta. So here's what we're going to do. I will be at my desk tomorrow morning at eight a.m., Eastern. The moment I walk into my office, I want to hear something. Do you have any idea what it is I want to hear?"

"Uh, no?"

"I want to hear the sound of the office fax machine, just a humming and a chirping as it spits out your full report on the dirty little secrets of Roberto Huerta. And I also want to hear who got to Plambeck and how they did it. And then I want to see you standing in front of my desk, on my carpet, by no later than three p.m. tomorrow afternoon. Do you have all that?"

He didn't wait for an answer, slamming down the phone, cracking the plastic casing.

***

President DeWitt was also watching the program, propped up in bed with several pillows.

It had been a couple weeks since his follow-up appointment and MRI at Bethesda Naval Hospital. The tests confirmed what he already knew. The cancer had spread. Several small tumors lined the lower third of his small intestines. Larger ones dotted his liver and large intestines. Doctor Watterson said the outlook was grim.

DeWitt had already lost 15 pounds and expected to lose more. It was already too late for chemotherapy; treatment would most likely have been in vain, anyway, and the best they could work for now was pain management as the disease ran its course over the next several months.

The liquid morphine suspension Watterson had provided could be taken discreetly, and it dulled all but a leftover hint of the pain. DeWitt decided it also clouded his mind.

After all, didn't he just hear that Plambeck asshole agree that Huerta would be a fine vice president?

30

Congressman Kleskowicz's local office was housed in a small complex across the street from a neighborhood park. On Friday, Anniston's producer secured permission from the City Department of Parks and Recreation to do a live broadcast from the park.

On Monday morning, Anniston and his remote crew set up a broadcast booth and several loudspeakers directly across the street from the congressman's office. As soon as the network news finished at 6:05 a.m., Anniston opened his broadcast.

"Welcome to a Monday morning on 'Anniston's Alley!' This is your friend Stan Anniston. It's a nice morning, a little chilly perhaps. We're right across the street from the office of Congressman Stu Kleskowicz. The congressman no doubt isn't in the office yet, but if you saw the notice in the Sun-Times, then you know he'll be in his office at eight o'clock. That gives you two hours to have a cup of coffee and a donut, get yourself dressed, and get down here to Humboldt Park. We're going to tell the Congressman how we feel about the foot-dragging going on regarding the confirmation of the new vice president. If you're one of the hundreds of people who have called my show demanding that Congress get moving and approve the president's choice of Bob Huerta, then I invite you to join us. Maybe we can make enough noise that the congressman will actually hear us."

For the next two hours, listeners made their way to the park. By eight a.m., no fewer than 1,500 were gathered. Some brought signs with slogans that included: *Get Off Your Ass, The People Are Speaking,* and

We Want Huerta.

By 8:15, Anniston had the crowd chanting in unison: "We Want Huerta! We Want Huerta! We Want Huerta!"

By 8:45, Chicago Police were on the scene, demanding that the broadcast stop and that the people disperse.

By 8:55, Stan Anniston was in handcuffs, seated in the back of a police cruiser.

It took until noon for police to clear the park. Congressman Kleskowicz stayed away from the office. Anniston was booked for disturbing the peace and released.

Word of the demonstration was picked up by the Associated Press. An article appeared in the following day's USA Today.

By the end of the week, no fewer than 134 congressional offices were beset by similar broadcasters with hordes of angry listeners chanting "We Want Huerta." Callers to programs on CNN and MSNBC angrily demanded that Congress move on the nomination.

In his Capitol Office, the Speaker of the House realized things were beginning to get out of hand. But Jimmy Langston said he had learned something interesting on his trip to Texas, so maybe all wasn't lost quite yet.

31

Jimmy Langston studied his scuffed shoetips as the Speaker of the House unleashed a string of profanity and invective at him, his work ethic, the vice president-designate, the president, the turncoat Plambeck who shit on everyone and then changed his cellular phone number, the jellyfish formerly known as the chairman of the House Judiciary Committee, that mewling bitch of a Senate Majority Leader who said "it was about time the House did its job," and the capricious nature of cruel, cruel fate.

But by the time the meeting was over and Langston had revealed his juicy little Texas plum, Wantner's mood was decidedly improved. Langston had new marching orders. This time he would travel – first class all the way – to Corpus Christi, Texas.

It wasn't often that Langston found himself in Wantner's good graces, so he decided to play it for all it was worth. And Wantner didn't need to know that the harvesting of his plum had come about accidentally.

During his week in south Texas, in and around Brooks County and surrounding environs, Langston had spoken to people from all walks of life – the high and mighty in local politics, the low and ignoble who dwelt from time to time in the Falfurrias jail, the coffeehouse waitresses, the truck stop mechanics, the schoolteachers, the newspaper editors, the police beat reporters – even the occasional homeless man or a woman in the town's church-sponsored shelter. Nobody, not a single soul, had anything particularly negative to say about Congressman Roberto

Huerta.

Some thought that he was, perhaps, a tad high-minded and holier-than-thou. A few felt that his public expressions of humility were little more than a charade, but even they had nothing real to pin on the congressman. Most spoke in glowing, almost fawning terms about a man who would likely have a job for life on the county board, if he so chose.

Langston learned from one county commissioner – who was less than cordial to a snooping outsider – that over $70,000 of Huerta's annual congressional salary was being pumped directly into the county's "Mr. Mentor" program.

Ultimately, the worst and most damning piece of information, the most telling bit of dirt he could dig up came from a truck-stop waitress, the cutie who answered Langston's cellular phone and barely missed catching the brunt of the speaker's anger. She said that, as sheriff, Huerta was a frequent diner at the truck stop restaurant. "He says he likes the apple pie," she said. "But he always winks and smiles at me, and he always leaves a nice tip. I thought for a while that he might have a crush on me."

But try as Langston might to get her to say that Huerta ever did anything more than smile and wink – he even offered her a nice sum of money to make up a story if she felt so inclined – she refused.

"If I didn't know better," she said, as she dried off after a shower in Langston's cheap motel room, "I'd think you were out to get our boy Bobby."

Langston was ready to give up, travel back to Washington and face the wrath of Speaker Wantner. But what the waitress said shortly after Langston's talk with Wantner changed everything.

"I don't know why your boss wouldn't want Bobby to be the vice president," she said. "Bobby is one of a kind, a real gentleman." Then she shook her head sadly. "How he ended up being married to the biggest slut in Corpus Christi is beyond me."

Langston reacted as if he had been slapped in the face.

"Janelle Huerta? You say his wife is a slut?"

The girl looked at Langston, and a look of understanding came over her face.

"Of course you don't know," she said. "It's not something they talk about down here. Heck, I tried telling some folks, but nobody wants to hear about sweet little Janelle Swenson! They just don't want to hear about anything that might reflect badly on Bobby."

For the next two hours, the young waitress laid out chapter and verse about a skanky slut who happened to be a classmate of her older sister when they lived in Corpus Christi, and how that same little slut went on to marry the most popular man in Brooks County, Texas.

The next day, as Langston relayed the information to his boss, it was all Wantner could do to keep from dancing a jig. Still, there were details that needed checking. The story would have to have at least some basis in fact, Wantner decided, before it could be made public.

So that very afternoon, Langston found himself on a airplane to the Texas Gulf Coast community of Corpus Christi. To Langston's way of thinking, Corpus Christi beat the hell out of Falfurrias. Unlike that rat's nest, Corpus Christi had fine hotels, a lovely beach with the requisite bikini-clad beauties, and some fabulous steak houses.

Langston saw this mission as historic. He and he alone was going to come up with the information that would deny the vice presidency to an individual who was most certainly unfit for office, no matter what the flabby-handed nincompoops in the national media thought. And a mission of historic nature required certain perks at the taxpayers' expense. A presidential suite at the Holiday Inn, for instance. The two-pound porterhouse at K-Bob's Steakhouse and Salad Wagon. Langston saw it as his due.

Of course, he intended to earn his reward. A visit to the courthouse was all it would take. That's where he would dig up proof that a young woman named Janelle Swenson had been hospitalized at Corpus Christi General Hospital in 1973, where she gave birth to a little girl who was immediately turned over to the Little Sisters of the Poor Orphanage and Girls' School.

Langston smiled at the courthouse clerk as she copied the records for him at the low, low price of five cents per page. He thanked her graciously and walked to the rental car waiting in the parking lot.

As he flew back to Washington, Langston decided that Texas really wasn't that bad of a place after all. One just had to visit someplace relatively civilized.

32

Huerta hung up the phone and buzzed the outer office. "Michelle, could you come in a minute?"

A moment later, she was there.

Huerta rose from his desk, walked to his chief assistant and gave her a big hug.

"Have you told Janelle about us?" she asked as Huerta released her.

"No way," Huerta laughed. "She'd no doubt tell Franklin. You think I want your big, tough boyfriend kicking my ass up and down Constitution Avenue?"

Riolas put her hands on her hips and scowled.

"You can knock off that 'boyfriend' crap," she grumped. "Just because I have learned to spend ten minutes in the same room with Donald Franklin without succumbing to nausea doesn't mean we're looking at honeymoon resort brochures."

"Give it time," Huerta said.

Riolas walked to a chair next to Huerta's desk and sat.

"I assume you called me in here because you had something to tell me?"

"I just talked to Franklin," Huerta said, a huge smile on his face. "The ice jam has apparently broken. Congress is getting ready to hold hearings."

Riolas smiled.

"One thing I'm starting to learn about our friend Donald Franklin," she said. "When he says he's gonna do something, he does it."

Huerta shook his head, amazed at Franklin's handiwork. "I'd love to know how he got Plambeck to turn around like that."

"No you wouldn't," Riolas said, with a sardonic smile.

"I would," said the voice at the door.

Huerta and Riolas turned to find Speaker Wantner at the office door.

"Clovis Plambeck has been, until now anyway, a very reliable individual," Wantner said. "He's not the sort of person who would flip-flop on such a vital issue without good reason. Someone must have said something to make him change his mind. I can't imagine for the life of me what that something would have been. Can you?"

"Maybe he just realized that Congressman Huerta is the right person for the job," Riolas said. Huerta smiled at her display of loyalty.

"Oh yes," Wantner said. "I'm sure that's exactly what happened."

Wantner stood silently for a moment, apparently waiting for Huerta to dismiss his assistant. He didn't.

Wantner turned to Riolas and flashed a cold smile.

"Mind if I speak to the congressman — alone?" Wantner finally asked.

"Actually, I mind," Huerta said. "I'd just as soon Ms. Riolas stay right where she is, if that's all right with you, Mr. Speaker. See, the last time we spoke privately, I got this odd feeling that you might have been asking me to do something that I felt was, well, shall we say, unethical. I'd like to have her take on it should I get such a feeling again."

Wantner shrugged.

"Well, sir, she's your employee. Far be it from me to tell a man how to handle personnel decisions. Still, she might find our discussion to be somewhat — uncomfortable."

"Nah, I'll be fine," Riolas said. "Don't you worry about me. These office chairs are nice and soft. Have we ever thanked you for these nice, soft chairs?"

Wantner sneered.

"Mr. Huerta..."

"Please, call me Bob," Huerta interrupted.

"MISTER Huerta," Wantner continued. "No doubt you have already heard that Congressman Gilbertson's committee is prepared to hold the hearings. Now, while I have been impressed by your tenacity during this ordeal, there comes a time when even the fiercest and most tenacious of warriors must realize that the battle is over. That time has come for you, Mr. Huerta."

Wantner sat on a chair next to Huerta's desk. Huerta noticed that Wantner was holding an envelope in his right hand.

"I want to give you one last chance, one gentleman to another, to withdraw your name from consideration before irreparable damage is done to your reputation and, dare I say it, to your family situation."

Huerta felt the hairs on his neck bristle.

"OK, last time you tried to bribe me. This time you're threatening me?"

Wantner held up a hand and smiled, shaking his head.

"Oh, it's not a threat, Congressman Huerta. It's a promise. A promise to help you avoid a potentially embarrassing and humiliating public exposure of some very, well, nasty information."

"What, did you find out that professional wrestling is fake?" Riolas snickered.

"It is?" Huerta gushed. "My God! Is my face red!"

Wantner shook his head.

"No, Mr. Huerta. Nothing quite so drastic. In fact, our thorough investigation into your background has found nothing incriminating in any way, shape or form. You are apparently what you appear to be — an honest, trustworthy individual."

He took a deep breath and shook his head sadly.

"It's a shame that the same can't be said about your wife."

Huerta felt a sudden flush of heat in his cheeks and heard the blood pounding in his ears. He stood, placed both fists on his desktop, and leaned toward the Speaker of the House.

"You investigated my wife?"

"That's not out of the ordinary, Mr. Huerta. After all, with all due respect to your wonderful assistant here, a man's wife is usually his closest advisor. The American people deserve to know whether or not a public official's closest advisor is an honorable person..."

"Explain yourself, man," Huerta hissed through clenched teeth. "And be very, very careful about the words you use."

Wantner smiled, crossed his legs and laced his fingers under his chin. He smiled as he spoke.

"The words are all in this report, Congressman Huerta," he said, his voice as sweet as a Carolina ham. He placed the envelope on the desk.

"All the facts and figures are here," he said. "These are copies. I have the originals. And I assure you that as much as I would dreadfully hate to have to release this information to the media, I feel I may have no choice but to do so. The American people have the right to know that the wife of the man who would be vice president is, shall we say, of loose moral character?"

Huerta lunged toward Wantner. Riolas lunged as well, throwing her arms around Huerta's neck from behind, stopping his progress. The Speaker of the House stood his ground, his arms folded across his chest. He was smiling.

"Don't do it, Bob," Riolas said. "You touch him, he wins." She released her hold on Huerta, and he stood with his arms at his side, his fists clenched.

"You filthy bastard," Huerta seethed. "You had to make it personal, didn't you? It's not enough to attack me. That much I can understand. But to attack my wife, a woman who has never done anything but good in her life, that's just going too far."

"Boy, didn't your daddy ever tell you not to go bear huntin' with a switch?" Wantner asked, sneering. "You really are not equipped for this, are you?"

Wantner turned and walked toward the door, speaking over his shoulder as he went.

"Read the report, Congressman," Wantner said. "Read the report, then call me. Call me before eight a.m. tomorrow. If I haven't heard from you by eight a.m., I will call the media and share this information with them. Read the report, Congressman Huerta."

Riolas shook her head in amazement as he left.

"I think I'm beginning to develop a sincere dislike for that man," she said.

Huerta opened the envelope. His eyes grew wider as he read, then narrowed into slits. He dropped the report on his desktop, stood and walked toward the door.

Riolas raised a hand to get his attention.

"Bob, we have a meeting with Franklin at four..."

"Cancel it," Huerta said in a low voice.

"Are you sure that's a good..."

"CANCEL IT!" Huerta shouted, turning on his heels and facing his assistant. "Cancel it, cancel everything else for today, cancel everything for tomorrow, cancel everything! Everything!"

He walked through the door and was gone.

Riolas sat alone and in shock. Then she picked up the report and read it. "Sons of bitches," she whispered. She picked up the phone and dialed Franklin's number.

33

As the makeup lady finished dabbing the flesh-toned pancake powder on his face, Stan Anniston had to chuckle a little.

"You've got a good face for radio," his old boss, Cal Kramer, used to say. "Shit, if I had a dog that looked like you, I'd shave its ass and teach it to walk backwards." Then the diminutive station manager would chuckle as if he had invented that particular little jape and walk away like a lion abandoning a cleanly picked gazelle carcass.

"If Kramer could see me now," he thought. Then it occurred to him that he just might.

The WGN-TV floor manager stuck her head into the makeup room and smiled at Anniston.

"We just got the call," she said. "The network will come to us in five minutes. We need to get you on the set."

Anniston raised one of his bushy red eyebrows at the makeup lady. She nodded as if to say that she was just about finished with him. The TV folks agreed that instead of caking Anniston's bald pate with powder, they would have him wear one of the new "Anniston's Alley on AM 720 WGN" ballcaps currently selling like the proverbial hotcakes in the station gift store. The lighting people agreed it would be easier to make sure his rotund face was well-lit instead of dealing with the glare from his dome.

The floor manager led Anniston to his chair. The lights were already on, hot and blinding. She told him to sit down and stop squinting. He told her he'd give it a try, but that he was making no promises.

"This is why I prefer radio," he quipped.

"Oh. That's why," she said with a sardonic smile.

Anniston faced the oppressive TV lights and fought to keep his eyes wide open. He found it helped to look at the oversized monitor situated to his right. The floor manager told him not to — to look at the camera instead. But his eyes were smarting, so to hell with what she thought, he decided.

"Ten seconds," the floor manager said. Anniston watched the monitor as two cuddly teddy bears bounced up and down on a fluffy pile of towels.

Then the theme music started, and the "Veepstakes" logo appeared on the screen. That was what MSNBC called the Huerta saga. CNN called it "the Huerta Headache" while the conservative, staid Fox News referred to the drama as "the Beltway Brawl."

The jovial face of host Nester Knoll appeared onscreen.

"The Republican leadership in Congress will shortly hold hearings on the Huerta nomination," he said. "Polls show that upwards of fifty-five percent of those asked say that Congressman Huerta should be approved as vice president. Public opinion seems to be solidifying behind the plucky former wrestler. To a large part, that may be because of the way the nomination is being talked about on America's airwaves."

Anniston blinked as he suddenly saw himself on the right side of a split screen. Out of the corner of his eye, he could see the floor manager frantically gesturing for him to stop looking at the monitor and start looking at the camera. He decided she might just be right. The image he was seeing looked like an overfed chipmunk caught in the glare of a flashlight.

On the other side of the screen was a rather priggish-looking woman of indeterminate age who looked like she would require major reconstructive surgery if she attempted to smile.

"With us today to discuss that aspect of this drama are two of America's foremost radio talk show hosts," Hold said, off-camera. "Representing the anti-Huerta faction is Gloria Honicutt, from the conservative-leaning Freedom Forever Radio Network. She is joining us here in the studio. And on the other side is Chicago talk-show host Stan Anniston who joins us this afternoon from WGN-TV in that picturesque city on Lake Michigan. You may recall that it was Anniston who led a huge pro-Huerta rally in Chicago earlier this week. Good afternoon to you both."

"Good afternoon, John," Anniston said. The woman merely nodded.

"Gloria, let's start with you," Knoll said, his image once again filling the screen. "You and other conservative pundits are continuing to beat the drum against the Huerta nomination even though the public clearly is saying, 'Hey, let's at least give this guy his day in court.' Why are you so dead set against Roberto Huerta? What are you afraid of?" He lifted a waggish eyebrow.

Honnicut smirked as her image appeared alongside Knoll's.

"If we're afraid of anything, Nester, it's of having an inexperienced former professional wrestler sitting a heartbeat away from the presidency. Just because it's a popular choice doesn't mean it's the correct choice. I'm sure you'll agree that Hitler was a popular leader at first, but one could hardly think that he was a good leader."

"How about it Stan?" Knoll said. Anniston suddenly saw his own image next to Knoll's. He forced himself to look at the camera. "Do you really think President DeWitt believes that Congressman Huerta is the best-qualified person for the job?"

"I do, Nester," Anniston said. "I'm sure that's why he picked him. And maybe it's because he is inexperienced that he's such a good choice. There are a lot of experienced politicians in Washington, and look where they've gotten us."

"What are your callers saying, Stan?" Knoll asked.

"They're saying that the president has the right to choose whoever he wants to sit in that chair," Anniston said. "And they're not buying all this crud about Huerta being unfit because he's a former pro wrestler. Heck, look at the job a former wrestler did as a governor! Sure, he quit after just one term, but even though he wasn't as popular as he was at first, his decline in the polls wasn't because people were afraid their governor was going to go house to house body-slamming folks."

"That's ridiculous," Honnicut interrupted, and now it was her image filling the screen. "As important a job as governor of a state may be, it pales in comparison to the presidency. Do we really want a person learning on the job at that high a level? DeWitt had a lot of capable, experienced people to choose from and instead he chose a freshman congressman for no other reason than to embarrass the Republican leadership."

"What's ridiculous, Gloria, is a Republican leadership that until recently ignored the clearly stated wishes of the people they pretend to represent," Anniston said. "Nester, you mentioned that rally we held here in Chicago. Thousands of people showed up to demand of one of our congressman that he at least give Huerta a fair shake in the Judiciary Committee. Nobody wants more than that..."

"What you want, Stan, is to tie up the government with a protracted committee hearing that the DeWitt Administration knows is doomed from the start," Honnicut said, interrupting again.

"And what you want, Gloria, is for President DeWitt to get even sicker than he already seems to be so that your boy, Al Wantner, can become president without ever having to face the voters — who would most certainly reject him as the slimy piece of political pond scum that he is. What you want is things to go on the way they have been, with partisan bickering, name-calling and mud-slinging, and with nothing being accomplished. I mean, good God, just because your party has the majority doesn't mean it has the right to grind government to a halt..."

"God, I just love talking to you radio types," Knoll interrupted, slapping his knee. "You're so restrained in your opinions. Be that as it may, perhaps Gloria has a point here. Maybe she is correct in saying that the vice presidency isn't the sort of job you give to someone just for helping little old ladies across the street and getting his name in the paper."

"I seem to remember reading somewhere that he saved that woman's life," Anniston said, with as serious an expression as he could muster. "That's more than any of your suit-wearing monkeys on the far right have done recently. They're so busy kissing up to their wealthy white contributors, they wouldn't help their own mothers if they were being mugged in front of a police station..."

"Oh, please," Honnicut said, rolling her eyes. "That's just the sort of class-warfare baiting claptrap we've been hearing for years from you liberals."

Anniston opened and closed his mouth as he tried to think of a way to say what he wanted to say to Honnicut without using the word "bitch." Knoll cut them both off.

"And that's just the sort of spirited give-and-take folks are hearing on the nation's airwaves as Congress gets set to begin hearings on the nomination of Roberto Huerta to be the next vice president." He thanked Honnicut and Anniston for being on the show, promised to answer phone calls and e-mails after the break, and disappeared.

"Good job," the floor manager said, giving him a smiling "thumbs up."

"Thanks," Anniston said, wondering if anything had been accomplished other than raising his blood pressure and making his face look like an overripe tomato with a beard.

34

As reluctant as he would be to admit it to anyone, Tommy Huerta was actually starting to enjoy life in Blair House. For one thing, the satellite TV receiver pulled in a hell of a lot more channels than he could get from the regular cable service back in Falfurrias. And here, he had a full-sized console TV with stereo speakers right in his bedroom. And a stereo. And a direct phone line for long distance calls at taxpayer expense.

As far as Tommy was concerned, this was living.

He spent most nights calling his friends back in Falfurrias. The only thing better than having a bunch of cool stuff at your disposal was being able to rub your friends' faces in it.

"I'm starting to think that having Superman as my father might not be such a bad gig after all," he said.

His friend Mark, on the other end of the line, chuckled.

"No, really," Tommy said. "It's like we're fucking royalty or something. Check it out. If I want a sandwich, I press a button and someone comes in and takes my order. I've got something like 130 channels on the TV in my bedroom, and that includes the Playboy Channel! And when school starts up this fall, I'll be going to a private high school. A whole new class of geeks to terrorize!"

Mark agreed that Tommy was probably the luckiest guy in the world.

"Well, it's not perfect," Tommy said. "For one thing, the Secret Service robots tail you wherever you go. There's a music store about four blocks from here. I wanted to walk over there yesterday just to take a look around. These two muscle boys in black suits and sunglasses forced me to get into a limo so they could drive me. Then they stood behind me scoping out the dangerous music store crowd just so I could scan the CD rack without fear of being assassinated or kidnapped. That part is a drag."

Mark concurred, though confessing that he thought it'd be cool for a while.

"Then there's the problem with the 'rents," he said. "Dad is, well, Dad. So nothing new there. He's out there trying to save the world as usual. But Mom is starting to act like one of those society ladies. She used to be so... normal, I guess. Now she's wearing fancy clothes and makeup. The other day she called me 'Thomas.' I thought I was going to puke."

Mark agreed that it was a sad state of affairs.

Tommy was about to launch into a discussion on whether the son of a vice president would, by the very nature of the position, be considered a babe magnet, when he heard his father shouting in the next room.

"And when were you going to tell me about this, when I'm on my death bed?"

Tommy strained his ears, but could hear no more.

"Gotta go," he said into the phone. Then he hung up.

He walked to the bedroom door, eased it open, and glanced into the hallway. No one was there. But he could hear noises coming out of his parents' room.

He walked down the hall and stood next to their door. From there, he could hear everything.

***

"Twenty-six years we've been together," Huerta seethed. His wife sat on the corner of the bed, sobbing. "Twenty-six years, and you would think at some point in all that time you might have mentioned that you had a child before we were married! You would think it might have come up in dinner conversation. 'Honey, there was a sale on watermelons at the Winn-Dixie today, and I stocked up on that flavored coffee creamer you like and, oh, by the way, I had a baby when I was sixteen.' At least then I would have heard about it from you, not from that slimy cocksucker!"

"It was another lifetime," Janelle sobbed. "It has nothing to do with you."

"IT HAS EVERYTHING TO DO WITH ME!" Huerta shouted. "It's an issue of trust, Janelle! This is not the sort of thing a husband needs to hear about from his enemies!"

Huerta put his face in his hands and rubbed his eyes.

"There's nothing about me you don't know," he said, softly. "I'm not proud of everything that's happened to me, everything I've done! I told you about how I almost cheated on you that night in Galveston, and how I backed out at the last minute. I didn't have to tell you, but I did because I never wanted you to hear about it from someone else. That would have been very painful, wouldn't it, hearing about something like that from someone else? Don't you think?"

He plunked down on a chair near the dresser, his face as red as a beet. Janelle sat and cried.

"You know all the details from the night Julio died. You know what I did and what I almost did. I've held nothing back from you. How can you justify not telling me about the most important thing to happen to you before we met?"

"I have no explanation other than what I already told you," she sniffed. "I was at a party with my boyfriend. He put rum in my Pepsi. I passed out and he raped me. Then some of his friends raped me. I could barely walk the next day! I missed two periods and told my mother. I had the baby, gave her up for adoption, and tried to get on with my life.

Then you came along. You were so noble and high and mighty and sure of yourself. You had all these moral standards. We were the only couple I've ever known that waited until their wedding night to have sex."

"Bullshit, Janny," Huerta barked. "My ethics have nothing to do with this. I have never been anything but straightforward and honest with you, and now it turns out that you've been anything but with me!"

"I wanted to tell you," she sobbed. "I planned to tell you, but I never found the right time or place. As time went on, it became easier and easier to not tell you."

"And now fucking Al Wantner throws it in my face," Huerta hissed. "Do you think that was the right time, the right place? Do you think he's telling me this because Father's Day is coming up? Or do you think he's going to leak this to the press to destroy me?"

Janelle erupted.

"IS THAT ALL YOU CAN FUCKING THINK ABOUT? HOW THINGS AFFECT YOU?"

"Don't you dare turn this around," Huerta said. "Don't you dare make this my fault!"

"IT IS YOUR FAULT," Janelle screamed. "If you were still a sheriff, then no one would give a shit about your past! You could have merrily gone on with your life without ever knowing about this. But no! You weren't satisfied with saving the poor people of Brooks County from the sins of the world! You had to save the whole fucking world! And now, the high and mighty Roberto Huerta finds himself in a position to share his goodness and light with the whole United States of America!"

"YOU KNOW I DIDN'T WANT THIS JOB!" Huerta shouted. "YOU KNOW I WAS PERFECTLY HAPPY AS SHERIFF!"

"Were you? Were you really?" Janelle said, her hands clenched into fists, her face coated with tears. "There wasn't a little, bitty part of you that felt justified when the committee chose you as a congressional candidate? There isn't a chunk of your soul that really and truly believes that you not only deserve to be vice president, but that you are being used as God's tool of salvation so that you can shine the light of holy righteousness for a sick and sinful age?"

"What the fuck are you talking about?"

"I don't know, Dad. Sounds like Mom might be pretty close to the truth."

Huerta and his wife turned to see Tommy standing at the bedroom door.

"Get out of here, Tommy. This has nothing to do with you," Huerta said.

"No, Dad. I don't think so. I think I'm going to stay right here."

Huerta's eyes narrowed into dark slits. "Young man, you'd better get the hell out of this room or..."

"Or what, Dad? You'll kill me? Like you did Julio?"

Huerta stood there with his mouth open. Then he sank to the bed and sat on the corner facing away from his wife and son.

"Tommy," Janelle said after a moment. "That's not fair and you know it."

"Then what is fair, Mom? What's fair? You and Dad screaming at each other is fair? Some kid in Texas being raised by strangers not knowing that her real mother is going to be the Second Lady? That's fair? My father being too busy raising every other kid in the county to spend time with me? That's fair, too, I suppose. And how about my cousin bleeding to death through holes in his chest that my father put there? That's fair? And now you two are at each others' throats because some silver-haired asshole wants to mess with Dad's political career? Fair? If that's fair, then fair sucks!"

Tommy turned on his heels, walked to his bedroom and slammed the door behind him. A moment later, a barrage of angry alternative rock music filled the hallway. Huerta sat on the corner of the bed looking at his socks.

Janelle eased to the corner of the mattress and put a hand on her husband's shoulders.

"I should have told you, Bob," she said. "I should have told you a long time ago. It's my fault that Wantner is in a position to use this."

He turned and looked at his wife. Then he took her in his arms.

They held each other for what seemed like hours.

"Tomorrow I'm going to call it quits," he said. "I'll call Wantner and say it's just not worth it. Then we'll go home together."

"I'm behind you all the way, whatever you decide to do," Janelle said.

35

When the alarm went off at 6:15, Huerta sat up on the edge of the bed. At first, he was surprised to see that he was still fully dressed. Then the events of the previous evening came flooding back.

"Fuck," he whispered, not wanting to disturb Janelle.

She lay on her side, breathing deep and soft. Her long, black hair cascaded over the pillow. She was also wearing what she had on the night before.

She could sleep through an earthquake, he decided.

He sat there for a moment just looking at her. In his mind's eye, he could picture his wife as a 16-year old girl, passed out from alcohol. He could picture her thug of a boyfriend unbuttoning her blouse, lifting her bra, pulling down her pants as his buddies stood in line and...

No, he decided. *I'm not going to go there. Not this morning.*

For one thing, he had a headache that made his skull feel fit to split. For another thing, there was the sure knowledge that there would never again be a day in his life when he didn't think those very thoughts, where the image of his wife – young, drunk, naked and being raped – wouldn't pop into his mind when he least expected it.

No sense looking for trouble, he thought. He stood, stretched, and headed for the bathroom. After a shower, he felt somewhat better. Nowhere near good. But better.

Janelle was still asleep. He dressed quietly and took a look at the clock. It was almost seven a.m. He had an hour to call Wantner. Then there would be travel arrangements to make. He realized that if he and the family left without saying anything to anyone, it would seem like they were sneaking out of town. But frankly, at this point, he didn't care what other people thought.

Huerta looked at himself in the dresser mirror. Everything was in order. Washington, D.C. may have destroyed his infant political career, but maybe that would turn out to be for the best. There might still be some good to come out of this. He was getting out relatively unscathed. No one needed to know about his wife's secret. He was starting to feel like he could deal with it himself. And now he'd have more time to work on his relationship with his son.

He opened the bedroom door and stepped out.

Huerta stood still in the hallway, not quite believing what he was seeing. Blocking his path, sitting in a folding chair, his arms folded across his chest, was Don Franklin.

"Mornin' Bob. Big day ahead?"

Huerta frowned.

"I'm sure you know the whole story by now. And if you don't, I can fill in the details for you later. But right now, you'll have to excuse me. I have a phone call to make."

"Yes, I know the whole story," Franklin said. "Michelle called me. She read Wanter's report to me. Interesting reading." He didn't move.

Huerta frowned. "Don, I have to get past you. I'm going to get past you, so let's not start something that neither one of us wants to finish."

"Oh, I forgot," Franklin said. "You're a tough guy." He shook his head and smiled.

"From what I'm seeing, you're not much for finishing things you start these days, Bob. So excuse me for not being worried about what a rough, tough son-of-a-bitch you think you are."

"You don't even know what you're talking about," Huerta said angrily. "I didn't want this job in the first place. And I'll be damned if you, Englund, or even DeWitt can make me do something that will hurt my family"

"How is it going to hurt your family, Bob?" Franklin said, still seated, still with his arms folded across his chest. "How can Wantner hurt you any more than he already has? Do you think Wantner's going to call a press conference to unveil your nasty little family secret? Do you think he's going to stand on the podium and pass copies of your wife's hospital records out to the assembled throng of media? Of course not! Not that he wouldn't if he really thought it would help, but this would hurt him, and he knows it. Therefore, it's not the sort of thing he'd do."

"His threat was perfectly clear."

"It was a threat, Bob! God, sometimes I forget how fucking green you are. Oh, sure, he'll wave it under your nose and hope that you'll do just what it looks like you're planning to do. He's hoping you'll tuck your tail between your legs and run back to Texas, pissing yourself like a scared little puppy. But he wouldn't dare be seen as the one to bring you down with something so sordid as a sex scandal, especially when it involves your wife and not you!"

"This isn't a poker game, Don."

"That's exactly what it is! If he goes on TV and proclaims that the Great Roberto Huerta's wife was raped at the age of sixteen, became pregnant as a result of that rape and bore a child out of wedlock, he looks like an even bigger scumbag than he already is. Of course, he could release his information to somebody in the fringe right-wing press or one of his puppet geeks with an Internet newsletter. But the mainstream press will stay away from the story in droves, Bob. Even if it does get reported, if we spin it right, you and your family look like Mister and Mrs. Mother Teresa! For Christ's sake, Bob! Your wife was a victim of a brutal crime. But instead of having an abortion, she did a remarkable thing by bringing the child into the world and giving it up for adoption. Very sympathetic shit!"

"But it's just not worth it to me, Don! It's not worth dragging my family through the shit pile to..."

"This is bigger than you, Bob!" Franklin shouted. "And frankly, it's bigger than your family. It's a battle of ideas, and we think ours are better than theirs. If you cop out, we lose. If you hang tough, we might lose anyway. But we might just win."

"Fuck all that!" Huerta shouted. "As far as I'm concerned, every man, woman and child in America should look out for themselves! I will not let these assholes hurt my family."

"Who gets hurt?" Franklin asked emphatically. "You? Your wife? Hell, you're already hurt! Quitting now won't make the hurt go away. It'll make it worse! Anyone else get hurt by this? The child Janelle had when she was sixteen? I don't think so! If it were possible for Wantner to learn the kid's identity, he would have waited until he had the information so he could wave that in your face as well. The child will go on blissfully unaware that she is anything more than the adopted child of a kind and loving family!"

"He has a point, Bob."

Huerta wheeled around. Janelle stood there, wrapped in a bathrobe. Her eyes were puffy from crying the night before.

"How much did you hear?" Huerta asked.

"Just about all of it," she said. "Look, last night I wanted you to quit. The thought of cutting and running and just going back to Texas sounded too good to pass up. But we're foolish to think that things will ever be normal again, Bob. Even if we did go back, the damage has already been done. What's been said can't be unsaid. And eventually you're going to resent losing out on this opportunity. Whether you act on it or not, you'll focus that resentment on me. And the more I think about it, the more I hate the idea of letting that rat bastard get away with this."

"The woman is making incredible sense, Bob," Franklin said.

"Maybe you should listen to her."

Huerta took his wife into his arms.

"If we leave, Wantner wins. It's as simple as that," she said into his shoulder.

"But what about Tommy?" he asked. "What are we going to do about Tommy?"

"Leave Tommy to me," she said. "I have an idea."

He looked into her eyes and realized how much he really loved this woman, how little anything else really mattered. Then he turned to Franklin.

"Let's have a chat with the Speaker of the House," he said. Franklin rose from the folding chair and took Huerta's hand, shaking it vigorously.

"I've said it before, and I'll say it again," Franklin stated. "You da MAN!"

***

Wantner's secretary had been alerted to expect the call. She connected Huerta to the Speaker of the House with minimal delay.

Huerta punched the speakerphone button so Franklin could hear both sides of the conversation.

"Good morning, Congressman Huerta," Wantner said. "I appreciate your promptness. Eight o'clock on the nose."

"I pride myself on being prompt, Mr. Speaker. Shall we cut to the chase?"

"I just want you to know that there is nothing personal here, Roberto," Wantner said, in syrupy sweet Southern tones. "I'm sure you are a perfectly wonderful person. And if circumstances were different, I'm sure we could have worked together for the good of this nation."

Franklin jotted a note on a piece of paper and held it up so Huerta could see it.

Magnanimous fucker, ain't he? the note read.

Huerta had to stifle a laugh.

"I understand, Mr. Speaker," Huerta said. "I understand perfectly. You're only doing what you feel you have to do. That's all any of us can do in the final analysis."

"I'm glad you feel that way, Roberto," Wantner said. "And if there's ever anything I can do for you in the future, I hope that you'll give me a call."

"Thank you, Mr. Speaker," Huerta said. "I'll remember that."

There was a moment of silence. Finally, Wantner spoke.

"So, are we going to set up that press conference?"

"Which press conference?" Huerta asked, smiling.

Wantner sounded a tad flustered.

"Which press conference? The press conference where you will withdraw your name from consideration for the vice presidency. What the hell do you think we've been talking about?"

"I thought maybe you were going to call a press conference announcing that the Republican leadership was going to stop dragging their feet on my nomination. After all, a minute ago we were talking about cooperation and not being personal and working for the good of the nation and doing what one feels one has to do, so I just assumed that's what you meant. As far as withdrawing my name from consideration, no can do! I'm obliged to fulfill my commitment to the president of the United States. What were you talking about, Mr. Speaker?"

Franklin held up both thumbs and grinned.

"Are you stupid or just suicidal?" Wantner hissed. "I told you what I was going to do with this sensitive information..."

"You do whatever you feel you have to do," Huerta said. "That's what I'm going to do. There are people in my office right now listening to this conversation on the speakerphone. And I don't know this to be a fact, but one or more of them might have accidentally left a personal pocket tape recorder running or something. And if you should feel so obliged to drag my family's personal business into the debate, these people in my office will no doubt feel obliged to share what they've heard this morning with their own contacts in the media. Now, I'm no lawyer, Mr. Speaker. But it seems that so far in our association we've had conversations that sounded like they could be construed as bribes, and now blackmail. Is that an unfair characterization on my part?"

The line was silent.

"Smug little asshole, aren't you Huerta? You've had your chance to behave like a professional. That chance has expired."

There was a click, and the connection was severed.

"It's gonna take him all day to get that knot out of his underwear," Franklin laughed. "Don't worry. He can't hurt you this way."

Huerta could only smile weakly. "I hope you're right," he said.

36

In the final analysis, Donald Franklin was right as rain.

Wantner couldn't directly leak the information he had on Janelle Huerta. He could, and he did, deliver it to Langston, who delivered it to an underling, who delivered it to another underling, who saw to it that copies were distributed to the media without attribution to the Speaker's Office.

But as it turned out, respectable publications chose to overlook the information, since it had no bearing on Huerta's fitness for office. Those who chose to remark on the information at all merely waved it away as speculation and rumor. Those that gave it significant coverage remarked that it reflected favorably on the would-be Second Family that Janelle carried the child for the full term of her pregnancy. And the extreme right-wing media and Internet newsletters that were critical of the Huertas were not taken seriously by anyone other than conspiracy kooks and survivalist types.

The political damage was nil.

It took all the pressure he could bring to bear, but somehow Wantner was able to delay the start of confirmation hearings until mid-July. The United States of America had been without a vice president for more than two months. Word on the Hill was that President DeWitt was still having a tough time recovering from his gall bladder surgery and was under orders from the doctor to cut back on his activities. Other than a few "photo ops" with visiting heads of state from Third-World countries (the president was always shown seated and smiling), there were no public appearances. Talk began to circulate that DeWitt was, in fact, in failing health.

Congressman Gilbertson set aside three days for hearings. It turned out that only one day was needed. Public demonstrations held outside congressional offices around the country continued to support the nomination. Most callers to talk radio stations around the country were behind Huerta. And after Clovis Plambeck announced his support of the Congressman, calls started flooding the members of the committee, running five-to-one in favor of confirmation.

The session was broadcast live on CNN, Fox News, MSNBC, CSPAN and all three networks. Huerta looked resplendent in his dark gray suit and tie. Don Franklin added just the right touch of color with a rainbow bow tie and a warm smile.

Gilbertson came charging out of the blocks, attacking the few liberal votes (against the WIC cutback, for instance) Huerta had recorded in his brief time on the House floor.

Huerta countered with good humor and a smile, saying that he always voted his conscience — that even though the Republicans were the majority, the minority still had the right to be heard.

"It takes two wings for a bird to fly," Huerta said. "The right wing," he said, pointing at Gilbertson, "and the left wing," which he indicated by placing his open palm on his chest. "A bird with only one wing ain't much of a bird. Wouldn't you agree?"

It was as corny as Grandpa Jacob's south forty, but the public ate it with a spoon.

At the opening of the second day of hearings – after the congressmen involved had a chance to check with their overnight polling data – the chairman asked if the members had any additional questions. None did.

Huerta was excused, and the committee voted almost unanimously to recommend confirmation by the whole House. Gilbertson felt he owed enough to Wantner to vote no, although he said he would support Huerta in front of the House.

On July 20, the House of Representatives – after a cautionary speech by Speaker Wantner warning of the danger the Republic faced when its elected leaders bowed to the capricious whims of uninformed public opinion – voted 333-102 to approve the nomination.

The ball was now in the court of the U.S. Senate, which wasted only a day discussing the issue. (Senators get overnight polling data as well.) At nine a.m. on the morning of July 21, the Senate confirmed the nomination of Roberto Orlando Huerta to be the next vice president of the United States, by voice vote.

Plans were set in motion for a joint session of Congress, to be convened at eight p.m., wherein Huerta would take the oath of office. The event would be highlighted by the first public speech by President DeWitt in almost two months.

37

Tommy Huerta made it perfectly clear that he had no interest whatsoever in attending his father's coronation.

"No way," he said. "I'm not going to be there. End of story."

Michelle Riolas smiled.

"This is the last thing you want to hear right now, sweetie. But you are so much like your father that it actually makes me want to laugh."

"I'm nothing like him," Tommy protested. "And I never will be."

"Is that right?" Riolas said. "Well, for one thing, you're wrong. You're hot-headed, self-righteous and cocky, just like he is."

"Oh yeah?" Tommy said. "And I suppose I'm also a cold-blooded killer with a heart of stone who only cares about his career."

"Cold-blooded killer? Your father? Are you just pissed off or are you really that stupid?"

Tommy looked at Michelle Riolas in a way that said he couldn't believe she was talking to him this way.

"What do you know about it, anyway?" he asked. "And why should I listen to anything you tell me? You work for him! You're his *employee*." He said the word in the same way one would say "whore."

"I knew your father before you were born, kid," she said. "I knew him when he was a wrestler. I knew him as a cop. And I know what happened the day he killed your cousin. You gotta get this chip off your shoulder, *vato*! It's affecting your posture."

"HE KILLED MY COUSIN!" Tommy shouted. "HE SHOT HIM TWICE AND THEN JUST STOOD THERE AND WATCHED HIM

BLEED TO DEATH."

"And then he put the gun to his own head and would have shot himself just as dead if Deputy Martinez hadn't tackled him and taken the gun away," Riolas said quietly.

Tommy stood there, his mouth open.

"Bullshit," he finally said.

"Nope. Dead-on truth. And since I am not your mother or your father, you had better damn well keep a civil tongue in that filthy mouth of yours or I will slap that cute little face clear around to the back of your head."

"He never said anything about..."

"What was he going to say, genius? 'I was so overcome with grief that I nearly took my own life'? That's not your dad and you know it. He reacted to a moment of insanity with an insane gesture. Thank God someone was there to stop him."

Tommy looked like he was trying to think of something to say. Riolas beat him to the punch.

"Fact of the matter is, hotshot, you've been beating your father up all these years for doing something he had to do. He didn't know that it was his nephew holding the gun. And good thing he didn't, because he might have hesitated a moment and Deputy Martinez would have been killed. Your cousin was full of 'angel dust' when he and his friends broke into that store. He didn't know what he was doing. But he was responsible for taking the drug. And as a result, he was responsible for what happened to him. Not your father, and not you."

Tommy just sat there, looking at the carpet.

"Now this isn't really any of my business, young man, but in my opinion you've been behaving like a spoiled, selfish little shit. Falfurrias isn't exactly the garden spot of south Texas. But you've had it pretty damn good. Better than most of your friends, I dare say. Your parents have busted their asses to make your life better than they had when they were kids. And this is the thanks they get? A surly, smart-mouth little punk with an attitude? Is that the way it should be, or do you think they might deserve a kid who shows a little bit of gratitude every now and then?"

"You don't know what it's like being his son," Tommy said. "Everyone measures me against him. Everyone expects me to be just like him."

"Well there's a real shocker! It's the same for all of us with parents that do anything worth a damn. It's up to you to be your own person. You can't live in your father's shadow, and you are only making yourself and everyone around you miserable when you try to act as if his shadow isn't there!"

Riolas sat down next to Tommy and put a hand on his knee.

"Look, kid. I know your father better than I know any of my own brothers. He's full of himself, that's for sure. He has an ego as big as Texas. But he loves you and he loves your mother and there's nothing he wouldn't do for either of you. But you have to meet him halfway, cowboy. If you don't want him for your hero, at least let him be your father."

Tommy hung his head and wiped his nose as the tears started falling.

"Now, if you don't want to be part of the hoopla tonight, that's up to you. But I think it would mean a lot to your mom and dad if you were there. What do you think?"

***

"Are you believing this yet?"

Huerta turned to his wife. She looked stunning in a full-length formal dress, complete with gloves that went all the way to her elbows. Her hair showed the effects of three hours in a beauty salon, all under the watchful eye of her own Secret Service agents, a new fact of life she would never get used to. In her own words, she was about "as gussied up" as she had ever expected to be, this side of her own wake.

Huerta, on the other hand, wore a plain gray business suit with a red and white tie. His thick black hair had been dealt with by the White House barber, and his sideburns and mustache had been evened out, their natural wild spirit tamed for the time being.

"No, I am not believing this," Janelle said. "I know it's happening, but I am not believing this at all."

They were seated, side-by-side, on a couch in what would have passed for a "Green Room" in the U.S. Capitol Building. Events around them were proceeding apace, and – even though Huerta knew himself to be the centerpiece of the evening's festivities – there was nothing for him to do now but wait until he was summoned into the House chamber at ten minutes after eight.

There was a knock at the door, answered by one of the ever-present Secret Service agents.

"Hi, kids!"

The familiar basso profundo of Don Franklin brought a smile to Huerta's face. He was dressed to kill in a tuxedo. Riolas stood by his side in a formal dress. Huerta remarked to himself that the two of them looked amazingly good together.

"Got room in here for one more?" Riolas asked.

She opened the door wider, and Tommy walked in. He was dressed in the only actual suit he owned — something his mother purchased earlier in the year just in case there was a funeral or something.

"Do I look like King of the Geeks or what?" Tommy said sheepishly.

He walked to his mother and hugged her tightly. Then he turned to his father and held out his hand.

Huerta took his son by the hand then pulled him close and hugged him tightly, his eyes welling up.

Janelle smiled at Riolas and silently mouthed the words "thank you."

Riolas smiled and winked.

"Our work here is done here, Wonder Woman," Franklin said to Riolas as he slowly closed the "Green Room" door.

***

While Roberto Huerta and his son were busy getting reacquainted, President John DeWitt studied his reflection in the mirror.

The starched blue collar of his finest dress shirt hung loosely around his neck. His face, apple-cheeked and jolly when he took office, now looked pale and drawn. The only color came from the dark circles under his eyes.

"I look like hell," he said out loud, even though he was alone.

He patted his breast pocket. The envelope was there. On the desk was a copy of the speech he was not going to deliver.

DeWitt walked to the desk and pressed the intercom button. "Send in Mr. Englund," he said. "And thank you for everything," he added.

38

Don Franklin and Michelle Riolas were seated side-by-side in the visitors' gallery, well above the House floor. Franklin gazed around the chamber with a small pair of binoculars as the room began to fill with congressmen, senators, cabinet members and Supreme Court justices.

"Damn, this makes me nervous," Riolas said. "You realize the whole damn government of the United States is here, right here in this room, all in the same place at the same time?"

Franklin was busy spying on a conversation between Al Wantner and Senator Bilson. He couldn't read lips very well, but he could certainly read expressions. Wantner was being as sweet as sugar, while Bilson regarded the Speaker of the House as if he were some giant species of bug.

"Why do these gatherings make you nervous?" Franklin asked. "You are, without a doubt, the most attractive individual in the chamber — except maybe for Wantner, but that's only comparing hair styles. He spends a little more time on his than you do."

Riolas ignored the joke, and gestured around the room. "In about ten minutes, this place will contain the entire government. What if some lunatic decides this is the perfect time to attack? The entire government — gone in a single stroke!"

Franklin shook his head lovingly.

"I think you've been reading too many Tom Clancy novels," he said. "This is the real world, in case you hadn't noticed."

***

Jim Englund was, perhaps for the first time in his political career, absolutely speechless.

He watched, his mouth hanging open, as the president regarded his image in the mirror, straightening his tie.

"How long have you known about it?"

"Since waking up in my hospital room the day of the surgery. I had gallstones, all right. But the ultrasound imagery showed a rather large lump on the pancreas. It was already too late. So I haven't really done myself any harm by waiting as long as I have. The final chapter had pretty much been written when I had the surgery in February."

"And you're absolutely sure this is how you want to handle this?"

DeWitt assured Englund that he knew what he was doing. He reached into his coat pocket, withdrew the envelope and handed it to his chief of staff.

"Do me a favor, would you Jim? Just wait here in the Oval Office."

***

The Sergeant-at-Arms of the House marched down the aisle and announced, "Ladies and gentlemen, the vice president-designate of the United States of America."

Huerta entered the chamber and proceeded toward the podium. He was met with a standing ovation. Even Wantner was standing, smiling sweetly, clapping politely.

Huerta shook hands with those who reached for him as he walked toward the front of the chamber. His eyes searched the visitors' gallery for a sign of his wife and son. He saw them, seated next to Michelle and Don. He blew his wife a kiss, which she immediately returned.

Upon reaching the podium, he was greeted by the Speaker of the House.

"Well, Roberto," he said, through smiling lips and clenched teeth. "I'll just bet you thought this day would never come, did you?"

"No more than you did, at first," Huerta said, through a smile of his own. "But hey, can't win 'em all!"

Huerta took a seat to the right of the speaker as the Sergeant-at-Arms made the next announcement.

"Ladies and gentlemen, the president of the United States of America."

The gallery doors swung open as the president, followed by members of his cabinet, entered the chamber.

DeWitt looked about as hale and hearty as Huerta had seen him since the whole ordeal began in May. The White House makeup artist had done her usual splendid job. He was smiling, waving, shaking hands, lingering a moment with some of his legislative favorites from both sides of the aisle.

At length, he reached the podium and shook hands with the speaker.

"You're looking well tonight, Mr. President," the speaker said.

"Yes, I am," DeWitt replied.

He moved past the speaker and clasped the hand of the soon-to-be vice president.

"This is going to be a big night for you, Bob. Even bigger than you planned. You'll never forget it. Just remember one thing. Trust in the people. Not these stuffed shirts. The people were there for you, or else you wouldn't be here tonight. The people will never let you down as long as they believe in you. Don't you let them down."

This struck Huerta as an odd sentiment to be sharing at this particular time. Before he could make a comment, the president moved to a chair next to the podium.

Speaker Wantner banged the gavel, asking for quiet. It was time to get this show on the road. But first, there was a matter of protocol to be attended to.

"Ladies and gentlemen. I have the high honor and extreme privilege of introducing the president of the United States of America."

Again, the chamber erupted in applause. Again, the president took the speaker's hand. He motioned for the speaker to lean over the railing so he could whisper something. The speaker complied.

"Thanks, Al. You almost sounded like you meant it that time."

Wantner opened his mouth to ask why all the hostility, but the president just walked away and took his place at the podium.

"Ladies and gentlemen," the president began as the applause receded. "Members of Congress. Honored Justices of the Supreme Court. Members of the Cabinet. Honored guests. Thank you for being here this evening to join me in honoring an extraordinary man, our new vice president. I will keep my remarks short this evening. After all, I don't wish to bore you all to distraction. And besides, just about everything that can be said about Roberto Orlando Huerta has already been said – time and time again – as we pursued the lengthy process of House and Senate confirmation."

He turned toward Huerta and smiled.

"If we may break a little from the planned protocol, I'm going to suggest a little change in the way we do this tonight. I know that Mr. Huerta has prepared a brief address. But I'm wondering if he'll give a small indulgence to an old man. I wonder if he would be so kind as to allow me to conclude my remarks after he is sworn into office. I promise to be brief, but I think this country has waited long enough for this fine man to assume the office of vice president, and I don't want to make him wait any longer with a bunch of hot air from an old windbag like me. So, if the Chief Justice would step this way, Bob, step down here, and we'll put this mule in the barn, in a manner of speaking."

Huerta rose from his seat and moved to a point to the right of the podium. The Chief Justice of the Supreme Court faced him from the left side. He extended a Bible in both hands.

"Mr. Huerta, are you prepared to take the oath of office?"

"Yes sir, I am."

"Then repeat after me."

And repeating after the Chief Justice, line for line, Huerta said ...

"I, Roberto Orlando Huerta, do solemnly swear that I will support and defend the Constitution of the United States; that I will bear true faith and allegiance to the same; that I take this obligation freely, without any mental reservation or purpose of evasion; that I will well and faithfully discharge the duties of the office on which I am about to enter. So help me God."

The Chief Justice lowered the Bible and extended his right hand.

"Congratulations, Mr. Vice President."

Once again, the chamber erupted in applause. From the gallery, Janelle stood and extended both arms in a long-distance hug. He saw her and pressed both hands to his heart. Tommy gave his father a double "thumbs-up," which Huerta promptly returned. Franklin and Riolas hugged each other. Wantner stood in front of his chair, smiling a tight-lipped smile, applauding politely.

After a moment or so, Huerta turned to the president. He thought he saw a tear glistening in DeWitt's eye.

"Sir, you had more to say?"

Huerta motioned toward the podium. Wantner took Huerta by the arm and led him to the chair reserved for the president of the Senate, the only vice presidential duty specifically assigned in the Constitution.

The president of the United States moved slowly toward the podium and waited for the applause to die down. Then he took a long, slow look around the chamber.

"First, my sincere congratulations to Vice President Huerta," DeWitt said when the cheering died down. "Pardon an old war horse for waxing eloquent and sentimental for a moment, but it is my true belief that the framers of the Constitution pictured people like your new vice president when they drew up the supreme law of the land."

He paused for a moment, regarding the assembly.

"Sad, isn't it, how far away we've evolved from the original vision our founders had for the governing of the country they created, the vision of a citizen's legislature? If one reads the writings of the Founding Fathers, one cannot escape the conclusion that the concept of a career politician was the farthest thing from their minds when they drew up the blueprints for our government. Yet today, the only way one can reasonably hope to win election to the House or Senate, not to mention the presidency, is by being a long-standing political functionary. Favors rendered for favors owed.

"A congressman makes what these days? Something over $150,000 per year? And yet how many of you spent upwards of two or three million for the privilege of serving your home districts? It seems that every new session we kick around the idea of campaign finance reform. But nothing ever gets done, because people don't like cutting their own throats.

"The American public would demand nothing less from us if they actually understood what we do here in the home town of their government. Every two years, 435 House seats and at least 33 in the Senate are put up for sale to the highest bidder. And before the spending ends for one election, it begins for the next. And that money has to come from somewhere. No wonder a vast majority of the American public refuses to have anything to do with the process. They stay away from the ballot box in droves. They have come to feel that it doesn't really matter what they say, what they do or who they vote for. Each and every one of you – and I include myself in that number – would do and say whatever it takes to get reelected, to get that extra dollar of campaign finance money, promising to do whatever for whoever has the biggest bag of cash."

DeWitt paused, and for the first time it was apparent that the president was sweating heavily. His makeup was seeping into his shirt collar, leaving a flesh-tone stain.

"Whose fault is it? Who is to blame for the fact that our government has been stolen from the people it purports to represent? There's enough blame to go around, I suppose. But in my humble opinion, the biggest portion of the blame rests on the seventy or eighty percent of the American public that couldn't be bothered to watch these proceedings here tonight."

DeWitt stared directly at the TV camera in front of him.

"Of course, you won't hear that from any of us here in Washington. Hell, we like it when you folks at home stay stupid. It works to our benefit that you're either too bored or too disgusted with the whole process to pay any attention to it. That suits us just fine! We nod our heads and smile when you say you want term limits. That's because we know that you're not talking about your congressman, your senator. It's the other guy's congressman, the other guy's senator who's the problem. You like your person in Congress! He's the one who got your district that multi-billion dollar defense contract! She's the one who got the budget cutters to spare that subsidy you count on. It was your congressman, your senator who managed to keep that military base open."

A low murmur rose from the assembled members of government. Some began to shift nervously in their seats.

"We may be a lot of things here in Washington, folks. But we're not idiots! We like our cushy jobs! And we know what it takes to get elected and re-elected. We know that if we can keep delivering the federal groceries to our home districts, that the good, civic-minded folks therein will keep sending us back to get more and bigger slices of the federal pork pie!

"And it really doesn't matter what party we belong to. Democrats are just as bad as Republicans in that regard! Try to shut down a pork-barrel project in a Republican's home district, he'll yowl just as loudly as the most wild-eyed liberal Democrat."

The new vice president shifted in his seat, wondering where this rambling diatribe was leading. He looked to his left. Wantner was staring at him, one eyebrow raised, as if he were asking Huerta what the hell was going on. Huerta shrugged.

"The sad truth of the matter is this — as long as we don't cause too much trouble, as long as you don't have to take out a second mortgage to pay your taxes, then you folks at home could honestly care less what we do here in Washington. And you'll keep sending the same kinds of people to represent you because that's the way you've been led to believe it should be. You'll send lawyers. You'll send politicians who are looking to move up from the county or state scene to the federal government where the big money really starts to roll in.

"Consider for a moment the career of our new vice president," DeWitt continued. "Almost two decades in law enforcement. He built a reputation of honesty. When there was an opening in his congressional district, his local party members nominated him by acclamation. He ran for Congress with no PAC money, no special interest money, just a few thousand dollars for radio, TV and newspaper ads in the last two weeks of the campaign. Yet, when I submitted his name into nomination, what did we hear from the so-called political experts up here in Washington? 'The man doesn't have enough political experience,' we were told. 'He's a rookie. He'll never make it.'

"Well, my friends, he did make it, didn't he? And now he is the vice president of the United States of America — but only because the previous occupant of that office died while having sex with a Japanese prostitute."

There was an audible gasp in the chamber.

DeWitt smiled and paused, enjoying the effect of his next-to-last political bombshell.

"Yes, I know it's been widely whispered and rumored but never confirmed, until now. And I only do so for two reasons. For one, Eugene Walters – rest his fornicating soul – died a bachelor. He left no family behind to be embarrassed by this sordid bit of news. And I also choose to reveal that nasty little fact to make a point. Walters, capable as he was, was a career politician. He paid his dues, kissed the correct asses. The vice presidency was bestowed upon him as a reward for long and faithful service to the Democratic Party.

"A regular working person like your new vice president would never have a chance to get that far in government without selling his soul to the highest bidder. If Mr. Huerta had been in office much longer, who knows, maybe he would have succumbed to the lure of corruption, as have most who dwell within this hallowed chamber. But our thorough investigation proved that he has not, as of yet, answered the call of easy money. He is a political rarity. He is truly innocent."

Huerta's face blushed beet red. Wantner wondered how long he should allow the president to ramble on like this before someone, in a kindly fashion, escorted the doddering old fool from the podium.

"I have complete and total faith in the integrity of Roberto Huerta," DeWitt continued. "And in the days and weeks to come, so will the rest of you. And by that, I mean the folks watching at home, not these overpaid, overstuffed turkeys here in the House Chamber. It's time that the American people reclaimed their government from the lawyers and professional politicians. And that's just what I intend to happen tonight.

"I truly believe that the only way the American public will ever accept the fact that a 'regular guy or gal' can serve in government will be when one such person is forced upon them and they can see, after a period of reflection, that such people are capable administrators of the public trust. So that's what I'm going to do. I'm going to force you to accept it."

DeWitt reached into his vest pocket and withdrew an envelope.

"According to procedures set forth in Article II and the twenty-fifth Amendment to the Constitution of the United States of America, when a president is deemed unable to carry out the duties of his office for any reason, he has the duty to convey that condition in a letter to the Secretary of State."

He paused, smiling, to survey the crowd.

In the balcony, Franklin felt the blood draining from his face to his feet.

"Son of a bitch," he whispered.

"I so deem that I, John Samuel DeWitt, due to a condition known as terminal pancreatic cancer, am unable to serve as president of the United States. That opinion is backed up by that of my personal physician. My full medical records will be made available to the media after my departure from Washington."

DeWitt gestured to Secretary Montgomery, who, unlike Englund, had not been briefed in advance. Montgomery rose self-consciously and moved toward the podium.

"Mr. Secretary, the Constitution dictates that I deliver this letter to you."

He pulled at one of Montgomery's lapels and deposited the letter inside his jacket pocket. Then he gave Montgomery a genial slap on the shoulder, and returned to the podium.

"I hereby resign the office of president of the United States of America, effective immediately."

DeWitt turned to the Chief Justice.

"Mr. Chief Justice, it would seem that your work here tonight is not yet done."

39

Bedlam reigned in the chamber as DeWitt stepped down and exited through the door behind the podium. His escape had been planned and coordinated with several key Secret Service agents from the day Huerta's confirmation first appeared imminent.

The agents whisked the former president through the hallway into a waiting limo, then off to Andrews Air Force Base, where a helicopter awaited to ferry him to his home in Fort Walton Beach, Florida.

In the confusion, nobody paid attention to his escape path. All eyes were on Huerta. He moved down the steps to the podium, where he met the Chief Justice and the Secretary of State.

Montgomery had already opened the envelope. Written on a single sheet of White House stationery was:

> *Jim,*
>
> *I hereby resign the presidency effective immediately. Sorry about all the confusion. Don't worry. Everything will be fine.*
>
> *John DeWitt.*

Montgomery looked first at Huerta, then at the Chief Justice.

"Okay," he said

The jurist reached for the Bible that had been lying on the floor next to his chair. His voice was shaky. Huerta could barely hear it over the confusion in the chamber.

"Are you ready to take the oath, Mr. Huerta?"

"Hell no, I'm not! I'm not ready to be the president of the United States! That wasn't part of the deal!"

He felt a hand on his shoulder, turned around, and faced the Speaker of the House.

"And that's a very wise decision, Roberto, if I may say so. It takes a brave man, a patriot, to know when he's being asked to do something he isn't capable of doing. You're looking out for the welfare of your country, sir, and I applaud you for it."

Huerta stared at the speaker.

"All you have to do now, sir, is resign the vice presidency. Then the order of succession passes to the Speaker of the House. Once you've officially resigned, then I shall reluctantly, and with all humility, take the oath of office as your president. Then and only then can I truly reward your remarkable patriotism and forbearance in what is, no doubt, an impossible situation for you."

Wantner began searching his pockets and then looked around for help.

"Does anyone up here have a pen and paper so the vice president can write a proper letter of resignation?" he asked.

Jim Reigel, Huerta's personal Secret Service agent, was on the podium by then.

"Get my wife and son out of here, now!" Huerta barked.

Reigel repeated the order into his lapel radio.

"Be ready to move as soon as I finish," Huerta said to Reigel. Then he turned to the Chief Justice and placed his right hand on the Bible.

"Give me the oath," he ordered. Wantner grasped Huerta by the shoulder and turned him around. Reigel moved toward the Speaker of the House and would have put him face down on the floor if he hadn't have been restrained by a look and an upraised hand from Huerta.

"You are out of your mind," Wantner hissed, his eyes glinting. "You can't go through with this! You're not qualified. Don't be a fucking fool."

Huerta regarded the speaker for a moment, then returned his attention to the Chief Justice. The Bible trembled in the jurist's outstretched hands.

"Give me the oath. And do it quick, before I change my mind."

He repeated the 35-word presidential oath – his second oath of the night – and was hustled out of the chamber, leaving pandemonium in his wake.

On the way to his limo, Huerta issued his first presidential orders.

The military was ordered to Defcon 3, just in case some international wise guy had a notion to take advantage of the national confusion. (Huerta had seen this done in a Tom Clancy movie, and it seemed like the right thing to do.) His wife and son were to be taken to the White House — it seemed like the safest place, in Huerta's mind. Franklin and Riolas were summoned to the White House.

And someone was to find John DeWitt and bring him, drag him if necessary, to the Oval Office.

During the five-minute drive to the White House, Huerta was silent. Park Police and Secret Service agents waited with weapons drawn. The throng of reporters gave them wide berth, but shouted questions as the limo passed through the gates.

Moments later, Huerta stormed into the Oval Office and found Jim Englund waiting for him.

The new president of the United States strode to his new assistant and punched him in the nose. Englund dropped to his ass on the blue and white carpet, a trickle of blood staining his white shirt.

"You knew about this, you fucker! Knew about it and didn't say a fucking thing!" Huerta stood, quivering with anger, as Englund regained his feet.

"I didn't sign up for this shit, Englund! This is not what I agreed to."

Englund withdrew a clean white hankie from his jacket pocket and dabbed at his injured nose. "Yes, I knew about it, but only for the last hour or so, and I didn't say anything because I was ordered not to. And yes, Mr. President, you did sign up for this shit. Part of being vice president is being ready to assume the presidency with no warning whatsoever. If DeWitt keeled over from a heart attack it would be the same thing."

"But if that would have happened, at least it would have — happened," Huerta steamed. "This was planned! Like a fucking practical joke, and I'm the patsy." He walked toward Englund, who retreated two steps.

Huerta realized the impression he was making – that Englund was retreating in fear of another punch – and felt ashamed. He reached toward Englund, placing a hand on his shoulder. "Sorry about the haymaker," he said. "Are you okay? Should I call someone?"

Englund sniffed. "It'll be all right, Mr. President. Nothing broken, I don't think. Just another souvenir of government service."

"Stop calling me Mr. President," Huerta snarled.

"But you are the president," Englund said, his own anger beginning to show. "You are most assuredly the president of the United States of America just as if you had been elected. And, unless you'd care to resign and hand over this office to that creepy little fuckwad from South Carolina, you'd better start acting like it."

Huerta turned to Englund, his eyes wide with shock. "Fuckwad?"

"Yeah, well, getting bopped in the beak must have jarred the vocabulary center of my brain," Englund said huffily. He took a seat in front of the ornate desk that was the centerpiece of the room. Huerta was reluctant to sit in the high-backed chair behind the desk. Instead, he sat on the chair next to Englund.

"There are things that have to be done, the sooner the better," Englund said. "You will need to go on TV, and say something to calm everyone down. I'll help you with that. We've already sent messages to our military commanders in the field and the CIA and FBI to be on the alert for anyone who might want to take advantage of the situation. Fortunately, most of the global hot spots have been pretty much in a state of remission for a while, but you can't be too careful. The Secretary of the Treasury has already put controls on the stock market, but look forward to a huge drop across the board come morning. Everything else, believe it or not, will continue as if nothing extraordinary has happened. Or at least we hope. The most important thing right now is to get you on TV, to show the world that you are confident – a bit miffed at being thrust into the office like this – but it's a job you are capable of handling."

"How soon can we do that?" Huerta asked, his head swimming.

"Within the hour. It's late here, but it's still early out west. Figure that most Americans – even the seventy percent of viewers who were not watching the televised joint session – now have some embryonic idea about what has happened. They'll be waiting on official word from you."

Englund reached into his coat pocket and withdrew the envelope DeWitt gave him earlier. "Before we do anything else, you might want to read this." He handed the envelope to Huerta, who regarded it for a moment, then opened it and withdrew the letter inside.

> *Bob.*
>
> *I'd tell you I'm sorry, but I'm not. Well, maybe a little for the way it happened. I couldn't bring you in on the plan. You were hesitant enough at being offered the number-two job. No way would you have gone along with the ultimate goal of my little scheme. I'm sorry about how it happened. But not for <u>what</u> happened. It*

may be the best thing that has ever happened to our country.

In the couple months leading toward your eventual confirmation, how many times did you express your frustration over the way things work in Washington? Well, now you're in a position to do something about it. You've got the ear of the American people. They'll be paying close attention to you over the next few weeks. They're not used to having a political rookie in the White House — no way it could ever happen on its own. But there you are, as close to "a regular guy" as has ever trod the fancy carpeting of the Oval Office. It will be up to you to show the nation that you can get things done, that government of the people, by the people and for the people has not perished from the Earth (as another president, far wiser than I, once said).

Think for a moment what it would be like if all elected offices were occupied by "regular" guys and gals, instead of professional politicians. Is it possible, or is it just the wishful thinking of a dying old man? I don't think I'll be around long enough to find out.

Will you be?

-John-

Huerta's face was wrinkled in an expression of utter confusion. He flipped the note to Englund. "What in the fuck is he talking about?"

As Englund perused the note, the intercom on the big desk buzzed. Huerta walked over to the desk and looked at the phone as if it were from another planet.

"Press the bottom button, the red one," Englund said without looking up from DeWitt's note.

Huerta did so.

"Yes?"

"Mr. Franklin and Ms. Riolas are here, sir."

"Tell them to come in," he said. "Thank you."

The door opened. Franklin breezed into the office, Riolas on his heels.

Franklin saw the bloodstains on Englund's shirt, Englund's swollen nose, put two and two together, and put his hands out in front of him.

"Hey, man. I knew nothing about this."

Huerta smiled.

"Don't worry, Don. I'm done punching people for the night."

Riolas walked to her boss and hugged him.

"Good God almighty," she whispered. "I can't believe this is happening."

"Oh, it's happening all right," Huerta said. He turned to Englund.

"You making any sense out of that letter yet?"

"More or less," Englund said. "It goes to the core of a subject he and I have talked about from time to time — how the government has gotten away from the 'citizens' legislature' the framers of the Constitution intended. He told me once that he would have liked to call a Constitutional Convention to change the way legislators are chosen — to take the money, graft and corruption out of the process. He was a tad unrealistic about it, I thought."

"Still, it's a nice idea," Franklin said.

Huerta thought about the way Wantner had tried to bribe him into withdrawing his name from consideration for the vice presidency. "How unrealistic of an idea is it, really?" he asked.

"Oh, incredibly!" Englund said. "Two-thirds of both houses would have to agree to it. Try getting these guys to vote for anything that would cut their own throats. Remember when they voted on campaign finance reform? It can't happen."

"What if it could?" Huerta asked. "Suppose we could convince both houses to go along with it. What then?"

"Well, assuming for the sake of argument that such a thing could happen, which it couldn't, then two-thirds of all state legislatures would have to approve it. If that was accomplished, each state would send representatives to the convention, they'd argue for – oh, I don't know – about twenty years or so and come up with a document that makes the IRS Tax Code look like 'Good Night Moon.' Then two-thirds of both houses would have to approve the document, then two-thirds of all state legislatures, and our great-grandchildren would see their grandchildren living under a new Constitution. Look, we're wasting our time. We have to get you on TV."

40

Transcript of President Huerta's televised address:

Good evening, ladies and gentlemen. Let me begin tonight by telling you that no one was more surprised than me about what happened tonight. I can only hope you will believe me when I tell you that I had no idea President DeWitt was going to do what he did. If I had known, I most assuredly would not have accepted his offer of the vice presidency.

However, what's done is done. As callous as it may sound, like it or not, I am the legal president of the United States. It is not a position I sought. But it's an obligation, and I intend to see it through for the rest of this term — God willing.

First, let me address myself to those around the world who are watching right now. If you are a friend of the United States, please be assured that our friendship is as strong – and as valuable – as ever. Although the country's leadership has changed, not much else has. All agreements reached in the past will be honored. All agreements currently being negotiated will continue as if John DeWitt were still president.

One of our great strengths as a nation is the fact that one person does not dictate the military strength and foreign policy of the United States. Our forces remain strong and in place, both internally and externally. Any nation or individual that attempts to harm our country or its citizens or interests will feel the sure and swift retribution of the most powerful military ever assembled. Let a word to the wise be sufficient in this regard.

Now, I would like to address myself to the people of the United States. I know this has all been somewhat unnerving. Please rest assured that, although I am new to this position, I am surrounded by the best political advisers in the country. And I am a fast learner. Jim Englund, who served as President DeWitt's chief of staff, has agreed to stay on the job. Don Franklin, who was the former vice president's chief of staff, will also assist me. And my entire congressional staff, headed by Michelle Riolas, will be on hand as well.

It is traditional for members of the president's cabinet to turn in their resignations after a sudden change in the presidency. I will ask that we all just forgo that tradition for the time being. Those serving under President DeWitt will remain at their posts to ensure the continued smooth functioning of government.

So, you see, about all that has really changed is the name on the door.

I'll be talking to you again in a few days. In the meantime, let's all stay calm. Go to work tomorrow like you always do. This is still the United States of America. In this country, you are the boss. We'll be discussing that aspect more in the future. For now, good night, and thank you for listening.

***

Transcript of Speaker Wantner's televised address to the nation, same night:

What has happened tonight was clearly planned from the onset, from the moment Roberto Huerta's name was submitted into nomination. It was purely the product of unbalanced thinking from an ill and elderly man, and the avaricious ambitions of a congressman from a tiny district in Texas who saw his chance to grab power and took it. Had not President DeWitt withheld from the American people the full extent of his illness, if we had known that his condition was, in fact, terminal, then I can assure you the Congress would have been far less likely to confirm someone without the slightest qualification for the vice presidency.

Tomorrow, I will ask the House Judiciary Committee to determine whether there is sufficient evidence to hold impeachment hearings. If you will recall from the vice presidential confirmation hearings, President Huerta declared – under oath – that he had no desire to serve as president. If this is determined to be a lie, if it can be proved that Huerta knew of the president's illness and its extent and said nothing about it, then he will have perjured himself, an act which recent history has shown to be an impeachable offense.

The American people will not sit idly by as their government is stolen from them. In the last several elections, the people have chosen the Republican Party to look out for their best interests in Washington. It is a solemn responsibility we take very seriously. We will not renege on our promise to the American people, no matter who is currently occupying the White House.

Thank you, and God Bless and Protect the United States of America.

41

The new president of the United States had to ask someone to show him to his living quarters. Agent Reigel – who knew the interior layout of the White House as well as anyone – escorted Huerta to the third-floor residential area. Janelle and Tommy had been taken there directly from the madhouse scene at the Capitol. Janelle greeted her husband with a hug.

"And to think your high school yearbook lists you as the kid most likely to do time in the pen," she said.

"They weren't off, it seems." He held her close. "What a fucking kettle of fish," he moaned.

"Tell me about it," Janelle said.

There was a knock at the door.

"WHAT?" Huerta bellowed, still clutching his wife.

The door opened, and Englund entered. "We need to talk about tomorrow."

Huerta wheeled around. "Do you live here too, Jim? That's convenient! Which side of the bed do you prefer?" he snarled.

Englund ignored the remark.

"We're starting with a clean slate. DeWitt's schedule doesn't apply, so we're starting over," Englund said. "We'll get you up at six. That reminds me," he said, reaching into his pocket for a pen and pad of paper and scratching a note to himself. "It would help if the kitchen staff had an idea of what some of your favorite meals might be. Breakfast tomorrow will probably be a smorgasbord of sorts, but the cooks will get it narrowed down eventually. After breakfast, you'll have a taped interview with a pool reporter. That interview will be shared by all the major networks. I'm not sure who's doing it yet, but it'll no doubt be a heavy hitter. We'll go over that during breakfast. Then you'll have an introductory meeting with the Cabinet at eight, followed by a meeting with the House and Senate leadership at nine-thirty. You have a telephone conference set with Russian President Smirnov at eleven — it means he has to stay up late, but he's willing and ready to talk to you, to get to know you. He knows what's happened — he's baffled by it, of course, but he's aware. If time permits, we'll get some of our other allied heads of state on the line for you — Britain, Germany, Japan, Canada and the like. They're all very nervous and will need to have their hands held. After lunch, you'll meet with the National Security Council. They'll get you up to speed on the world situation and current operational intelligence. The Joint Chiefs will sit in. That will take most of the afternoon. Then, after six or so, you and I will get together with SecState and SecDef to help them get a sense of your positions on foreign and military affairs."

Huerta's head was swimming. "Gee, no time for miniature golf?"

"I wasn't quite finished, sir," Englund said. "After dinner, just a private dinner for you and your family, I would like to sit down with you and chart out some sort of embryonic legislative agenda. There's still a year and a half left in this term. We don't want inertia to set in."

"Oh, heavens no!" Huerta sneered. "Sounds like I have a busy day planned. Do I get to go to the bathroom at any point during this hectic little schedule you've assembled?"

Again, Englund remained stonefaced. "Sir, this is my job. My job is to help you do your job. Your job is to be president of the United States. I know you are not happy about the current situation. If it would help you to punch me again, I would only ask that you aim for the stomach this time, as my nose is still quite sore."

He smiled. Huerta returned his smile, despite himself.

Janelle regarded her husband with a mixture of scorn and amazement. "Bob! Did you punch this man in the nose?" Huerta grinned sheepishly and shrugged his shoulders.

Englund came to his rescue. "Not much of a punch for a former grappler, I must say. Didn't break a thing." He wiggled the tip of his nose with a forefinger and smiled.

"You and your temper," Janelle said. "It's gonna get you killed someday."

"You'll have to check with Jim on that," Huerta said. "I don't think I have time to get killed." He turned to his chief of staff. "So, is that it then?"

"Pretty much," Englund said. "Except for one thing. After we work on a basic legislative agenda, we'll discuss one more item. You might want to start thinking about it right away, if you'd like."

"And what would that be?"

"Who are you going to nominate as your vice president?" Englund asked with a wry smile. "You're going to need one, you know."

42

In his dream, El Luchador Mysterio was wrestling for the South Texas Championship against El Rey del Infierno ("The King of Hell").

El Rey had him in a fierce headlock and he was struggling to get his breath, to turn from his back and get on his knees, thereby to get on his feet and take some of the pressure off. But El Rey had him in a death grip. The script called for the two of them to tussle back and forth for about 15 minutes before the match came to an end in a double count-out. El Rey was playing his part with unusual vigor.

"Hey, fella," El Luchador whispered in Spanish. "Ease it up a bit! This match isn't even being televised." El Rey answered by applying the grip even tighter.

El Luchador felt his left eyeball pop right out of his skull. It made a squelching sound. He watched it sail over the top rope, landing in the lap of an old lady in the first row. She wiped the orb on her dress and put it in her purse. A souvenir!

The loss of his eye, dream or no, was just about enough to piss him off.

El Luchador worked his way into a sitting position. Then, with great difficulty, he made it to his knees, then his feet. Finally, he was able to pry his throbbing skull out of the vise-like grip of his foe.

Fuck a whole bunch of this, he thought, still in Spanish, as he flung himself against the ropes, using the spring action to launch himself at his masked opponent. He struck El Rey with the full force of his outstretched forearm, right across the chest. The blow sent his adversary to the mat.

Wants to improvise on the script, does he? he thought. *Two can play at that game.*

He reached toward the head of his prostrate enemy and gripped the woolly top of his mask. This would be the ultimate insult, the unmasking of an opponent in the middle of the ring. It just wasn't done, unless it had been previously approved and scripted. But he no longer cared.

Fucker popped out one of my eyes, and that demands payback. It probably meant that he would not receive his share of the purse tonight, but that was just tough titties.

With a single motion, El Luchador swept the mask from his opponent's skull, holding his trophy high in the air. The crowd booed, not at El Rey, but at El Luchador. Their reaction shocked him — he had long been a fan favorite.

No, that's not quite accurate. They weren't just booing, they were mocking him.

"You're a fraud!" they screamed. "Faker! You don't belong in there! Get out of there, you loser!" El Luchador stood in the middle of the ring, stunned.

The referee motioned for the ringing of the bell, announcing that El Luchador del Huerta had been disqualified

El Roberto Mysterio crossed the ring, grabbed the referee by the shoulders, spun him around to argue face to face, and found he could say nothing. The referee was John DeWitt. The crowd was now chanting his opponent's name — "Rey! Rey! Rey! Rey!"

El Presidente Luchador turned around, just a moment too late. El Rey was now perched on the far corner turnbuckle, his arms outstretched. For the first time, El Huerta realized that El Rey del Infierno was none other than Al Wantner.

El Wantner leaped from the top of the ropes and caught El Mysterio

Roberto in a full cross body-block, pinning him to the mat. The former president of the United States fell to the mat and slapped it three times. It was the end of the match, but Wantner, or El Rey, or whoever he was, would not release the hold. He kept El Luchador Huerta pinned to the mat, pressing against him so hard he could not draw a breath.

He struggled and heaved and pushed, but without the ability to draw oxygen, the struggle merely accelerated his loss of consciousness, and El Roberto del Luchador felt the world slip away from him as the former president laughed and the Speaker of the House laughed and the audience laughed, but somewhere, not too far away, a woman was crying softly. Very softly.

Huerta sat up in bed, blinked – realizing he still had a full complement of eyeballs – and saw that the sniffing, snuffling sounds he heard in his dream were coming from his wife.

"Are you okay, hon?" he asked, rolling over on his side and putting an arm over her blanketed form.

"Swell," she sniffled without turning. "Now I've gone and woke you up. I'm a great big help."

Huerta reached for the bedside lamp and switched it on. "Want to talk about it?" he asked.

"Not really," she said, wiping her leaking eyes. "I'm just being selfish, that's all."

"You? You don't have a selfish bone in your body," Huerta said, pulling her close to him under the covers. "Now give! What's up?"

She was quiet as she considered her words. Then the waterworks opened up for real and she sobbed into his shoulder.

"I don't want to be the First Lady! I'm not cut out for that sort of thing. It's not me! I don't want to identify with a cause and say stupid things like 'Just Say No.' I don't want to hold fundraising teas and socials and hob-nob with the hoity-toity people who walk around with their noses in the air and think their poop doesn't stink because they have a little money. I just want to be your wife."

Guilt stabbed at Huerta's heart as he realized yet again that he wasn't the only one being inconvenienced.

"Hey," he said softly. You don't have to do anything or say anything or be anything that you don't want to! This ain't something I'm going to do the rest of my life, babe. Just the next year and a half, and then we're out of here."

"You make it sound like it's no big deal, but it is a big deal," she sniffed. "We can't just be regular people any more. You're the president. I'm the First Lady. And think about what this is going to do to Tommy! Good God, if he wasn't maladjusted before, this is gonna do the trick just wait and see!" Janelle snuggled her head into her husband's soggy shoulder. "You will forgive me, I hope, if I don't turn out to be particularly politically correct. I'll try not to say anything to embarrass you, but if someone shoves a microphone under my nose, I'm apt to revert to the vocabulary of a Texas country girl. And heaven forbid anyone should stick a microphone under your son's nose..."

"It was your propensity toward profanity that first attracted me to you, my love," Huerta said. "And Tommy is Tommy. He'll always be Tommy. The press corps will just have to watch out for itself!"

He pulled her close and kissed her softly. For the better part of the next hour, the First Couple gave little thought to the affairs of state.

43

That morning, newspaper headlines screamed the news about the abrupt change of command in Washington. The editorial pages presented divergent views, but mostly came to the same conclusions.

From the New York *Times*:

> While we sympathize with the former president and the terminal nature of his illness, this is not the way things are done in a civilized democracy. President DeWitt should have been straightforward with the American people. The way he chose to leave office damaged the institution of the presidency. It will be up to the current occupant of that office to determine whether or not that damage will be permanent.

From the Washington *Post*

> Roberto Huerta finds himself faced with a monumental challenge. Unfortunately, for Huerta and the nation, it is a challenge for which he seems to be thoroughly unprepared.

From the Chicago *Tribune*

> While Speaker Wantner's cries for impeachment hearings border on the ludicrous, his outrage has been echoed by countless Americans who feel like they've

been the victims of an incredible practical joke. If President Huerta was aware of DeWitt's condition, he needs to step forward now and take his medicine.

From the San Francisco *Chronicle*

Clearly, Roberto Huerta is not prepared to be president of the United States. Sadly, his ego (no doubt bolstered by all the recent media attention) prevented him from seeing the opportunity to bail out of this hopeless situation when it presented itself. After President DeWitt's astonishing resignation, Speaker of the House Al Wantner was heard over the open microphone making a very reasonable suggestion to Huerta that he resign the vice presidency, thereby turning the vacant presidency over to the experienced congressman from South Carolina. Huerta ignored the suggestion and took the presidential oath. It reminds us of the old saying, "Act in haste, repent in leisure."

***

The "heavy hitter" pool reporter assigned to interview the president on his first day in office turned out to be Don Samuelson from ABC.

This was not good news, Englund said, because Samuelson was the sort of reporter who would shout questions at the Pope during the celebration of a High Requiem Mass. There was little likelihood that he would afford the new president anything resembling kid gloves.

"Stick close to the question," Englund advised. "Don't wander too far afield, or Samuelson will find some way to turn your words against you. You have a tendency to get a little too verbose. You're going to have to change that. Word economy. That's the thing for you to remember from now on. Say what you have to say, but in as few words as possible."

"OK, word economy," Huerta said. "How's this? 'Fuck you!' Two words, meaning conveyed."

"Nice," Englund said dryly. "You're a quick study."

The interview was staged in the Roosevelt Room. Samuelson stood to greet the president. Huerta took the reporter's hand but couldn't tear his eyes away from his cartoonish hairpiece. It was slick, black and shiny, and seemed to be made of vinyl. Huerta found himself wanting to touch it.

"Thank you for agreeing to talk to me today," Samuelson said in a deep, thick voice. "I know this hasn't been an easy time for you."

"That about sums it up," Huerta said. He wondered if Samuelson's scalp got hot under that thing.

Press Secretary Hamilton butted in. "You get ten minutes, Don, then we pull the plug. The new president has a busy schedule in front of him."

Samuelson nodded his agreement and cued the cameraman.

"Good day, ladies and gentlemen. I'm ABC News Correspondent Don Samuelson in the White House with Roberto Huerta, who, through extraordinary and remarkable circumstances, suddenly found himself thrust into the presidency after last night's Joint Session of Congress. Mr. President, thank you again for agreeing to this interview."

"I would say it is my pleasure, Don, but I don't want to start out by telling a lie," Huerta replied.

"Let's recap a little," Samuelson said, referring to the notepad on his lap. "A year ago from this moment, you were the sheriff of Brooks County, Texas. Last November you were elected to your first term in Congress. After you heroicly rescued a woman in front of her Washington apartment, you were selected by former President DeWitt to replace the late Vice President Eugene Walters. After being confirmed, you were sworn in during a Joint Session of Congress during which President DeWitt abruptly resigned, turning the reins of the White House over to you. Are you ready to face this challenge, Mr. President?"

"About as ready as anyone can be with a few minutes notice, Don,"

Huerta said. "There's a lot I don't know about the job as of yet. But President DeWitt was surrounded by a team of capable, experienced staff and cabinet members. I will be counting on their help for the next little while."

"How will a Huerta presidency differ from a DeWitt presidency?"

"It's really too early to answer that, Don. I only stepped into the job last night."

"But you must have some sort of idea about areas where you would have done things differently than Mr. DeWitt. In your confirmation hearings, you said you thought the president was too quick to roll over on welfare cuts. Will your administration mean a return to more spending on social welfare programs?"

"Again, Don, it's too early to say. I will meet later today with key administration officials, and we'll start charting a course. But don't worry, we'll keep the press informed along the way."

"Mr. President, Al Wantner, the Speaker of the House, is coming right out and saying that you knew DeWitt was terminally ill and that you withheld this knowledge during your confirmation hearings. Is there any truth to that?"

"None whatsoever, Don. And the Speaker needs to be a little more responsible with his allegations. Like most of us, I thought the president was having a slow recovery from his gall bladder surgery. And the Speaker of the House should know better than to trumpet false accusations at a time like this. The country needs to come together, and the Speaker is sounding a divisive tone. The nation deserves better than that."

"Will your administration be able to deal with Speaker Wantner?"

"I certainly hope so," Huerta said. "but that depends, to a large degree, on whether or not Mr. Wantner wants to work with the administration. Past experience has shown that he pretty much has his own agenda, and that his agenda doesn't always mesh with that of his own party, not to mention the rest of the government."

"That sounds suspiciously like a gauntlet being thrown down," Samuelson said, arching one of his massive eyebrows.

"It is nothing of the sort," Huerta said. "It is a statement of fact. If there's one point I'd like to make clear during this interview, it's this. I am new at this job, yes. But I didn't just fall off the cabbage truck. During whatever time I may be tasked with this burden, I will continue to operate the same way I've always operated. I will be straightforward with the American people and call it as I see it. If I should happen to encounter political obstacles set in my path by those who feel inclined to take advantage of the situation, I will identify those obstacles, call them what they are, and tell the American people all about them. This administration will move forward, with or without the Speaker of the House and the Republicans in Congress."

"I see we are just about out of time. Just one more question, Mr. President. Are you at all concerned that this job might be too big for you? We all heard Speaker Wantner suggest that you resign and turn the office over to him. Are you putting your personal ego over the welfare of the nation?" Samuelson settled back to await the response.

"Frankly, Don, I would be lying if I told you that I felt anywhere near prepared to be president of the United States. But the situation is what it is. If I felt that the Speaker of the House was better suited for this job, then I would have resigned on the spot. But that would have given the Republican Party control of the White House and both houses of Congress. Now don't get me wrong. They are good people and, by and large, they are concerned with the welfare of the nation. But I think their policies are misguided. And, when I took the vice presidential oath, I swore that I would faithfully execute the office. Part of that office includes the possibility of being forced to step into the presidency if need be. I made a promise to the people of the United States when I took that oath, and I intend to fulfill that oath."

Off-camera, Hamilton made frantic "knife-across-the-throat" gesticulations. Samuelson made it clear he received the signal by raising another massive eyebrow.

"Well, I know you have a busy day ahead of you, so I'll just say thank you, Mr. President," Samuelson said.

When the camera crew and Samuelson were gone, Huerta met with Englund, who appraised the president's first media performance. "All in all, not too shabby," Englund said. "You were a bit over-the-top with Wantner, however. Do we really want to be in a pissing contest with the most powerful man in Congress?"

"What's the matter, Jimbo?" Huerta asked. "Think it's a fight we can't win?"

"It's not the winning or the losing that concerns me right now, sir," Englund said. "It's just that the person who picks the fight is generally the one who is thought of as the bully. And that's not who you want to be seen as if you want the people to rally behind you."

44

The cabinet meeting was helpful. Each department head delivered a brief status report. Nothing really earth-shaking was going on in any single department. Defense was busy with turmoil in the Middle East and the seemingly never-ending dance with Iraq. State was also working on the time-honored Mideast imbroglio. Education was just about to come out with new computer-based curriculum guidelines. And so on. And so on. And it was good. It all gave Huerta a feeling for what was going on, a sense of being connected.

The meeting with the congressional leadership was more troubling, though it did leave the new president with the germ of an idea. For one thing, Wantner refused to even show up.

"The president (he fairly sneered the word, Englund reported) knows how I feel," Wantner said. "I don't see where another little face-to-face chat is going to do us any good at this point."

The rest of the leadership, however, showed up at the appointed time. From the Senate, Majority Leader Grace Bilson and Minority Leader Hal Rosen. From the House, Majority Leader Eddie O'Hara and Minority Leader Billy Montana. Each with his or her chief of staff. All were gracious, all were sympathetic to the new president's dilemma.

But not much of anything got done.

"I'm sure you realize this has been just as much of a shock to me as it was to you," Huerta told the assembled lawmakers. "I'm still trying to get used to the idea. Hell, I'm still trying to get used to the idea of being *vice* president!" This brought a smile to most faces.

"I just want you to know that DeWitt's people have all agreed to stay on the job for now," he said. "Except for the obvious, things are pretty much the same right now as they were this time yesterday. We put the military at Defcon three for awhile, but if anyone was thinking of doing anything unfriendly, they've apparently thought better of it. We're back at a regular military alert status now. So, other than the new name at the top of the organizational chart, it's still pretty much the same corporation you've been doing business with."

"Not that we've been doing a lot of business with that particular corporation," Congressman O'Hara said. The beefy legislator from New Hampshire had challenged Wantner for the Speakership at the beginning of the current term. He wasn't quite the ideologue that Wantner was, but he was Republican through and through.

"Well," Huerta noted, "it's hard to do business with anyone when the major players can't even agree to meet in the same room. I only wish I could have persuaded Mr. Wantner to meet with us today."

"I wish you could have persuaded Mr. Wantner to stand in front of a speeding Mack truck," Congressman Montana quipped.

Huerta frowned. "Billy, that's not helpful. The Speaker of the House is a competent spokesman for his particular wing of the Republican Party. While I am president, all viewpoints will be treated with respect in this office, no matter how much I may personally disagree with them. It seems to me we should be working on bringing divergent views together, not engaging in pointless partisan sniping." Montana regarded his shoetips, accepting his chastisement.

Huerta raised his voice a little to make his point. "I will go on record here and now saying that I will do whatever it takes to open the lines of communication between the White House and the Hill, but that has to work both ways if it's going to work. Think you could convey that to your boss, Ed?"

"I'll see if I can't catch him in a receptive mood," O'Hara chuckled.

"You can't expect partisan differences to disappear overnight just because you're the president now," Senator Bilson said. "The two-party system has been a good thing for this country. I think it was you, Mr. President, who painted that picture with your 'two-winged bird' analogy during your confirmation hearings."

She smiled. Huerta felt the warmth of that smile, and it gave him an idea.

"We are adversaries, true," she continued. "But we all want the same thing — most of us anyway. For the time being, anyway, I think you'll find a lack of overt hostility in the Senate."

Huerta dismissed the leadership, but asked the two Democrats to remain.

"I'm going to be relying on you two," he told Montana and Rosen, knowing full well that both men felt cheated by events. Each felt the vice presidency should have been his, and thus the presidency. He wanted to instill them with the sense that they were needed. "The things we stand for as Democrats are more important now than they ever have been. Can I count on you?" They each, in turn, assured him that he could.

"May I ask," Rosen posed, "if you have begun to give consideration to your choice for vice president?"

"All things in due time," the president replied.

He had begun consideration, but felt it would be prudent to play his cards close to the vest.

***

"Mister President!" The cheerful voice of Russian President Genady Smirnov boomed over the phone. "I do not even know your first name! Some reports refer to you as Roberto. Yet others as Bob. Which is it, may I ask?"

"Please, Mr. President, call me Bob," Huerta said.

"So, your reporters are incorrect when they call you Roberto?"

"My real name is Roberto, but my friends call me Bob. And we are going to be friends, I hope."

"Oh, I certainly hope so as well, Bob. But much of that will depend on what happens in the near future. As you can imagine, we are all a little apprehensive about what your President DeWitt said and did last night. We think of a stable America as being a good thing for the world. If America is unstable, then we feel the world must be a little shaky as well."

Huerta smiled as he gave the Russian president the same assurances he had given the congressional leadership and the American people at large: the DeWitt team was still in place, but the team had a new captain. And that was all.

If Smirnov was buying it, he sure didn't sound like it, Huerta thought.

"Yes, time will tell," Smirnov said. "And I do hope we will be friends. But remember something, a little advice for your benefit. When there is a big watchdog in the neighborhood, the neighbors all rest easy. But when that watchdog starts acting strangely, then the neighbors start to wonder which is more to fear — the burglars, or the watchdog itself. Be well, my new friend Bob."

***

Even though he hadn't eaten since breakfast, Huerta picked at his dinner. The spread was sumptuous – traditional Mexican favorites like chicken mole – but he was simply too tired to have much of an appetite.

For the first time in hours, he was alone with his wife. She did her best to make conversation.

"How was my day? Well let's see," Huerta grumped. "I got grilled by some bozo with plastic hair who edited the living shit out of our conversation and produced a broadcast interview that made me sound like I was spoiling for a fist fight with the Speaker of the House. Then I listened to chapter and verse about who's doing what to who with what amount of tax dollars and yada yada yada from the cabinet, held a nifty little rah-rah session with the congressional leadership where they all looked at me like I have a horn growing out of my forehead, got threatened by the president of Russia, and heard all about how the very fucking Sword of Damocles is hanging by that proverbial camel's hair over the United States of America and it's my job to keep every asshole with a grudge and a pair of scissors as far away as possible or else the whole shit-a-ree is gonna come plunging down on all of our heads. And you?"

"TV," Janelle said. "I watched a lot of TV. They've got televisions in almost every room in this place. It's kind of scary."

Huerta nodded in commiseration. A thoughtful expression crossed Janelle's face.

"Tommy seems to like it, though," she said.

***

After dinner, Huerta spent almost a half hour in the bathroom. (*Even in here, a TV*, he thought.) He sat on the toilet with his eyes closed.

His first presidential bowel movement. He let his mind wander over the events of the day.

The most disturbing part of it all? The constant feeling of being managed. He always understood that a president had a staff of advisors, but he never realized how controlling those advisors could be.

Is this how it was with all presidents? he thought. *Did they make their own decisions, or did they just bow to those advisors best at presenting their advice?*

He came to a conclusion, an understanding with himself. It was simple, actually. Like it or not (and he didn't!), he was in charge now. *Time to start acting like it,* he decided.

He resolved not to rely simply on the "best advice." As much as was possible, he would set the tone for his own administration, however short-lived that administration would be. The decisions would be his and his alone, for better or worse. And if that meant shaking things up a little, then so be it.

About an hour later, he met in the Oval Office with Englund, Secretary of State Montgomery, Riolas and Franklin.

"Time to start cranking out a little domestic policy," Englund said. "Nothing too drastic to start with. You're going to want to take things slow and easy at first. I'm sure you'll want to stay the course on several of President DeWitt's initiatives."

Riolas noticed the look on Huerta's face. She had seen it before. She was the only one in the room who knew what it meant. There was an explosion coming.

"Fellas," Huerta said. "And you, Michelle, even though you'll always be a 'fella' to me — no offense. I have a few things to say. Jim, you said this morning that I have to start concentrating on the world economy. So, with that in mind... FUCK 'slow'! FUCK 'easy'! And FUCK doing things the way DeWitt would have done. DeWitt bailed on his responsibilities and his country! Yeah, he was sick. Yeah, I feel sorry for him. But he turned tail and ran and dumped this whole banana factory on me. Well, kids, it's on my lap! Not DeWitt's! Not Wantner's! Not yours! Mine! And we're going to do things my way! Questions?"

"Just one," Montgomery said. "Are you out of your mind? This sudden burst of independence is laudable, but is it practical? Do you want to go down in history as having accomplished anything at all?"

"That was three questions, Bill," Huerta said. "But since I like you, I'll answer them all. Am I out of my mind? Perhaps. Am I being practical? Who the hell knows? Do I want to go down in history? Ask anyone who knows me — I give a rat's ass about my place in history! But I do care about the people! And it's time the government started working for them, not for itself!"

Englund closed his notebook. "Mr. President, what you're talking about is just dandy as hell. But this isn't Falfurrias, Texas. You can't get things done here by the sheer power of will like you could down there. The force of your personality, as powerful as that may be, will not be enough to carry the day in Washington. Like it or not, there is a game to be played here. There are rules. And a president – even a president like Bob Huerta – disregards those rules at his own peril."

Huerta regarded his chief of staff. "Maybe I'm not being clear, Jim. I don't want to play the game. And, unless this is all just a horrible dream from which I will soon awaken, it seems to me that I don't have to play the game! Inasmuch as I currently own the ball we're playing with, it seems to me that they have to play my game!"

Franklin eased back on the couch, crossed his legs and smiled. "I think I know what you're getting at," he said. "Mind if I take a stab at it?"

"Please do," Huerta said.

"Thank you. I believe I shall. Unless I am mistaken, which I seldom am, what you are saying is this: 'I wasn't elected to this office. I didn't want this office in the first place. I do not at this moment anticipate seeking election to this office. Therefore, I feel the freedom to act without regard to my own political viability. I can try to do things that I think will make things better all around, even though such actions do nothing for my popularity in the Senate Cloak Room or the Steam Bath at the Official Congressional Massage Parlor on Eighth Street.' Does that about sum it up?"

"You're smarter than I look," Huerta said.

"That's all well and good," Montgomery said. "But you're ignoring the realities. Things get done a certain way here or they don't get done at all. Go around stepping on every legislative pecker that gets wagged at you and you're not going to have a single friend on the Hill. Hell, Bob. You weren't there for long, but you were there! You know how it goes!"

"That's because the people who set up the system have a vested interest in making it as confusing and bureaucratic as possible," Huerta said. "No one challenges the system because they all benefit from the system. Well, la de da! For whatever reason, God or Fate or Divine Providence has thrust me into this position. I do not intend to benefit from the system. In fact – and listen closely here, kiddies – I intend to bring down the whole ever-fucking system I can!"

"You da MAN!" Franklin shouted.

"Now, I don't expect everyone in this room to agree with me," Huerta said. "That is your right. If you see it differently, then I will reluctantly accept your resignations. But here's what's going to happen in the next year and several months. Starting with the selection of a vice president. Take notes, and smoke 'em if you got 'em. By tomorrow morning, I want what I'm about to say to be second nature to all of you."

For the next two hours, President Roberto Orlando Huerta outlined his vision of American Government, the Way it Oughta Be.

First order of business: the selection of a new vice president. Secondly, a speaking tour. A little old-fashioned political revival, a series of "tent meetings" to get the word out to the average American that the government again belongs to them — that all they have to do is exercise their civic responsibility.

At the end, no one clapped him on the back and called him a genius or a visionary. But then, no one offered to resign, either.

"So, who's in the mood to take a little drive down to the Capitol?" Huerta asked.

45

Jimmy Langston had friends in New York. He had friends in New Orleans. More than any place else, he had friends in Chicago.

These were not the sort of friends one talks about in polite circles. They were, however, the type of friends one goes to when one needs a favor. They were the kind of people one seeks out because they always know someone who knows someone who will do something for you if the price is right.

It started with what could have passed as a casual remark if shared by two people who didn't know each other, an innocent comment from an angry person who felt slighted by cruel fate. Speaker Wantner should, by all rights, have been president of the United States. The clumsy beaner in the White House knew it, the American people knew it, and Jimmy Langston had no doubts whatsoever.

"The time will come," Wantner raged. "He will soon realize the width and depth of his mistake! He had his chance to do right by his nation, and he chose the wrong path! He will realize this, and he will come to me asking for help. And I will tell him to shove it up his ass! I will tell him to forget any cooperation on anything! No budget! No presidential initiatives! No vice president! None of it will happen. I won't allow it! This is going to be a very, very long year for Roberto Dogfuck Huerta!"

It was then that Langston raised the point about the current order of presidential succession. "It was just a trick of fate," is how he put it. "If Gilbertson hadn't crumbled when he did, and that cunt Bilson hadn't gotten up on her high horse like she did, then the spic would have never gotten the confirmation. Then we sit back and watch as DeWitt gets eaten up by tumors and you polish up your speech for his funeral."

He paused. "Just a trick of fate, is all. That's the thing about fate. You can't trust it to go the way you want it to. Take Huerta, for instance. He probably thinks he's fucking pre-ordained for this job. But that might just not be the case! Maybe, just maybe, this is fate's way of getting someone else into the Oval Office. Ever think of that?"

Wantner marveled at the sudden sagacity of his chief aide, a man he usually considered as little more than a higher form of ape. "So, what you're saying is that this is not the end of the game, but perhaps just the beginning of another inning?"

"Could be," Langston said. "Say Huerta slips on a bar of soap and cracks his skull. Or steps in front of a truck. Or some other unfortunate accident befalls our new president before he can name a veep. The end result is the same. You're the president."

Wantner mused silently.

"Well," he said, trying to push his aide a little further, "that's the tricky thing about accidents, isn't it? They're just so unreliable."

"That's why they sell insurance," Langston said. He knew where his boss was going, and he wanted to get there as cautiously as possible. "Some of my friends sell insurance. To hear them talk, accidents happen all the time. It's just a matter of predicting when, where, and to whom they're gonna happen."

The buzzer on Wantner's desk intercom sounded. He punched the "transmit" button.

"I said no calls," he barked.

The door to his office swung open, and the president of the United States walked in, followed by Donald Franklin.

"Hope I'm not interrupting anything," Huerta said, smiling.

"Why of course not, Mr. President," Wantner said, rising to his feet and extending his hand. Huerta responded by jamming his hands into his jacket pocket.

"Might we have a word alone — without your..." he nodded toward Langston.

Wantner looked at Langston, who rose to his feet, shrugged his shoulders, and stalked from the office. Franklin followed him to the door. When Langston stepped through, Franklin closed the door and made his way to a chair near the president.

Wantner raised his hands in a questioning gesture. "When you said 'alone,' Mr. President, I thought you meant 'alone.'"

"Ah," Huerta said. "But I'm the president. I'm never alone!"

Wantner smiled, realizing there was no percentage in waging war over whose assistant got to stay and whose had to leave.

"As you will, Mr. President. Would you like some coffee?"

"No thank you," Huerta said. Franklin, however, raised his hand.

"I would," he said. "Cream, two sugars please." He smiled broadly.

Wantner returned the smile. He walked to his desk and punched the intercom button. "Jimmy, a cup of coffee please for the president's... assistant."

Huerta took a seat near the speaker's desk. The door opened. Langston entered with a cup – emblazoned with the seal of the House of Representatives – and handed it to Franklin. Franklin took the cup and acknowledged Langston with a smile and a nod. Langston merely turned and walked back to the door.

"Uh, Jimmy?"

Langston turned at the sound of the speaker's voice.

"Those people we were talking about? Make some calls."

Langston looked puzzled for a moment. Then he smiled, nodded, and exited.

Wantner turned his gaze to the president.

"And to what do I owe this most surprising visit?" he asked. "This is most unusual. It is custom for the president to send for the speaker, not vice versa..."

"Well, that was then and this is now," Huerta said, cutting off Wantner. "A lot of things are going to be different now. Change is good for the spirit, don't you think?" He smiled.

"Why, I couldn't agree more, Mr. President," Wantner said.

"Good. Because I've been doing a lot of thinking ever since President DeWitt laid this god-awful egg in my lap. I've been thinking that if I am forced to be president, then I shall be the kind of president I want to be, not the kind of president I'm expected to be..."

"You can be whatever kind of president you want to be, I'm sure," Wantner interrupted.

"I'm most assuredly the kind of president who doesn't like being interrupted by a congressman," Huerta said with a smile. From across the room, Franklin placed a finger to his lips in a "shush" motion.

"I just want to know one thing from you, then I'm going to leave," Huerta said. "You are well known as being the kind of person who doesn't work or play well with others. I just want to hear, from your own lips, if you plan to work or play well with this administration."

"It depends on the game you're asking me to play," the speaker said with a smile.

"Ah yes, the game. It is a game to you, after all."

"Life is a game, love is a game, politics is a game..." Wantner started.

"And Scrabble! Don't forget Scrabble!" Franklin added.

Huerta suppressed a smile.

"The game, Mr. Speaker, is the welfare of the American people. Do we give a rat's ass? Do we want to make things better? Or do we pretty much like things the way they are?"

"Well, sir," Wantner said after a moment. "Things could always be better. What did you have in mind?"

"Specifically? A program to return the reins of government to the people. Where they belong."

For the next few minutes, as Wantner stared blankly, Huerta outlined his program.

"And I just want to know if I can expect any sort of cooperation at all from the House leadership," Huerta said in conclusion.

Wantner continued to sit and stare. After another moment, he spoke.

"May I speak freely?"

"Please do," Huerta said, sitting back and crossing his legs.

"I think you are dangerously naive," Wantner said, rising to his feet. "I think it shows how thoroughly unprepared you are for the job you are pretending to hold that you would even approach me with such a moronic scheme. And now that I've heard what you have to say, I will ask you to leave."

He sat down at his desk and turned his attention to some papers on the desktop.

"This was just a courtesy call, Mr. Speaker," Huerta said. "I just wanted to see if there was an ounce of cooperation in you. I expected this reaction, but still I hoped. I gave you a chance to work with us." He stood. "But it's your decision. Now I'm going to take my case to the people whose opinion matters."

"Oh please," Wantner blurted, laughing. "If you're talking about the Great American Electorate, save your breath! They just don't give a damn!"

"It's that easy for you to write them off?" Huerta asked.

"Even easier than that," Wantner said, looking up. "Go, tell them your little story. Tomorrow, I'll tell them another story. Then you can go on TV and tell them how wrong I was! Then I'll go on TV and tell them how wrong YOU were. And we'll go back and forth and back and forth until people stop paying attention. And in the final analysis, I win!"

Wantner stood and leaned forward on his desktop.

"You, Bob Huerta? You're just the president! You don't even COUNT! I have the House of Representatives! And nothing gets done without the House, or its speaker!"

He sat down again and resumed his paperwork.

"But please," he said without looking up. "Feel free to stop by any time."

Huerta turned toward Franklin. Franklin wore a "told-you-so" expression.

The two men stood and left the office. When they were gone, Wantner punched the intercom button.

"Langston! In here. Now."

The stakes had been raised. He had been wrong to underestimate the opponent. Huerta had a game plan. And it would be best if that game never got started.

Langston poked his head in the door.

"Those phone calls," Langston said. "Already made."

Wantner paused. The gravity of what they were talking about, roundabout way and all, started to sink in. Instead of feeling repulsed by the idea of assassination, he felt...

Renewed? Excited? Maybe. The possibility was there.

"Keep on it," he said, as Langston nodded. "Maybe you should talk to those friends," he suggested. "Those insurance friends of yours. Have them consult their actuarial charts. See what they predict. And one more thing. You'll be on your own for this one. I never want to hear the word 'insurance' issue from your lips again."

Langston understood perfectly. He had the ball and was free to run with it. But if the plan went "tits up," so would Jimmy Langston.

46

"Ten seconds, Mr. President," the floor director said.

"Thank you," Huerta responded. He had been president just a few days, and here he was getting ready to make his second nationwide television address from the Oval Office. Odd, he thought, that he wasn't more nervous.

The floor director gave his cue, and President Roberto Huerta talked to the people.

Ladies and Gentlemen, good evening.

I told you the night I unexpectedly became your president that I would be in touch with you on a regular basis. I told you that my staff and I would be hard at work on an agenda for the country. Our agenda is beginning to take shape, and I have a few ideas I'd like to propose to you tonight.

When President DeWitt gave his speech to the joint session of Congress before resigning, he gave us all a pretty good scolding. I've been reviewing his speech in my mind. And I can't take issue with what he said. We have let it get away from us. Either we're too bored to care or we think that it doesn't really matter, so why bother? And that's why things have gotten to where they are in your government.

That's right, folks. YOUR government. Not mine. Not Speaker Wantner's. Yours! Everyone who sits in elected office tonight is here because you put us here. Nobody showed up in DC with a satchel full of Armani suits and just decided to become a congressman or senator. You elected each and every member of Congress, each and every Senator, and yes, indirectly, even me.

So is that a problem? Of course not. It's called a representative democracy. Other than coming up with some sort of forced servitude, like a national jury duty, it's the best way to make sure the people have a representative voice in the affairs of their government. And every other year, you, as voters, have a chance to tell us how we're doing. And every two years, you fail to live up to that obligation.

Why? Money! The system has gotten so tainted by money that you probably don't have much of a reason to pay attention. After all, who is your congressman more likely to listen to? You with your little phone call of outrage, or some slick lobbyist with a sack full of money?

There's only one way to change this scenario. And frankly, what I'm going to say right now will not be welcome news for career politicians.

The only way to give government back to you is if we take the money out of it. Tomorrow, I will present to the House of Representatives a five-point plan that will take the process of selecting your government representatives away from the professional politicians and give it back to you, where it belongs. Here are the highlights.

First. We would eliminate campaign contributions from institutions of any kind, and by this I mean corporations, unions, nonprofits, political parties, special interest groups and every other kind of organization. Organizations aren't citizens, just concentrations of power. Only actual, living, breathing human beings would be able to contribute to political campaigns, and their contributions would be limited to a collective $5,000 to any one candidate of any political party. Institutions would, of course, continue to be entitled to free speech and could publish their views anywhere they can afford, just like they do now, but their expenditures and the source of their funds would need to be disclosed. That way, you would know who they are representing.

Secondly, we would push for a constitutional amendment instituting term limits. Our friends in the Republican Party used to beat the Democrats over the head with this particular issue until suddenly, one day, they found themselves in the position to be harmed by such limits. This bill would give the issue to the states, and if two-thirds of the states agree, term limits would be the law of the land.

Third. Money for races in a given state can only come from citizens within that state. All too often, Alabama candidates get money from Tennessee political action committees, candidates from Kentucky get money from New York millionaires, and the people of a given state are not heard!

Fourth. All candidates for national office would be nominated through a caucus system in each congressional district. This would mean the end of the traditional smoke-filled room selection process where special interest groups funnel money into the campaign coffers of the candidate of their choosing. It would mean a level playing field. And speaking of that...

The fifth part of this bill would make it easier access for new political parties to become involved in the process. All parties – no matter how small – would be granted dollar-for-dollar funding in federal matching grants that traditionally go to only the two major parties.

In conjunction, although we cannot call ourselves a free country and then compel such a move on our media, I would encourage America's broadcasters and print publications to work with us in coming up with some way to level the advertising field so a candidate with good ideas and a small bank account has as much access to the battlefield of ideas as those with millions to spend.

These five points define the core of this administration's domestic policy. There will be many details to be worked out. It is my hope that the entire nation will really come to understand and discuss these five points so that we may refine these primary objectives into a workable program to return this government to the control of the citizens that pay for it. I don't want to sound bossy coming out of the chute, but one fact is clear. If you do not participate in this dialogue, your voice will not be heard.

My fellow Americans, I assure you that I have not made any friends here in Washington by what I've just said. I've already presented this plan to the leadership of the House of Representatives, but suffice to say, it didn't get a warm response. In fact, soon you'll be hearing from those who disagree with this plan. They'll probably tell you that it's too idealistic, that it could never work. They'll tell you that I am much too naive to be president, that I don't know how things get done in Washington, that I have to learn how to "play the game" if I want to get anything done during my time in office.

But that's not my job, is it, to play a game? My job as your president, as I understand it, is to ensure that every American has equal access to an idea we all grew up to believe in: "The American Dream."

Congress has turned a deaf ear to this plan. But if you – in bulk – care enough to call your congressman, your senator, and tell them you think there is some merit to this plan, they cannot turn a deaf ear to you! If you care enough to take government back from the people you've allowed to take it away from you, then we can get it done.

It's entirely up to you!

Now, to underscore my belief that government of the people means government by the people, I'm planning to travel around the country to spread the message I've just shared with you. We will soon have an itinerary to consider. All I ask is that, in the meantime, you give some serious consideration to what I've said tonight.

I'll be talking to you again soon. Thanks for your time, and good night.

47

"So, are we going to meet like this often?" Senator Bilson asked. "People are going to start talking."

"Let them say what they want," Huerta replied with a smile. He rose from the high-backed chair and walked to the couch, seating himself next to the Senate Majority Leader. Englund sat silently in a corner.

"Grace, when we all got together the other day, you said something about partisan differences not disappearing overnight. Let me ask you a question. Do you think there will ever be any hope of both parties working in concert for the good of this country?"

She studied the question.

"Given the current situation, no. I'm sorry, Mr. President, but there is just so much divisiveness and bad feeling out there right now. Especially in the House. Hell, there isn't all that much unity among Republicans. We've got all these factions pulling in their own directions. I don't know how anyone can hope to ever pull them all together."

"It would take something big, all right," the president said. "Something big, indeed. Even then, it might not work. But at least it could be a start."

The matriarchal senator from New Jersey folded her hands on her lap and turned to face Huerta.

"Mr. President, might I ask what you are talking about?"

"Yup, it would take something big to pull the various factions together — even a little bit." Huerta stood and walked back to his desk.

He sat on the corner. "Do you believe in leading by example, Senator?"

"It's a good method, I suppose," she said, after a moment's reflection.

"That's good," Huerta said. "So do I." He paused for a moment and studied her face. It was a good face, open, friendly. "We call this system of ours a democracy. But is it, really? It can't be when the people we represent don't participate in the process. They increasingly want nothing to do with their own government. They automatically assume that their elected leaders are crooks that are more concerned with feathering their own corrupt little nests than with serving the public interest. And year after year, we prove them right. I submit that if we could find a way to restore America's faith in its government, then more people would start paying attention. More people would get involved. But we have to be the ones to set the example. Someone has to be willing to take that first step."

Huerta noted that Bilson was nodding in agreement as he spoke.

"Ever since I came to Congress earlier this year, I've often wondered why we can't lay down the rancor of party politics and try to find a way to work together," Huerta said. "It's really frustrating. There are so many people out there – both in government and out – with so many good ideas that just aren't being heard. Why? Several factors. Could be they don't belong to the right party. Maybe the idea is coming from someone without any particular political capital to trade on, no favors to call in."

He paused for a moment, like the skilled fisherman who knows the fish is considering the bait. "How many times, Grace, have you heard of an idea someone in the Senate had that you couldn't even consider because the person wasn't a member of the majority party?"

"More times than I can count," she said. "It's part of the game."

"It's amazing how many times I've heard that analogy," Huerta said, shaking his head. "But is it a good game? Is it a necessary game?

Is the game good for the country? Or does it just serve the interest of its players, and no one else?" Again, he waited for an answer.

Bilson shifted in her seat. "Mr. President, I agree that the system is horribly constipated. But we can't just wish it away."

"Can't we?" Huerta asked. "Or are we just afraid to try?"

After a moment's silence, Bilson asked, "And what would you propose, sir?"

Huerta smiled and told her.

Almost an hour later, Senator Bilson called several key GOP lawmakers and asked them to meet with her — immediately. Actually, it was more of a demand than a request. They picked up on the urgency of her call.

Once the leaders had gathered in her office and the doors were shut, she related the details of her meeting with the president.

"And you told him 'no,' of course?" Speaker Wantner asked, scowling.

"I said I'd think about it," she replied.

Wantner exploded. "Land's sakes, woman! Don't you know when you're being played for a prize fool? Divide and Conquer! That's what he's trying to do! You should have spit in his eye, kicked him in the gonads and told him to shove the vice presidency up his ass!"

Bilson's eyes flashed with anger. "Yes," she hissed. "That would have been the grown-up thing to do, after all."

"I think the Speaker was speaking metaphorically," Congressman O'Hara said. The House Majority Leader's considerable girth took up a large portion of the couch in Bilson's office. "And I agree with his analysis. What Huerta is doing smacks of Machiavelli's admonition — 'Keep your friends close, but keep your enemies closer.'"

Bilson paced the floor between the two congressmen. "I just can't help but think there may be some sense to the idea," she said. "It would go a long way toward breaching the gap between the parties. It would…"

"That's just wishful thinking, woman," Wantner interrupted. "Wishful thinking and your own ego talking."

Bilson felt her hands balling into fists and decided that if the oily little creep called her "woman" one more time, she would explore the backs of his eye sockets with her fingernails.

"Well, I don't know if it's ego," said Senator Harold McGee, the number two Republican in the Senate. "That might be a bit harsh, Al. But I do think the idea is a tad fanciful."

"A tad?" Wantner blurted. "It's ludicrous! 'Bridge the gap between the parties?' Who in hell thinks the gap needs to be bridged? That's just another way of saying we should compromise our principles. We should sleep with Satan, try to see things from his point of view for awhile, walk a mile in his hooves! If we do things your way, Grace, then we will be expected to countenance each and every boneheaded scheme that floats down Pennsylvania Avenue! Should we have a legitimate problem with some new presidential initiative, we'll be blasted for not going along with the new spirit of peace, brotherhood and harmony! Bullshit! It's a bunch of new-age claptrap, and I will not stand for it. I will not cooperate with it. And I will not allow it to be considered for even one moment on the House floor."

The Speaker rose from his seat, bowed in a perfunctory fashion to the Senate Majority Leader, and stormed from the room.

His departure was marked with a moment of silence, followed by some audible exhaling.

"He certainly is the intense one, isn't he?" McGee whistled.

"That man is a profound asshole," O'Hara said.

"People like him are what is wrong with government," Bilson said. "I used to see that characteristic as unwavering dedication to a political belief. Now I'm not so sure. In fact, I think that sort of inflexibility — it's like a cancer. A cancer that must be stopped."

48

He had been studying the new president for a few days now, ever since receiving his orders in a coded classified advertisement in the morning newspaper.

The newspapers said that President Huerta was going to conduct a ten-state speaking tour over the next two weeks. The editorial writers speculated that, despite Huerta's denials, these public speaking engagements were the beginning of a full-fledged presidential campaign. He would speak at rallies held in public locations to bring in the largest amount of people possible.

The president would hold his Chicago rally at the United Center. A basketball stadium! All that open space; the very thought of it made the man smile. It was a scenario ready-made for what he had in mind.

The newspapers were being open with the president's schedule. They detailed when and where the president would speak and the routes he would take to each engagement. It was as if, in the heady rush of all this new openness, they had forgotten about security and overlooked the lessons learned in Dallas.

And that suited him just fine. Maybe he'd teach them a thing or two about Chicago.

***

People who work in the communications industry are among the worst when it comes to communicating among themselves. Which is why Stan Anniston found out that he had been selected to interview the new president when the Secret Service advance team descended on the studios of WGN Radio in downtown Chicago.

The agents researched entrances and exits, took a survey of personnel who would be on hand the day of the interview, and paid special attention to the man who would be doing the interview.

Anniston was impressed, but not surprised, by how much they knew about him. They knew about his previous brushes with the law — the time he chained himself to a dumpster to protest a garbage rate hike in Big Arm, Montana; and, of course, the pro-Huerta rally in Chicago. They asked him a battery of questions, most having to do with how he felt about things going on in the world today. Anniston didn't pull any punches. He said he felt things were, by and large, screwed up. He said he believed President Huerta had some good ideas, but that it would take more than good ideas to get this country out of the swamp in which it had been mired for decades.

Apparently, he didn't say anything to set off any alarms with the Secret Service. They shook his hand, thanked him for his cooperation, then notified station management when to expect the president.

***

Each day brought its own numerous little shocks to the new president. Today's culture shock — flying on Air Force One.

"Quite a bird, isn't it?" Franklin asked. He was more accustomed to this mode of transportation, having done some considerable globe-hopping during his tenure as Vice President Walters' chief aide.

"I should say so," Huerta said in a near-whisper. The airplane had everything. It was a regular White House in the Sky. Instant communications access — he could conduct a bloody press conference from up here if he wanted to. Teletype machines, faxes, phones, Internet access, you name it.

"This is a hell of a set-up," Huerta said. Riolas entered the presidential cabin, smiling excitedly. "Hey, they make a tasty margarita on this plane! Anyone want one? I'm buying!"

***

Huerta's first public speech as president was a marginal success. The sound system at Madison Square Garden was tricky. The Secret Service agents were nervous — they were against the idea from the start. Huerta rejected their demand that he speak from behind a shield of bulletproof Plexiglas. He said it would be a sign that the president was afraid of the people. They said to do otherwise was asking for disaster.

During the speech in New York, they positioned a ring of agents around the podium — too low to stop a bullet, but close enough to be able to deal with anyone who rushed the stage. Security was as tight as it could be for such a venue. Entrance was restricted to only four passageways; the rest were sealed and guarded. Metal detectors screened for weapons; purses were checked. The event passed without incident.

Turnout was disappointing — only 15,000 New Yorkers showed up to hear the president discuss what he referred to as "The New Responsibility."

The media gave the event wide coverage, however. Each subsequent newscast, along with the morning newspaper editions, touched on the high points of the president's address:

- Government was a servant of the people — a fact the people had better start forcing their government to acknowledge.
- Republicans and Democrats could retain their ideological differences and still work together. He called on the House of Representatives to quit stalling on the confirmation of Senator Grace Bilson as the next vice president.
- As much as they might not like to hear it, the American people shared in the blame for the quagmire in Washington. They needed to get involved, find out what was happening, take part in

their own government.

- Huerta once again outlined the high points of the political reform legislation that was currently stuck in a House committee. He exhorted the crowd – such as it was – to get involved by contacting their legislators and demanding passage.

The morning editorials gave Huerta credit for saying the things that needed to be said. Some questioned his political wisdom, saying that Walter Mondale's dismal performance in the 1984 presidential election should be enough proof for anyone that American voters don't want to hear what's wrong with their country. They much preferred the flag-waving, drum-beating, everything's-just-dandy theme of the Reagan campaign. The editors were skeptical, but stopped short of condemning Huerta's program.

***

It made him smile to think about it. Getting on the United Center security detail hadn't been much of a trick. His twelve years on the force and his impeccable record meant he was one of the most trustworthy police officers in the department. His word was golden as far as the brass at City Hall were concerned. It made him the perfect guy to call on when things needed doing — covertly, quietly and neatly.

He wasn't called on to perform these special extra-curricular activities with any great frequency, but when he was, it was for jobs that needed some extra finesse. Fingering a high-placed informant, for instance. Waiting in an alley for somebody who talked too much – or who might talk too much – to walk into a bullet fired from an unregistered gun, and then directing the subsequent investigation. It was a great way to earn some extra retirement income. Best not to be too ostentatious, of course. Squirrel it away in numbered Swiss accounts. Then, when he retired, he would vanish. His police pension checks would pile up in a neglected mailbox.

Retirement was coming sooner than he expected. He figured on giving it at least four more years, getting to the big 2-0 before he hung up his badge. After the job at hand, however, it wouldn't be wise to stick around.

It had to be planned just right. He knew there was a great deal of risk involved. And a lot of it depended on just how close he could get and how much confusion would be created in the aftermath. If he was careful and sly, getting away would not be much of a problem.

For one thing, a uniform and badge gives one-instant credibility. He would just be one more cop chasing after the guy who shot the president.

49

Huerta and his wife were in the presidential suite, no doubt asleep by now. The president had an early appearance in the morning at some radio station.

Christ, they were such regular people, Franklin thought. Normal folks! A regular Ozzie and Harriet in the White House. Bob had a temper, that was for sure, but Janelle was a calming influence. Neither one of them had a pretentious bone in their bodies. As he sipped his scotch, he had to wonder what sort of toll the presidency would take on them.

The White House was not known as a particularly happy home. He tried to remember the last time a truly loving couple lived there. The Fords, of course. They were the closest thing to "regular folks" to have ever occupied the Executive Mansion in recent history. The Reagans were affectionate enough, he supposed. Same for the Carters. The Clintons, that was another story. One could only wonder about the Bushes – George the elder and Barbara seemed happy enough, but George the younger's relationship with his wife Laura looked about as genuine and comfortable as a plastic-covered love seat. And the Nixons could barely stand looking at each other.

No, Franklin mused, the White House is not the best place to live when your marriage is on the rocks. And being close to the White House wasn't exactly a Marriage Encounter weekend, either. Successful relationships spawned in the heat of a political campaign had a very short shelf-life.

Only once had Franklin ever contemplated the possibility of marriage. That was back in the early '70s while he was stumping for McGovern. He and a fellow campaign worker, a jaunty warrior woman named Shantelle Washington, were quite the item. They kept steady company for four years. But when the 1976 election came around, he was a Carter man and she backed the more idealistic Sargent Shriver. And that was the end of the relationship. She accused him of selling out his core beliefs for the sake of political expediency. Half the time he thought about it, he agreed she was probably right. The rest of the time, he convinced himself that she was a dreamer, and that dreamers don't get anything done in the rough-and-tumble world of workaday politics. One had to be realistic, he told her. One has to accept what gains and successes can reasonably be accomplished. If you hold out for the whole ball of wax and aren't satisfied with anything less, then your life will be nothing but constant disappointment.

It made sense then. It made sense now. But it didn't make him any less lonely during those long nights when he hungered for her touch.

She was the last serious relationship. He saw her again, briefly, during the 1988 campaign. She was a Jesse Jackson delegate when he was a DNC organizer. She still hadn't lost the fire in her eyes. And she commented to Franklin how "old and sad" he looked.

Over the years, he managed to convince himself that men like him weren't meant to settle down.

He gulped down the rest of the scotch and asked the bartender for another.

"Let me get that one for you," said a familiar voice.

Franklin swiveled around on the barstool and smiled.

"What's a girl like you doing in a nice place like this?"

"Trying to ply you with alcohol, it would seem," said Riolas, taking the stool next to his. She addressed the bartender. "Another slug of rotgut for the stew bum and a white wine spritzer for the lady." She regarded Franklin's face and frowned thoughtfully.

"You're up late tonight, aren't you?"

"Couldn't sleep," he said. "So much going on, so fast. He's trying to do a lot, and I just have to wonder if it isn't all too much."

The bartender came back with the drinks. Franklin reached for his wallet, but Riolas swatted his hand.

"This one's on me, cowboy!"

The bartender smiled as Riolas paid him.

"Don't get the wrong idea about me," Franklin said. "Just because I let you buy me a drink doesn't mean you can have your way with me."

"Hah!" she snorted. "When I snap my fingers, you will be mine! Mere mortal, foolishly thinking yourself able to withstand my feminine wiles?"

Franklin smiled. Then he changed the subject.

"Pretty heady stuff, isn't it? Working for a president?"

It was a defense mechanism, changing the subject like that, and he regretted it immediately. Keeping the conversation on political – therefore safely impersonal – territory.

Riolas shrugged. "Busier, yeah. But he's still the same guy. He's holding up well. So is she. They should be good for the rest of the term."

"No more than that? He won't run again?"

"It would surprise me," she said. "But I guess I can't really rule it out." She sipped at her drink.

A few moments of silence passed between them. Then Franklin laughed out loud, a booming guffaw that drew the attention of the hotel bar's few patrons.

"Look at us. It's almost midnight, we're in Chicago — one of the most exciting cities in the world. And here we sit, two political functionaries, obviously attracted to each other, and all we can talk about is our big boss man who's currently sleeping with the woman he loves. And we're worried about how he's holding up?"

Riolas smiled and stirred her wine spritzer.

"He has a life," she said. "And our lives these days seem to be sitting on the proverbial back burner."

Suddenly, Franklin was tired of beating around the bush. He turned to look at her. "Wanna do something about that?" Franklin asked. He didn't have to elaborate.

"Let me finish my wine," she said.

She gulped it down quickly, wiped her lips with a napkin and turned to face Franklin.

"Do you have pay-per-view?"

"Yup."

"Good. Then we'll go to your room. Mine doesn't."

***

Police Sergeant Phil McCluskey was sound asleep. It was the sleep of a man who is confident and self-assured.

Tomorrow was all taken care of. He wouldn't take unnecessary risks. After all, the target had several more speaking engagements down the road, and there were others like him with orders to carry out. So, no sense getting killed. Still, if he got his chance, he'd take it.

He would be part of the security detail near the presidential platform. The president and his Secret Service agents would walk right past him on the way to the podium. Huerta would be shaking hands with well-wishers as he walks. It'd be the perfect place to execute the plan.

He already had his vacation approved. The personnel department thought he was flying from O'Hare to San Antonio. But if things went right, he would report to an airport locker and find a new Canadian passport, identification papers, and an airline ticket to Buenos Aires, along with $500,000 and the number to a new Swiss bank account with a $1.5 million balance.

50

The sound from the TV woke him up. For a moment, he thought he was dreaming. He remembered the night before, and decided if this were a dream, then he did not want to wake up. Ever!

Riolas was sitting up on her side of the bed with a pillow propped behind her back. She was wearing only the T-shirt she wore into the hotel lounge the night before. She was clicking the TV remote, going from channel to channel.

"I think I understand why you guys love these things so much," she said. "It's control. Power. You don't like what this multi-billion dollar television network has prepared for your entertainment? Boom! Switch to something else. Then something else! And all the channels vie for even a moment of your attention. If they only knew what it was you wanted, they would try to do it for you, to be it for you. But you don't give them a chance. You light up each channel, one at a time, and reject each, should it fail to catch your imagination at that first instant of connection." She turned to face Franklin, who was still struggling to wake up completely.

"And there, I have summed up the similarities between man's two most consuming fascinations — the pursuit of love, and the pursuit of something good on TV."

"Yeah, but there never is anything good on TV," he said, taking the remote from her hand and pulling her close. They made good morning love while, on the screen, the Teletubbies cavorted around their little grass-covered hill.

51

The presidential motorcade wound its way toward the stadium. The early afternoon sun glinted off the jet-black paint of the armored Suburban.

"I hate the fact that they have to shut down the freeway for things like this," Huerta said. "Rush hour is about twenty hours long in this city, and here we are making things worse."

"A necessary evil, Mr. President," Agent Reigel said. He used those words frequently, almost like a mantra, whenever Huerta complained about restrictions on his movements or inconveniences to others.

"How come I can't walk to the bathroom alone?"

"Why can't Janelle and I take a stroll in the garden without you bozos tagging along?"

"Why do people who I've been working with for months still have to be searched for weapons before they can come into the Oval Office?"

A Necessary Evil, Mr. President! A simple chant of penance, it covered many sins.

The interview at the radio station went well enough, Huerta decided. The host was an affable but somewhat scary-looking fellow named Stan Anniston. But he seemed pretty well-prepared, up on all his facts and figures. And despite the high-tech atmosphere of the billion-dollar radio station, Anniston had a small-town way about him that Huerta found refreshing.

But the first thing Huerta noticed about the burly talk show host was his Green Bay Packers ball cap.

"Isn't that somewhat dangerous?" Huerta asked. "I mean, here you are in the heart of the beast, as it were. I'll bet you get more threats on your life than I do!"

"That's probably true," Anniston laughed. "Truth is, I don't even start my car any more without checking under the hood to see if there's a pack of dynamite with a Bears sticker on it."

The men shared a laugh, and Huerta felt an immediate bond with him.

"You're one to talk, though," Anniston said. "I happen to know, sir, that you are a Green Bay fan yourself! Somehow, you managed to grow up in south Texas without having a mob of angry Cowboys fans rip you to pieces. By my way of thinking, maybe that's how you developed the courage you showed during the vice presidential confirmation process, not to mention the guts you showed when you found the presidency itself dumped into your lap."

Huerta smiled. "Yeah, this is a tough job," he said. "I didn't ask for it, but now I have it. So I'm going to do things the way I see fit and hope I can make things a little bit better for everyone in the process."

It was a short interview, only ten minutes. No calls were accepted. When it was over, Anniston shook Huerta's hand.

"Thanks for coming today, Mr. President. And thanks for coming to Chicago. I think there are a lot of people here who agree with what you've been saying on this tour."

"Thanks, Stan," Huerta said. He got up to leave, then – almost as an afterthought – he turned back.

"Are you going to the rally today?"

Anniston shook his head. "I wish I was, Mr. President," he said. "I didn't get an invitation."

Huerta frowned. "Well, I can fix that," he said. "That's one of the very few cool things about this job." He turned to Franklin. "Don, do you think we could get this man a pass?"

Franklin shrugged his shoulders. "I don't see why not. We've got a couple left."

"Fine," Huerta said. "See if you can get him one, please." He turned to Agent Reigel.

"Any problems with that?"

Reigel frowned.

"Actually, sir, yes there is. There are a few passes, but there's no place for the gentleman to sit. The seats are all taken."

Anniston smiled.

"That's fine, Mr. President. I appreciate the gesture, but don't go through any special..."

"It's no problem, Stan," Huerta said. He thought a moment.

"Tell you what. We'll get you a VIP pass. Then you meet up with Mr. Franklin there at the stadium. He'll bring you to wherever they have us waiting to go out to the podium. You can even hang with us if you'd like, if you don't mind just standing around on the podium looking stupid."

"No, I don't mind," Anniston said, grinning.

As the limo approached the stadium, Huerta smiled to think of how pleased the talk show host looked because of a simple gesture. It made him feel good. His spirits were buoyed further when he saw the approaching parking lot at the stadium. The place seemed to be packed.

There was no admission charge, of course. But that didn't bring out the hoped-for crowds in New York, Boston or Cleveland. Maybe the word was starting to get out.

The two heavily armored Suburbans with their companion Secret Service and support vehicles were waved through the police cordon and directed into the stadium proper.

With a ring of agents and police officers around him, Huerta was whisked to an inner office to wait for showtime. Janelle would watch the speech from the "Green Room." It was going to be carried live on local

TV with sound bites uploaded to New York in time for the evening newscasts. He looked around the room and took stock of the people.

Englund, was there, of course. So were Reigel and several other agents he knew only by their first names. A couple of city cops were standing outside the door and the hallway. But no Don Franklin.

"Has Don gone to find that talk show host?" he asked Englund.

"Yes sir," Englund said. "They agreed to meet at Gate Five right about now."

"Good," Huerta said. "When Franklin gets here, hold on to him. This is his town. I'd like to have him on the podium with me."

"I'll give it a go," Reigel said, and he put out word through his lapel radio.

***

They found Franklin and Anniston with Michelle Riolas at a concession stand. It was closed, a fact that caused no small amount of vexation to a native of the city's South Side.

"All this time I've been gone from Chi Town," Franklin moaned. "And I finally get back and I can't even buy a beer. Ain't this some shit?"

"No beer, I can understand," Anniston said. "After all, it would probably be better to keep folks sober for this thing. But no hot dogs? That's un-American!"

"We'll get you a hot dog later, little boy," said Riolas. "And a lollipop. Don't you cry now."

A Chicago cop walked up to them. "Either of you guys Don Franklin?"

"That's what my mother says, but she lies sometimes." Franklin felt uncomfortable around the Chicago police force — he had been involved in the great political upheaval of 1968, and some things you never forget.

The cop turned toward Anniston.

"That must make you Stan Anniston."

"Yes sir, nothing I can do about it."

"The president wants you and him," the cop said. "Come with me, please."

***

Sergeant McCluskey was part of the 1968 upheaval as well, but only through family connection. His father was a cop back when Mayor Daley ran the joint — not that snot-nosed kid of his, but the old man himself.

McCluskey's father had suffered great indignities during the rioting outside the Democratic National Convention of 1968. McCluskey remembered the smell of urine and feces on his father when he came home in the morning. That day, all he could talk about was the fucking hippies who had filled plastic bags with their piss and shit and threw them at the police. His father was never the same after that, especially with all the negative attention focused on the Chicago Police Department in the aftermath.

Now the same hippies who trashed Michigan Avenue in 1968 were running the Democratic Party. They thought they were all respectable now, but they still probably carried the stink of piss and shit on them. He had no way of knowing if it was true, but it was fun to think that maybe this spic president was one of the protesters who threw shit at his father. Not that it mattered. But it would be a nice touch of justice.

He was in position, about 15 yards from the steps leading to the podium. The field-level seats were full. Huerta would walk right past him.

The Secret Service and his fellow officers would struggle to hold back the surging crowd. Some, of course, would get through to shake the president's hand.

And he would be ready.

266

***

"So, are we under arrest?" There was just a hint of pique in Franklin's voice.

"Only if you want to be," the cop said. He looked all of 17 years old, Franklin thought. He also looked edgy. "I just got orders that the president wants you two guys with him. Can we go now?"

"Yeah, let's go," Franklin said, more than a little miffed.

"Whoa, wait a minute," the cop said. "They didn't say nothing about no woman coming with you. Just you two guys. Those were my orders."

"No sweat, Don. I'll meet you back in the hotel later," Riolas said, giving the cop a disdainful look.

"At last, something to look forward to," Franklin said. He and Stan followed the police officer.

Riolas watched Franklin walk away. She'd learned some time ago that she liked watching him walk away.

Minutes later, after passing through several security checks, Franklin and Stan were shown into the president's waiting room.

"Sorry about that, Don," Huerta said after Franklin detailed how he had been practically taken into custody. "I just wanted to have you here with me this afternoon, to be up there on the podium with me. This is your hometown. And none of this would have been possible without you. I just wanted you to bask in the glow a little bit, take some recognition for all you've done for me and for the country."

"Well, when you put it that way, it makes it kind of hard to stay pissed off," Franklin said.

The door opened. It was Reigel.

"Everyone ready to move?"

***

It was a moving ring of Secret Service agents and police with Huerta, Englund and Franklin at the core. Anniston trailed behind with some of the lesser celebrities.

The opening round of speeches by the Mayor, some local congressmen and other dignitaries had concluded, and now it was time for the main event. Franklin thought the whole thing resembled a prizefight at Madison Square Garden, with the contenders making their way to the ring — each fighter surrounded by his entourage.

The crowd surged forward to the rope and police barrier and thrust their hands toward the president. Reigel and the other Secret Service agents tried to eyeball each and every hand, ever on the alert for anything that could be used as a weapon.

Huerta reached through the protective ring of agents and officers and grasped what hands he could reach.

He loves this shit, Franklin thought. *He loves it, and I wonder how much that's going to change him.*

The podium drew nearer. The sound of the crowd was deafening. The Mayor of Chicago, a gaggle of aldermen, and a handful of congressmen stood on the platform, clapping their hands wildly. It was a regular love fest, Franklin thought.

Then somebody shouted "GUN!" and everything went to hell in a hurry.

52

Sergeant McCluskey watched out of the corner of his eye as the ring of protection drew nearer and nearer. He stood with his arms outstretched, his back to the aisle, holding back the upwelling wall of humanity that wanted to connect with their president, to touch him.

When the president and his protectors were mere feet away, McCluskey wheeled around and pointed to the far side of the aisle with his left hand. His eyes were open wide, almost bugging out of the sockets. His right hand went to his service pistol.

"GUN!" he screamed, pointing at a middle-aged man holding a video camera.

Secret Service agents moved rapidly in the direction of the perceived threat. His weapon drawn, held at hip level, McCluskey lunged toward the circle surrounding Huerta.

Automatically, agents grabbed the president by the arms. They were going to push him to the ground and cover him with their bodies. All eyes were looking in the direction the Chicago cop had pointed.

Two agents tackled the camera-toting man and wrestled him to the ground. McCluskey continued toward the president. The agents had him bent into a crouching position.

The cop's weapon was low, making it harder to see. It was pointed at the president's belly. His finger tightened on the trigger.

***

"GUN!" someone shouted, but Franklin didn't see who it was. He saw the agents starting to push Huerta to the ground. He also saw something they didn't see.

"That cop's going the wrong way," he thought.

Then he saw the cop was holding a gun, just about at hip level, close to the belt. Everyone else was looking to the left side of the aisle at a cameraman. No one else seemed to notice the oncoming cop with the gun.

Franklin moved without thinking. He launched himself at the cop and grabbed his right wrist. He tried to lift the wrist, point it in the air. It was halfway up when the gun went off.

"That didn't hurt much," Franklin thought. It was like a punch in the lower right part of his chest — all concussion, no pain.

"Nope, that wasn't bad at all," he mused just before the darkness took him down and away.

***

"GUN!" someone shouted, and the first thing Huerta realized was that he couldn't move his arms, and that someone was kneeing him in the small of the back. His initial reaction was to try and free himself, but the agents had him tight. He was heading to the floor, like it or not.

What is Don doing? he thought, in the instant that passed. His agents were concentrating on an area to his left, but here was Don Franklin moving to his right, looking like he was wrestling with a policeman.

Huerta was being pushed to the floor when he heard the muffled report and saw a small flower of red blossom on the back of Franklin's gray suitcoat. Then it felt like someone, one of the agents probably, punched him just below the right collarbone. And it hurt like a bitch!

He went face down to the floor and screamed.

***

Agent Reigel saw the video camera for what it was and paid it no heed. His eyes scanned the boiling mass of humanity for the real threat he knew would be there. Several agents had taken the cameraman down to the ground, others had pushed the president down on his face, but everyone heard the shot and Reigel was the first to see where the sound had come from.

The Chicago cop was wrestling with Franklin, trying to get the large man off of him. Someone was screaming. Franklin fell like a rag doll, and Reigel saw the gun.

The cop turned to run. Reigel started after him. But then someone grabbed the cop, wrapping his arms around the cop's ankles. The cop fell to the floor, the gun bounced from his grasp.

It took Reigel a moment to realize that it was the radio guy, Stan Anniston, who was holding onto the shooter's legs. Reigel moved toward the struggle, but his feet got tangled in the legs of the agents who were pushing the president to the floor.

He looked up to see the cop reaching for the gun that had bounced away from him as he was tackled. The radio guy was climbing the cop's body, fighting to keep the cop's arm pinned to the ground. He was screaming, trying to get the attention of the other agents.

"HERE! HERE! HERE!"

Before Reigel could get to his feet, the cop reached the gun, pointed it, and pulled the trigger a final time.

***

Anniston was looking toward the podium, scanning the faces to see if anyone from a competing radio station was there when he heard someone shout "GUN!"

Instinctively, he flinched and ducked into a crouching position.

271

Then he heard a popping sound. He was looking right at the cop as he struggled to push Franklin's bleeding body away from him.

The rest of it, he saw later, on videotape, not quite believing it was he who was doing these athletic, heroic things. He could not remember flinging himself at the shooter, wrapping his meaty arms around the man's knees, pulling him to the floor. But he could remember lying on the ground as he tried to hold the man down.

He saw the man – a cop, yet – lying face-down under him, reaching for the gun that lay inches from his right hand. He hoped someone else was seeing this and would at least try to kick the gun away. No such luck.

He used the shooter's body, climbing it like a rope ladder, and pinned the cop's right arm to the ground just as the cop grabbed the pistol in his right hand and slipped his finger into the trigger guard.

***

"Fucking nigger," McCluskey hissed.

The bullet was meant for the spic, but the nigger got in the way. *This isn't the way it was supposed to go*, he thought.

The plan was to scream the one word guaranteed to cause a commotion. He would point toward a likely suspect in the crowd. The Secret Service would take the word of a policeman with stripes on his shoulders. As they reacted to the misdirection, he would move in close and get off his shot unseen. He knew there was only time for one shot. Then, in the confusion he had created, he would be just another uniform in a surging sea of humanity. He would make his way to the perimeter of the stadium, into his squad car, and race to the airport. There was a change of clothes in the car and a small travel bag. He would get to the airport and be gone before the slow-motion television pictures had a chance to identify him as the shooter.

But the nigger fucked everything up. There might be time for a second shot, but forget any chance of getting out of here. Best to turn and run and right now. If he moved quick he could still get lost in the crowd.

Someone grabbed him by an ankle and he spilled to the floor. He looked back and saw some fat-assed civilian with a bald head and red beard climbing his body, screaming at the other cops and agents for help.

Well, that's the ball game, he thought as he reached for the gun. In a split second, the thought about the problem of surviving in a federal prison where the inmates might like nothing better than to torture a cop to death with whatever sharp things they could get their hands on. Not an attractive prospect.

The fat guy pinned his arm down at the biceps, but he could still bend his elbow. He brought the barrel of the gun to his right temple and pulled the trigger.

There was a small popping sound. The dust was kicked up around the dead cop's head. The bullet slammed through his skull, spraying nearby shoes with a shower of bone and bits of brain.

***

"Holy fuck!" Stan Anniston screamed as the cop shot himself. Large portions of the cop's brains were lying in a pink and white pile of clotted lumps to the left of his head.

Suddenly something hit him in the back, knocking him away from the dead cop. He rolled away a short distance and saw a Secret Service agent kicking the gun out of the dead cop's hand.

The agent looked right at him now.

"Are you okay?"

"Yeah," Anniston said, wiping his face. He looked at his hand. It was covered with blood and little pink chunks of the cop's brain.

He vomited. Then he fainted.

53

The Speaker of the House watched the events unfolding over a satellite uplink. He knew nothing about the particulars in advance. He didn't want to know.

It was enough that something had happened. And the video was clear as a bell. Huerta had certainly taken a bullet. He was screaming like a pussy. He could forgive that, he supposed. The slow-motion video showed that the bullet struck him just below the right collarbone. The spreading rosette of blood was impossible to miss on his clean, white shirt. There were major blood vessels in that area. It was probably a mortal wound. Hell, it had to be!

He punched his intercom button. There were arrangements to make. He had to speak to the nation he would soon be leading. They would want to hear from their new president. He would be appropriately somber, of course, when the time came. But for the moment there was plenty of time for some private cheer!

***

Michelle and Janelle saw the same thing Wantner saw, the same time he saw it. They stood in shocked silence, looking at the screen, then at each other. Janelle turned toward a cop at the door.

"Take me to him," she said in a calm, quiet voice.

The cop refused. "Ma'am, the shit is flying fast and furious out there, and nobody's going anywhere right now."

Riolas walked to the door, stood on tiptoes and hissed in the officer's face.

"Pal, if you don't take us to them right now, and I mean right fucking now, then you're going to be singing soprano in the police choir this coming Christmas, and I am not shitting you."

The police officer backed off, and said something into his walkie-talkie. He listened to the radio reply, then turned toward the women.

"The ambulances are waiting right out here. Stick close to me and the other officers and move quickly."

***

Huerta never lost consciousness. He was pressed under a pile of bodies, his shoulder ached and throbbed, but the worst of it – the thing that was making him scream in agony – was the bony point of a knee that was being driven into his lower back.

Through the bodies, he could hear several agents shouting. "SHOOTER DOWN! SHOOTER DOWN!" It was then that the president put everything together in his mind. He realized he had not been punched in the shoulder.

It was a bullet wound.

In the darkness caused by the pile of bodies, his mind's eye replayed the scene in slow motion — Franklin moving toward the cop, Franklin grabbing the cop by the wrist, the muffled "pop" followed by the spreading blossom of blood on the back of Franklin's suitcoat, the blow to his own shoulder. Then the second "pop," after which all he could hear was screaming.

It dawned on him that Donald Franklin would have been safe and sound if he, the president of the United States, had not wanted to show off the "local boy who made good" like a prize steer.

In short order, he was hoisted to his feet, and then back off his feet. He was being carried at a run by several agents, back down the aisle toward the stadium office they had been using as a "Green Room."

No, that wasn't it. There was an ambulance in the driveway door. A gurney was already out and waiting.

The agents dropped him, none too gently, on the gurney, and a swarm of medics began tending to him. His shirt was ripped off.

Huerta tried to look at the wound, but hands held his head still.

"You're going to be OK, Mr. President," people kept telling him. "You're going to be just fine." He wondered if they might be lying.

At that point, he realized that his wife had seen the whole thing on TV.

"Get on the radio, right now, call Janelle and tell her I'm all right," he shouted at Englund, who had suffered a bloody nose (this time it was broken) and a fractured little finger during all the shoving and pushing, produced a cellphone and dialed, wincing at the pain in his hand.

The medical people were astounded by the forcefulness of the president's voice. It meant the bullet hadn't punctured a lung. Another good sign was the overall lack of blood. There was none coming out of his mouth or nose. The hole in his chest bled, but not copiously. There was no exit wound on his back. Subsequent examination showed that most of the blood on Huerta's shirt was, in fact, Franklin's.

The president was trundled into the ambulance. Englund piled in after the gurney was loaded and secured. An oxygen mask was strapped into place over Huerta's nose. He brushed it aside.

"Jim, tell me about Don. Is Don going to be okay?"

"I don't know, Bob. It looked really bad." Maybe it was just the re-injured nose, Huerta thought, but Englund looked like he was ready to start crying. Huerta allowed the ambulance attendant to put the oxygen mask back in place. But he pushed it aside once more when Janelle appeared through the open back doors. She knelt by his side and kissed his cheek. He grasped her hand and told her he was going to be fine.

During the five-minute ride to the hospital, the bullet hole was closely inspected. It was determined that the projectile, much of its energy spent on its disastrous path through Don Franklin's chest, had probably only gone about an inch into the president's upper right pectoral muscle. This was confirmed by X-ray.

The bullet was extracted under local anesthesia.

***

In the same hospital at the same time, Donald Franklin was fighting for his life.

His body had taken the brunt of the damage from the bullet, slowing it down sufficiently to where it presented the president with merely a troublesome puncture wound.

Riolas sat next to his gurney during the ambulance ride, holding his hand, talking to him, joking with him, saying anything at all just in case he could actually hear her. She would not let him die thinking he was alone.

He's so pale, she thought. The skin tone of his face, usually a cheerful, warm mahogany, now was the washed-out gray of burnt charcoal.

At the hospital, the initial assessment was not encouraging. Franklin had a shattered rib bone, a collapsed lung, a large exit wound just under his right shoulder blade, and considerable blood loss. An attending physician found Michelle Riolas in a nearby waiting room.

"Are you his wife?" the doctor asked.

"For the lack of a better term, yeah," she replied.

The doctor explained that it would be touch-and-go for the next several hours. Luckily, the bullet hadn't severed the aorta, but there was a lot of vascular damage. He might lose the lung altogether. The biggest danger was blood loss. It would take hours of surgery to get that under control. Should he survive the surgery, his chances looked good.

But survival was by no means assured.

54

As it turned out, the thing that tripped up the Speaker of the House was his own lack of patience. Had he waited out the medical reports from the hospital, he would not have made the speech, or at least it would have been modified.

Instead, he went ahead on the assumption that Huerta was either dead or dying. He had good reason to hope. In the video of the attack, it was clear that the president's chest was covered with blood. Even if he had survived – which seemed unlikely to one unaware of the facts – he would at least be incapacitated. The Constitution contains provisions for what is to be done in such circumstances.

So, from the Communications Center of the U.S. Capitol, Wantner went on the air and said the following:

> Ladies and gentlemen of the United States of America, it would seem there has been an attempt on the life of President Huerta. We're still awaiting word on his condition, but the first reports from the scene of this dastardly attack make it appear that the president's condition is grave.
>
> The United States cannot afford to be leaderless in these dangerous times, especially with as much confusion as there has been over the past several months. Therefore, in accordance with the Twenty-fifth Amendment to the Constitution of the United States, I am officially assuming the duties of president of the United States pending further word on Mr. Huerta's condition. As there is no sitting vice president, Article II

of the Constitution clearly delineates the order of presidential succession. In the event of the death or incapacity of the president, and in the absence of a vice president, the Speaker of the House of Representatives automatically assumes the duties of the presidency. Now I will, of course, refrain from taking the Oath of Office for the present, at least until we get word on the president's condition. But I will be going directly to the White House after I'm done speaking to you.

I ask you to pray for me in the difficult days ahead. And, please, pray for Mrs. Huerta. Thank you, and God Bless the United States of America.

***

About two hours after the shooting, when Huerta had recovered sufficiently, Englund tuned in CNN for the president to watch. They were replaying Wantner's speech every half hour.

When the networks received word that the president's injuries were not serious, Wantner was afforded the opportunity to give a second speech. He refused, saying his duties during the president's state of incapacity were far too pressing to allow for such a thing.

With Janelle standing near the head of his hospital bed, Huerta seethed with anger. He addressed his chief of staff.

"I want a news crew, cameras, lights, everything. I want them right here, in this hospital room. I want them here in an hour. I'm going on TV, live, and I'm going to settle that little fucker's hash once and for all."

55

Transcript of President Huerta's September 19th address to the nation from Mt. Morency Hospital, Chicago, Illinois:

Good evening, ladies and gentlemen. This has been quite an unsettling day. But, to paraphrase Mark Twain, the reports of my death have been greatly exaggerated.

Yes, as you can see, I am in the hospital. I have an IV connected to me, and my right arm is in a sling. As you have heard by now, the bullet only went an inch or so into my right upper chest. I'm told I can leave here tomorrow morning. My life was saved by my good friend, Donald Franklin, who now lies in a surgical recovery room in this same hospital. I ask that you pray for him as he fights for his life.

The investigation into the shooting continues. At the moment, it appears to be the act of a single individual who took his own life as he was being captured. Yet, and I have no way of knowing this for sure, somehow I feel that this was a deliberate attempt to stop me from talking about the things I've been talking about in my recent travels — the program I've been calling "The New Responsibility."

As I look into this camera, here in my hospital room, it occurs to me that I am simultaneously speaking to millions of Americans and people around the world — I can say far more than the pre-digested sound bites most of you will hear on subsequent broadcast news reports. I wouldn't want to go through this trauma again, but, now that I seem to have your full attention there's something I need you to do tonight.

I want each and every one of you to call your congressman, right now. The toll-free number should be showing up at the bottom of your screen as I speak. Call your congressman, please, and tell him or her that it's time to bring an end to the kind of government we've seen over the past several decades. It's time to end the political divisiveness, the bickering, the back-biting and the rancor. It's time for good people with divergent viewpoints to come together instead of pulling apart. Tell your representative that it has to stop! It's time to pass the government reform legislation that's sitting idle in the House!

Now, I'd like to address myself to Albert Wantner, the Speaker of the House.

Sir, you may stand down.

I am in charge. I am not incapacitated. The provisions outlined in Article II and the Twenty-fifth Amendment to the Constitution do not apply. I never lost consciousness. I was treated with local anesthesia. I am in full command of my mental faculties. The medical opinion of the doctor in charge of my case will be borne out in a signed affidavit by the Secretary of State and my own chief of staff, James Englund.

Unless there is a clear indication, in fifteen minutes or less, that you, Mr. Wantner, are out of the White House and have resumed your lawful duties, I will use my powers to assemble Congress. I will ask them to immediately remove you as Speaker of the House. I will ask them to replace you with someone of their choosing, someone who understands the rule of law. Someone who knows that we do not govern by dragging our feet and fighting at every step, but by finding common ground in the areas in which we agree, and building consensus from that point.

You have fifteen minutes, Mr. Speaker.

Regardless of whether Mr. Wantner remains at the helm, I ask the House of Representatives to stop dragging their feet and approve Senator Grace Bilson as our new vice president.

We must take advantage of this unique opportunity to show the people of the world that we are serious about moving the country forward, that their government is ready to leave the bickering behind it as a footnote in the history books. A bipartisan Executive Branch — a Democrat as president, and a Republican as vice president. Working together, hand in glove, differing where we may, agreeing where we can, but all along moving this country forward.

Now, I address the American people. You have your own responsibility to bear in the running of your government. I've been talking about that a whole lot lately. I will have more to say about that in the near future. But, for the time being, I want everyone to know that I am okay, just a little sore. We will continue to keep Don Franklin in our prayers, and we ask that you do so as well.

Thank you, and good night.

56

It took Al Wantner just under seven minutes to reach CNN by phone.

"Well, it is certainly a relief to hear the president sounding so hale and hearty. Of course, I will stand down! And I look forward to working with the president, as soon as he is able, toward implementing some of the good ideas he has talked about."

That evening, the switchboard at the Capitol Building was swamped by phone calls. And faxes. And telegrams. And e-mails. A gathering of about 5,000 people carried signs in front of the Capitol. Two of those signs read, "Give Us Our Country Back!" and "WE are the GOVERNMENT!"

The following Thursday, the House of Representatives met in full session.

The only order of business was an immediate confirmation vote on the nomination of New Jersey Senator Grace Bilson as vice president of the United States, without benefit of committee hearings. This passed on a unanimous voice vote.

Later that afternoon, the Senate also approved the Bilson nomination, and yet another Joint Session of Congress was scheduled for the following night.

***

It seemed unrelated at the time, but on the evening after the failed assassination attempt, an assistant to an undersecretary at the Justice

Department got a curious phone call. The caller promised to deliver a box full of cassette tapes containing some incriminating information about a formerly high-powered Member of Congress who had just fallen off his high horse.

"My umbrella of protection has been removed," the caller said. "I have to cover my ass while I still have an ass to cover."

The only thing the caller requested was immunity from prosecution for any and all criminal wrong-doing that might be revealed during the blockbuster, red-letter investigation that was sure to follow.

The undersecretary promised to convey the request to his boss. His boss took the information to the Attorney General, assurances were given, and the caller was told how to deliver the tapes.

***

Huerta lay in his bed, feeling the ache in his shoulder. It wasn't a deep wound, but it was painful. Ibuprofen pills managed keep the ache at a level where he could deal with it. But it still hurt.

The bedroom door opened slightly, and Tommy poked his head into the room.

"Hey, Dadster," Tommy said.

"Hey," Huerta said. "Come on in."

Tommy opened the door all the way and stepped into the room.

"Some pretty exciting stuff, eh kid?" Huerta smiled.

"Yeah. Getting shot. Exciting."

Tommy looked like he wanted to talk about something but didn't know how to get started.

"Yeah, maybe 'exciting' wasn't the right word," Huerta said. "Maybe 'scary' would have been a better choice."

"Yeah," Tommy said. He sat on the edge of the mattress, looking at his father.

"Can I get you anything? Want some coffee or a soda?"

"Nah, I'm fine," he said. "How about you? How are you doing?"

Tommy thought about it for a moment.

"Well... Dad, I feel like shit right now."

Huerta decided to overlook the breach in language.

"Why's that?" he said.

Tommy looked down at the floor.

"This whole thing, you being president, you getting shot, it's got my head messed up a little. All this time I'm resenting the fact that I'm Superman's son, then one day I'm watching TV and I see that you've taken a bullet in the chest and might be dead."

Huerta saw tears in his son's eyes.

"You're gonna hate me..." he said as the tears started falling.

Huerta sat up and put an arm around his son's shoulders.

"That'll never happen," he said quietly.

"Wait until you hear everything," Tommy sniffed. "Back when we lived in Texas, after you killed... after you shot Julio... I used to pray that somebody would shoot you. I used to pray that you'd get the same thing you did to Julio."

Huerta smiled.

"God doesn't work like that, son. He'd be crazy to give teenaged boys that kind of power! If he did, dads everywhere would be dropping dead twenty per second!"

He patted his son's shoulder, then roughed up his hair.

"Son, you've done nothing that every other young man hasn't done at one time or another. I used to be pissed at my father all the time, mostly because he had the gall to die before I could really get to know him. Being pissed at your dad is part of becoming a man. You'll get over it."

Then he popped his son on the back of the head with an open palm.

"That is, you'd better get over it!"

Tommy smiled, leaned forward and hugged his father.

285

***

Stan Anniston hit fast-forward on his VCR.

The on-screen image sped along until the moment the Chicago cop pointed and shouted "Gun!"

"See?" Anniston said to his wife. "Right here is where it all happens. This cop shouts out that someone's got a gun, and the Secret Service reacts in that direction."

He hit the "frame forward" button, moving the image along one frame at a time.

"Now, while the Secret Service agents are getting ready to pound the shit out of some poor schmuck with a video camera, the cop pulls his piece and moves toward the president."

"Did the guy with the camera get hurt?" Abby, his wife, asked.

"Busted arm, I think. Now there's a lawsuit!" Anniston chuckled.

He advanced several more frames.

"Right about here, I start to see what's happening. I'm just about to move toward the cop when the big black guy gets in my way..."

"And takes the bullet that you would have taken if you got there first." Abby said, without a trace of humor.

"Yeah. That," Anniston said.

He advanced the tape through the part where Franklin got shot.

"Now here is where I grab the cop around the knees."

He advanced the tape and Abby pointed at something on the screen.

"Back it up a second, just a few frames," she said.

Anniston hesitated.

"I don't think it's necessary to..."

"Back it up!" she demanded. "I just noticed something."

Anniston did as he was told.

"Now, run it ahead one frame at a time," she said.

Again, Anniston complied. Abby broke into a booming laugh.

"You didn't tackle that guy!" she guffawed, tears streaming from her eyes. "You tripped and fell into him."

Anniston frowned.

"The point isn't how I tackled the guy," he said. "It's that I tackled him, and that he didn't get away."

Abby scooted across the couch and pulled herself onto her husband's lap.

"Well, give that man the Medal of Honor," she said as she wrapped her arms around his neck. "You did keep him from getting away, after all."

"Yeah, I did that, didn't I?" he said as he pulled her close.

Suddenly she snatched the remote from his hands.

"What are you doing?" he asked.

"I want to fast-forward to the part when you barfed and fainted," she said with a grin.

***

Riolas remained at Franklin's bedside the entire night. The nurses told her that he'd probably be out until morning.

She held his hand, stroking it. At least he was off the forced respiration machine. The bleeding had been halted. The damaged lung had been repaired — it would not need to be removed. It was a bad situation, but not as bad as it could be.

She felt Franklin's hand wrap around her fingers. His eyes were open and looking right at her.

"Hey there, lazybones," she said softly. "Nappy time over?"

Franklin looked around the room, then back at Riolas. The tube in his throat was still there, keeping his airway open, so speech was impossible.

"Are you just going to lollygag the rest of your life away, or are you going to get better so you can get back to work, you lazy sack of shit?"

287

Franklin smiled as best he could with a tube taped in his mouth. He lifted his right hand, extended the middle finger, and displayed it in Riolas's general direction.

"Welcome back, Donny," she said.

57

After taking the oath, Vice President Bilson was escorted to her seat as president of the Senate by Congressman O'Hara. This would have been Speaker Wantner's job, if he had still been Speaker.

Earlier in the evening, Huerta asked Bilson if she would agree to a slight modification in the swearing-in ceremony. She assured Huerta that she had no problem with his delivering a speech immediately after she was sworn in.

"Just as long as you're not going to pull a DeWitt on me," she said. He laughed and promised he wouldn't.

Bilson also agreed to something else, then further agreed to allow Huerta to make the announcement in his speech.

As the applause died down, Huerta spoke off-the-cuff, no prepared text.

"Ladies and Gentlemen, as I recall I had a statement prepared to deliver the last time we all met in Joint Session like this. I didn't get to deliver it then, and much of it is no longer appropriate. So, if you don't mind, I just want to say a few words from the heart.

"First, I would like to thank the Congress of the United States of America for its quick action in choosing a new Speaker of the House and the subsequent and speedy confirmation of Vice President Bilson. And I'd like to congratulate Senator Harold McGee on his election to the post of Senate Majority Leader. The new vice president and I will look forward to working with the congressional leadership in a the spirit of cooperation and bipartisanship."

Huerta paused for a moment, then smiled broadly.

"But I'd like to correct something that is being widely reported in the newspapers tonight. This will not be the first bipartisan administration in recent history. This will be the first nonpartisan administration ever. Earlier tonight, I presented your new vice president with an idea. I would revoke my membership in the Democratic Party if she would do the same with her membership in the GOP. She agreed, and in each others' presence, we burned our official party membership cards."

He paused for effect. "They made a lovely little flame in the Oval Office ashtray." This was greeted by laughter and applause throughout the Chamber.

***

Watching on a TV (this one in the spacious bathroom as she soaked in a bubble bath), Janelle Huerta blew a soap-bubble kiss at her husband's image on the screen. She had a special greeting in mind for him when he returned to the official residence.

***

"By taking this step," Huerta continued, "we are pointing out once and for all that the needs of the people transcend party considerations. From now on, you can be assured that your president and vice president are acting as independents. True, she is still possessed of a more conservative point of view than am I. And we will no doubt debate many points. But these debates will be conducted in a professional manner, with nothing but the welfare of the country at issue.

"Taking divisiveness out of government is just the first step in an even larger goal — namely, getting the American people interested enough to re-invest in their own government. I know I'm just beating the same old dead horse when I stand up here and talk about the ever-declining percentage of registered voters who bother to make it to the polls on election day. They tune us out, they assume we are all corrupt, and they want nothing to do with us.

"Well, folks, you've heard me say on several occasions that the American people share in the blame for the current state of government. Every two years, all 435 members of the House of Representatives and at least thirty-three Senators stand for election or reelection. And, as voters, we have the unfortunate tendency to elect those people who promise to bring the biggest bag of federal groceries to our doors.

"Think about that for a moment. Would you willingly vote for someone who promised to cut the fat out of a federal program that benefits your district? Would you vote for someone who pledged to take a good, close look at entitlement programs that you count on from month to month?

"Of course not! We have been told year after year that the other guy should sacrifice to balance the budget. If you're a corporate CEO, you want government to cut back on welfare, student loans, and the like. You don't want them to go after your tax loopholes. If you're a retired person, you want the government to slash federal spending in every area except Social Security, Medicare and other programs that benefit the elderly. Teachers resist cutbacks on educational resource spending. If I were a member of the military, I would insist on maintaining the defense budget. Our national motto is no longer 'In God We Trust.' It is now, 'Lay Off My Entitlements!'

"And your government listens! Oh, gosh how we listen! We won't think of cutting back on something that might affect you. We'll cut somewhere in some program that will affect someone else! Why? Because we want to get re-elected, that's why!

"Well, this is the government we have today and it's easy to feel that we're pretty much stuck with it. It's that kind of thinking that got us into this mess. We're going to look into it, to try to make it better. We'll need your help. We're up to the challenge. Are you?"

***

In a private Florida hospital room, secluded from the world, the old man watched the image on the television screen and smiled. It couldn't have worked out better if he had been pulling the strings himself. Here at the end of things, he felt a sense of peace and well-being. The medication pretty much controlled the pain. His mind was more-or-less clear. And now that it looked like things were working out the way he had planned, he was ready to go.

The former president looked at the man sitting by his bedside.

"Looks like we made a good choice after all, doesn't it, Jim?"

"I never doubted you for a moment, sir" Englund said.

DeWitt laughed until he gasped for breath. "Bullshit," he said weakly, reaching for his former chief of staff's hand. "I doubted, you doubted, everyone doubted. Except, maybe, him." He pointed at the image of the young president on the TV screen. "Somehow I'm left with the feeling that he never doubted — not once."

Englund smiled. "You weren't there when he punched me in the nose, Mr. President."

DeWitt laughed again. "No, but I wish I had been." He smiled.

DeWitt took a deep breath.

"It's going to be OK. I really think it is," he said, Englund gazing fondly at him.

Then he closed his eyes and died.

***

Jimmy Langston shook his head sadly as he clicked off the TV. The idiots were actually applauding! He knew perfectly well that the next day, the same fools who were clapping and congratulating the president would be looking for ways to stick knives into his back. He smiled at the thought.

Langston stepped outside his apartment and closed the door behind him. He had 15 minutes to get to the appointed meeting place. There, he would deliver the box of tapes currently secreted in the trunk of his car. He would turn them over only after being given unlimited immunity and a first-class ticket to the Caribbean island of his choice.

"Be prepared — the motto of a true scout," he said quietly as he walked to his car.

He unlocked the driver's side door, opened it, sat down, closed the door, and put his key into the ignition. Then he remembered his seatbelt. "Buckle up for safety," he said to himself as he clicked the belt in place. Then he twisted the key in the ignition.

The resulting explosion tore a chunk out of the pavement several inches deep. One person standing nearby was killed by shrapnel. Four were injured. The body and car were destroyed beyond recognition, and any hope of identification.

And so were the tapes.

***

Huerta looked out at the packed House Chamber. The audience regarded him in rapt silence.

"Well, I guess I've just about said my piece. There's a bit more than a year left in this administration. Soon, the vice president and I will decide whether we want to stick around for another four years of this. A lot depends on how things go. Should we decide to run again, it will be as an independent team without benefit of party nomination or affiliation. Should the parties decide to front candidates of their own, that will be their business. The more the merrier, as they say. At any rate, thank you for your attention tonight, both the folks here in the Chamber and those watching on TV, especially two very special folks who aren't here tonight but know who they are. Now, let's get busy and start running things the way the people want them run."

***

Hearing her boss speak, three words came to her mind. "The Huerta Manifesto," she said under her breath.

"What two people?" Franklin asked. "You suppose he meant us?"

"What's that?" Riolas asked. She held Franklin's hand as it dangled from the side of the hospital bed. The steady hiss of the oxygen apparatus made the TV hard to hear.

"He meant us just then, don't you think? I mean, the man couldn't find the crack of his own ass without his Donald and Michelle, now could he?"

Riolas eased onto the side of the bed and put her head on Franklin's shoulder. "Wouldn't surprise me if he did mean us," she said. She had no way of knowing that earlier that afternoon, Huerta had made a call to the Democratic Committee Chairperson in Brooks County, Texas. He suggested that the district would be well-served should a certain Ms. Michelle Riolas be considered as the party's candidate for the special election to select his replacement in Congress.

She lay there in silence as the president concluded his remarks. Then Franklin started laughing, and it scared her. She was afraid he would tear his stitches. "What are you laughing at, fool?"

"Him. Us. The whole thing," he said, his laughter dying out for lack of strength. "I recall once he said he didn't like Frank Capra movies. Shit, this whole thing has been a Frank Capra movie! 'Meet John Doe.' 'Mr. Smith Goes to Washington.' Old Frank couldn't have written a better script himself." He chuckled quietly.

"You know what they say," Riolas replied. "'truth is stranger than fiction.' Look at us! Who would have thought a blushing flower of a girl like me would ever end up with a roguish ne'er-do-well like you?"

They shared a quiet moment as the president and the new vice president shook hands at the podium.

"I'm not a marrying man," Franklin said at length. "But if I were that type, I'd ask you."

"That's nice," she said, snuggling closer. "I'd say 'no,' of course, but it's still nice to know that you think of me that way."

Franklin groaned. "See if I ever steal flowers for you again!"

THE END.

Dead End Street® *highly recommends these titles:*

A painful break-up/break-down chases high-tech marketing wiz Sandy Lowiltry from her Silicon Valley home. She comes to rest on the Oregon Coast, where she seeks solace in the opera-themed sanctuary of the Hotel

Bel Canto and the arms of a handsome eccentric who spends his days combing the beach for sea glass.

Sandy soon learns what the tourist ladies already know — it's easy to fall for Frosted Glass Man. Besides great sex and alarmingly intricate campsite cuisine, Frosty offers do-it-yourself mythologies that would melt even the coldest heart. But will it be enough to quiet the whisper of ambition, the voice inside Sandy's head that chides her for settling? Will she really leave behind Silicon Valley for love in such a strange package?

"...a most unlikely tale of discovery and passion. ...a shimmering fable, as delicate and whimsical as a handful of glass."
   – Debra Bokur, *Many Mountains Moving* literary journal

"A breezy, richly-textured romp through the inner circuitry of a postmodern heroine."
   – Christina Waters, PhD, *Metro* Newspapers (San Jose)

...available everywhere books are sold...

Also available in screenplay format!

Fifty-year-old Bill Harness is on a strange but seemingly benign journey, rambling across the country in an old Pontiac and anonymously leaving large checks with promising young opera singers. His fuel, however, is sorrow, and it isn't until he arrives on a small island outside of Seattle and befriends Gabriella Compton, a phenomenally talented soprano, that he is able to address the three great tragedies of his vocally gifted family.

"Michael J. Vaughn has turned out a beautiful, lyrical novel. I was caught up in the narrative within three sentences and was held spellbound by the story until the end. It is as captivating as a well-performed *La Boheme*, as tragic and triumphant as *Tosca*."

— Ani Harrison, *Tacoma Reporter*

"By turns rousing, lyrical and intoxicating, GABRIELLA'S VOICE is the work of a virtuoso."

— Calder Lowe, *The Montserrat Review*

"Vaughn performs the… task of invoking sounds from the silence of words on paper. Arias whirl from the pages… a treat for the ear as well as the mind."

— Gregory Harris, *BookPage*

…available everywhere books are sold…

Also available in screenplay format!

A Little Lower Than The Angels

Marty Gallanter

Basis For the Upcoming Motion Picture

Suzanne Rosewell is the youngest female partner in the history of her prestigious Wall Street law firm. She's a strong, driven woman with the will to succeed. Then she meets Elias Garner, an enigmatic black Jazz musician who carries an ancient golden trumpet and represents the even more furtive "Chairman" (whom we learn heads the most powerful corporation on earth).

Elias explains that God has always placed among us thirty-six righteous people – each of whom "knows the divine will" and all of which must be accounted for if humanity is to redeem itself. Five are missing from the Chairman's list and Suzanne is asked to set aside her career to search for them. If she is unsuccessful, it appears that the world cannot exist beyond the sunrise.

...available everywhere books are sold...

"Science can clone the body, but it cannot touch the soul."

To divert attention from its priesthood pedophilia scandals, the Vatican allows Doctor Marcus Leon to extract DNA from blood trapped in the Shroud of Turin. Dr. Leon then ignites a firestorm of controversy by announcing his plan to clone the image upon the Shroud — that of the man known by history as Jesus of Nazareth.

The experiment is a success, and the public embraces the clone as the Lord incarnate — not realizing that he is the Anti-Christ.

Led by Michael the Archangel, Dr. Leon must now build an army to defeat his greatest achievement and biggest mistake.

...available everywhere books are sold...

In the late sixties, the Zodiac serial killer terrorized the Bay Area, committing brutal, random attacks, and bragging about them in letters to the San Francisco *Chronicle*. In Santa Rosa, fifty miles to the north, investigators Manny Bruin and Mick Millian tailed potential suspect Byron Avion, an eccentric, portly man admittedly obsessed with the Zodiac. Bruin and Millian soon became convinced that Avion was the Highway 101 Murderer, a Zodiac-style killer who prowled the Santa Rosa area. But a decade-long investigation failed to connect Avion to the crimes. When the case finally broke, it re-wrote the book on homicide investigations and forever changed the direction of each man's life.

About the Author: Michael D. Kelleher is the internationally acclaimed author-scholar of *Profiling the Lethal Employee*, *Murder Most Rare: the Female Serial Killer* and *When Good Kids Kill*. His writing is truly exemplary, as is reflected by his long list of publishing credits for such venerable houses as Random House, Dell, the Greenwood Publishing Group, and Dead End Street®. Kelleher's work has appeared in the many of the country's major dailies, including the *Washington Post*, the *New York Times* and the San Francisco *Examiner*. He's a frequent guest on both radio and television, including a variety of national news programs.

...available everywhere books are sold...

Devastated that his wife and writing partner of 25 years left him on the eve of the new millennium, Lionel Rolfe set pen to paper in an attempt to make sense of the dance between men and women. But, as he began writing, a deeper understanding took hold – the Grim Reaper stopped by. And not just once, but again and again. The deaths of Carl Kessler, the unrepentant Stalinist and trade union organizer, and Nieson Himmel, a close friend and veteran nighttime police reporter for the Los Angeles Times, hit him hard. But it was the death of Rolfe's uncle, the great violinist Yehudi Menuhin, that turned his life upside down. In the end, the emotional ordeal was a blessing in disguise. After all, without it, the world would not have DEATH AND REDEMPTION IN LONDON & L.A. – an engrossing tale of one man's search for redemption in the only place it has ever been found... within the soul. Come along with the author as he strives to deal with a life half-lived and dreams perpetually deferred. You'll laugh, you'll cry. But most of all, you'll see the world through the eyes of a man truly in touch with his sensibilities; a man who'll change your worldview forever.

...available everywhere books are sold...

ANOTHER FINE OFFERING FROM

DEAD END STREET®

www.ingramcontent.com/pod-product-compliance
Lightning Source LLC
Chambersburg PA
CBHW031553240626
47153CB00002B/488